Time Passed o
Past

A collection of short stories

TIME PASSED
ON
TIMES PAST

A COLLECTION OF SHORT STORIES

CONTENTS

CONTENTS (cont.)

CONTENTS (cont.)

TIME PASSED
ON
TIMES PAST

A collection of short stories written by members of
Taunton u3a

Edited by M. J. Knight

INTRODUCTION

Anyone who lives in Somerset or travels regularly through the county will be familiar with the M5 motorway. There is no doubt that it has made travelling to other parts of the country much easier and much quicker but it has also brought problems for the county and its residents as well. Particularly at weekends and at holiday times the traffic can be very heavy on the motorway and any incident, however small, causes congestion which can mean hold-ups of 30 - 45 minutes. When there are serious incidents the motorway can be closed in both directions for investigation or to land the air ambulance. On occasions, the motorway can be closed for up to 12 hours and this causes traffic chaos and mayhem for miles around. Drivers these days rely on the GPS apps on their smartphones or satellite navigation systems in their cars to guide them to their destination. Motorway closures mean these systems direct the motorists to alternative routes. Somerset is notorious for its narrow winding 'B' roads and its high hedges along these routes. These hedges sometimes 'hide' stone walls within them so the opportunities for further accidents and congestion abound. Thus, the whole area for miles around the motorway becomes gridlocked.

The miserable motorist and his or her passengers stuck with nowhere to go for several hours is reduced to staring at the vehicle in front, playing games on their 'phones or tablets, watching DVDs or just keeping the kids in the back from throttling each other. Ultimately, many tire of these activities and resort to the age-old custom of storytelling. Whether it be on the motorway itself or on one of the lanes around, stuck between the proverbial rock and a hard place (usually another vehicle) numerous tales are told, just to pass the time and keep everyone sane.

This book contains some of the stories that u3a* members may have told while awaiting some sign of movement from the vehicles ahead of them. Some are true, some are not, many are a mixture of truth and imagination. Some are downright ridiculous but might make you smile. Our hope is that you find something to enjoy within these pages and, possibly, may even be tempted to pick up a pen or open up a laptop to write your own story.

*

TAUNTON u3a learn, laugh, live

https://u3asites.org.uk/taunton

- u3a is a UK-wide collection of 1000+ charities that provide the opportunity for those no longer in work to come together and learn for fun.

- If you would like to know more then please take a look at our website (the address is shown above).

One

After crawling less than a mile in forty -five minutes along a tiny lane bordered on both sides by high hedges the car driver turned to his passenger and sighed,

"I could always drive into a field, leave the car there and we could walk. It's only another three or four miles."

"I don't think so, it's too scary on these narrow roads," came the reply.

"Mmm, you're probably right."

After a few minutes the passenger continued,

"Have you ever been **really** *scared?"*

"I don't think so. Why?"

"Well I have," the passenger replied.

"Let me tell you a story."

WW X IS X ER X

AFTER DARK

It doesn't take much, does it? You just riffle through a pile of old photos and whoosh, you're back there again. The swinging sixties. Well, maybe in London, not nearly so much out here on the far-flung edges of a nondescript market town. When photos were still images on a piece of card and, of course, they never lied. Not like modern contraption 'Smart' phones, whose mini screens spew out incessant streams, no, flippin' great rivers, of puerile drivel, "fake news." What's that all about? Anyway, I digress. I meander. I do that a lot nowadays. But looking at those old photos set me thinking, so this is my tale for you. Hope you enjoy it. I'm talking about a night along while back.

In the end it had turned out to be a pretty fun night. Having been one half of a couple for so long, I was seriously out of practice at attending 'do's' on my own and, not having the first idea of how I would cope, I had been dubious about accepting the invitation. In my sane heart of hearts I knew the break-up had been right, but it hadn't been easy. It still wasn't. I guess after so long with someone you have, or need, to go through some sort of a grieving process until, hopefully, you come out the other side unscathed. Or relatively unscathed. My life certainly had been a tapestry so far, though my jury's still out over the 'of rich and varied hue' bit.

It was a big works do and, as it included a buffet rather than a sit-down meal, I reasoned that it might just be impersonal enough to enable me to mingle, to blend in and not look like a loner, a total loser. Also, it had been four months now and I really did need to get back out into the world again. Who knows, maybe I could even think about gently, oh so very gently, easing myself back into the world of dating, romance even. Well, they say that hope springs eternal. ('They' are so all-knowing and all-encompassing; don't 'they' just make you want to puke!)

As the day loomed closer, what had seemed like a mildly good idea at the time now began to assume terrors of gigantic proportions. The 'what-ifs' began. What if I can't hack it? What if I get drunk and start to blub? What if every single other person there isn't? Single, I mean. What if every other person is, in fact, not single but half of an idyllic loved-up partnership? What if?

What if? What if? Forget 'what if?' Therein lies madness. What had I let myself in for? Too late to back out. I've just got to launch myself in and get it over and done with. (Swift mental note to self: never accept another invitation for as long as you live).

As I started to think about getting ready, my pep-talk to myself went roughly along these lines. You'll enjoy it (huh!) Make sure you're squeaky clean. Smell fragrant. Wear your designer underwear. Dress to look the absolute best you can. Paste on a smile. Try to sparkle conversationally. Attempt to mingle. Possibly (but not definitely) flirt if the opportunity presents itself. Dance (maybe). Don't drink too much. Don't force-feed yourself because you can't think what else to do. Etc. etc. Ad nauseum.

Though not exactly on my doorstep, the venue was just about close enough to be within walking distance, a salient point as I had kept on the mortgage and money was a bit of a squeeze, to say the least. A taxi was a luxury I could ill afford.

In a funny, masochistic sort of way, I ended up enjoying the process of getting ready. I revelled in the long, hot shower, enjoying the luxury of not having to share, to use as much hot water as I wanted. I chose my toiletries with infinite care, erring on the side of, I hoped, sophisticated caution. I chose my clothes carefully, wanting to achieve a look that encapsulated casual but smart, somewhat cool even, no mean feat I have to admit.

Once dressed and ready for the off, I took a very long, very studied, look in the mirror, appraising myself more rigorously than I could remember doing for years. I was pretty chuffed with the result. I felt I had managed to achieve the look I set out to achieve. I knew I looked good and that made me feel good. Or a pretty close approximation of good. I set off with my head held high and my confidence pretty well intact. I'd counted on there being a fair crowd already by the time I arrived, a half-hour after kick-off. To my relief, I wasn't wrong. It wasn't crazily packed but crowded enough for me to feel anonymously comfortable.

I did all the things on my checklist I had said I would do, and some I hadn't even thought to mention to myself. I tried not to do the things I'd vowed to veto with, for the most part, a modicum of success. I helped myself to a touch more food than I had intended, though I hope I never allowed myself to look like a complete and total glutton. I drank a little more than was strictly sensible, getting a bit tiddly, but never coming anywhere close to the falling-down stage. I mingled, chatting inanely rather than sparklingly but, hey, so did everyone else. I flirted mildly, both of us knowing that there was never going to be any serious intent.

All in all, I did myself proud, even if I say so myself. Most importantly, I had broken my own self-imposed ice. I had taken the first tentative steps. I felt I was on the wobbly road to becoming a fully functioning member of the human race again. I left, alone, far later than I had intended to. It was creeping on towards three o'clock in the morning. I wasn't the last to leave, though, by any means. The disco was still in full swing when I started to wend my way home. The night was beautiful, with a tiny sliver of a moon, millions of stars, not quite cold enough to seriously impact, though cold enough for me not to want to dawdle. I felt a self-satisfied little rosy glow (alcohol induced, I'm sure) of contentment, that all was very much right with my world. The dark was almost pitch black.

The streets were totally deserted with not a soul about. After a few minutes the streets gave way to countryside; no pavements, just road. I was conscious of every single one of my footsteps bouncing deafeningly back to me from the iron-hard surface of that road. But apart from them, the silence was profound. Then, in a heartbeat lasting a lifetime, an odd sensation of extreme isolation and loneliness replaced my euphoria of a breath ago. Not for the first time, I was stunned by the lightning-quick caprices of the human brain. Then came the painfully slow, dawning realisation that mine weren't the only reverberations. Each of my steps was being echoed by someone else's. I wasn't alone.

Because I'd been in my own little reverie, the awareness of another presence had seeped through to me almost imperceptibly. One second I was on my own, the next I wasn't. I couldn't at first make out where the footsteps were coming from, whether in front, behind, to the left, to the right. Hedges rustled, contorting sound. Bit by bit, with me barely aware, those footsteps echoing mine had made their way into my consciousness, seemingly from out of the ether.

Whoever was sharing that pitch-dark country road with me on that pre-dawn morning was not a million miles away. OK, you read all sorts of horror stories about what happens to people out on their own in the dangerous dark, but I had always taken them with a gigantic pinch of salt. For goodness sake, we lived in a civilised society and I felt pretty sure that most of my fellow human beings were kind, considerate people wanting nothing more than to live in harmony with one another. So I wasn't overly perturbed. At first. Then, bit by terrifying bit, my stupid imagination started to run rampant, to get the better of me. It went into mega-overdrive. I began to envisage tomorrow's grisly front-page headlines, with my bruised and bloody corpse the main focus. It's true that when terror strikes, your heart really does beat so loudly you can't work out why it hasn't woken up the whole world. My loneliness and isolation intensified tenfold, a million-fold.

My thoughts were a maelstrom.

Sounds seemed to distort, become nebulous, deceptive, so that footsteps now seemed to surround me. It was difficult to differentiate between the two sets: even my own were no longer clear to me. I tried to concentrate, willing my attention to focus. I was shockingly aware that, although I wasn't drunk, I had drunk a little more than would be considered sensible. I wasn't absolutely stone-cold sober. I could stand up straight and walk a fairly straight line, but my sensibilities had erred just a tad too far from the side of caution. The hairs on the back of my neck were standing to attention. I felt exposed and vulnerable, that every one of my steps was being noted, weighed up and processed. For what seemed like forever, in reality probably only a few moments, I gave in to this horror state. My knees felt wobbly; my stomach was lurching all over the place. I was shaking with terror.

In the end I took a slow, deep breath, gave myself a huge mental shake and told myself to pull myself together, which I managed with some commendable degree of success to do. I could feel the adrenalin pumping. My concentration contracted to an awareness solely of sound. I willed my mind to identify the source of that sound, eventually concluding the footsteps were behind me. The brain works so much faster, so much more arbitrarily, than the ability to put thoughts into words. In the space of a split second, what seemed like a million disconnected questions raced around in my head. Should I slow down, speed up, loiter until the person had passed me, surreptitiously attempt to catch a glimpse of whoever was following me – no, not following me, simply walking behind me - speak to the person behind me? Should I go to the supermarket tomorrow because I've almost run out of toilet roll and deodorant? What should I do?

Two split seconds later I had managed to compose myself enough to make a rational decision. I would do nothing. Or rather, I would keep on walking exactly as I was doing at that minute, willing my focus on the person behind me, to remain aware of the pace of their walk, any deviation from that pace, whether their breathing pattern remained constant, whether their intentions were noble, whether I was safe. In short, I would try to surmise what was in my shadowy companion's mind. And that is what I did. We walked apart, in tandem, for about ten of the longest minutes of my life, neither of us deviating from the rhythm we had set up, until at last I gained my doorway.

In my relief, my knees almost buckled beneath me. It was only then that I finally snuck a glance at my nemesis. That glance sucked the breath out of me. She was barely your average 5 foot 2 inches and slightly built. You could almost have blown her away with one breath. It's not beyond the realms of possibility that she was at the same works do as me. Poor girl. It must have been a gut-wrenching experience to find herself imprisoned behind a stranger, a pretty muscular 6 foot 2 inches bloke who, as far as she was concerned, could have been all the hounds from hell rolled into one, wanting nothing more than to inflict the maximum harm possible on her. And how horrifyingly unnerving for her to realise that he seemed to be there for the duration, that there was nowhere she could escape to get out of his way, that she could only continue blindly on her chosen course. How I wished I could have told her I had felt exactly the same as she dogged my footsteps home. I didn't. Instead I gave just a very slight nod and a muted goodnight. Once inside it occurred to me that I should have made sure she got home safely. I spent a restless night, tossing and turning, riddled with guilt.

The weekend dragged mercilessly. The guilt never fully assuaged. Halfway through work on Monday, my terrors were alleviated. I breathed an internal sigh of relief as I spotted her walking down a corridor, too far away for me to speak to or acknowledge. I never did get to know her name. I've always wished I had.

Kaye Sirra-Sirra

Two

On a long journey from Wellington to Stoke on Trent on a weekend in the summer a family became stuck between junctions 24 and 23. The traffic was motionless and had been so for almost an hour when the driver, a man in his fifties, without warning startled his passengers, a woman and two teenage children by exclaiming,

"Let's talk about the meaning of life."

"What?" was the surprised response.

"Well, you learn about several religions in school, what do they have to say about life and its meaning?"

The woman in the front passenger seat who may have been the teenagers' mother, but, equally, may not, said quietly,

"Let me tell you a story."

"WHAT HAVE YOU LEARNT?" SAID THE MAN ON THE LEFT

Tom lived with his two brothers and a sister in the basement of a disused shop in Clapham. He had just turned nine. The shop had been empty for months.

It had been 6 months since their mother had passed, due to, they think, pneumonia. All they knew was she'd been very ill and they'd no money to fetch a doctor. When she died, they didn't know what to do.

Billy the eldest, organised them. "Right, if we stay here the authorities will lock us all up in the Workhouse. We had to do that when dad died. We know how bad that was, working for those vicious Bragans . We're not taking punishment like that again! Luckily, mum's cousin managed to get us out. We wouldn't be together, and we don't want that but we don't know where this cousin lives now, so she can't help us! We'd never get out of there! All agreed?."

"Aye" they said in unison. They'd told Nellie next door of their mother's death, asked her to notify the doctor, then they scarpered. They couldn't pay for her funeral so she'd have to have a pauper's grave alas. That was how they came to be living in the grotty basement. It was dry at least, and no colder than their house had been. Billy and Jack had been going out each day looking for work but had found none yet, not even the markets. They just got by for food by keeping their eyes open for fruit or veg that had fallen under the stalls. Sometimes, the stallholders gave them a penny or two for fetching, carrying and cleaning up afterwards. Every so often, they went to other markets and managed to get something to eat off a stall without anyone noticing. Bit risky mind! Tom sometimes went along with them, and amused himself, listening to the barrow boys calling, or just sitting playing with sticks and leaves in the gutters by the road.

On this particular day Tom was walking round the market when another boy, about his own age, came running towards him. Seeing Tom he ran over, grabbed Tom by the shoulder and then ran off, ducking behind a stall, and under the fence. Tom heard the blowing of a whistle as a Bow Street runner came hurtling into the market, followed by a smartly dressed gentleman.

“That’s him,” the man hollered, ’Thief!” The Bow Street Runner grabbed Tom. “This gentleman says you stole from his shop today!.”

“I never,” said Tom shocked. “I haven’t been to no shops Guv. I’ve been here all the time with me brothers. See, they’re over there!” Seeing Tom amidst all the commotion, his brothers ran up. The Runner stated that this gentleman has seen Tom in his shop and witnessed him pocket a valuable watch. Billy and Jack professed Tom’s innocence. He’d been at the market all day in sight of them.

“Well, this gentleman here is sure he’s the culprit. Empty your pockets son!” Tom felt in his pockets, his face aghast, he brought out a large silver pocket watch. Tom’s brothers looked at him in shock, mouths open wide.

“But I never,” Tom pleaded, “I’ve been here all the time. I promise ya.” The boys continued to profess his innocence.

“But there was a boy who ran up to me for no reason, held me, and then ran under that fence.” The Gentleman held Tom fast whilst the Runner investigated.

“No-one there lad, and no one here to corroborate your story, apart from your brothers that is.”

“I’m sorry but I’m going to have to arrest you for larceny. Theft to you boy. You’ll have to come with me and go in front of the judge tomorrow, unless any other proof comes to light.”

Tom was handcuffed, sobbing, and was pulled away by the Runner, with the Gentleman and his brothers following behind. Tom sat terrified in a cold cell that night without food amongst drunks and criminals. In the morning, he was hauled before the Judge. Billy, Jack and Nancy were present in the court room. It was all over in a couple of minutes!!

The Gentleman swore that Tom was the boy he'd seen in his shop, and who had stolen the silver pocket watch. The Bow Street Runner confirmed that the said watch was found in possession of Master Tom Jenkins, of no fixed abode. Case closed. The judge pronounced Tom guilty, and as there had been a spate of such blatant thievery in the area lately, and he believed that gangs of boys had been responsible for this, a clear example had to be sent out to all would be criminals.

"You, Tom Jenkins, have been sentenced to Transportation to our Australian colony for the period of no less than 20 years!" Down went the Judge's gavel!

Tom saw no more of his family as he was led in chains to the cells below. Tom and the other criminals were moved the next day to an underground jail in the centre of London, to await transportation. Water trickled down the walls, and rats scurried along the floors. Tom sat with his head down, crying.

"It wasn't me!"

A young man took pity on this young boy. Matthew stated, "Easier being with somebody else lad. You stick with me! I'll protect you! I've got a little brother about your age. The guards take great pleasure in kicking, hitting and depriving us of food."

No sooner said than the door opened and the guards laughed as they threw some bread in amongst the many prisoners. Not enough to go round. Matthew lunged forward and grabbed a chunk for himself and for Tom.

"See what I mean?" winked Matthew.

"Thank you," Tom replied.

Three weeks later, those held in the jail were taken in shackles to Portsmouth to await their ship. They had no idea where they were heading. Tom missed his family so badly but he couldn't read or write and his brothers and sister had no address. He had no way to contact them. Tom had never seen such a huge ship before, only the boats on the Thames. The ship was bound for Western

Australia, to help the Swan River Colony grow, founded by free men, but needing more labour. The treatment on the ship was harsh for even petty offences. Tom sat terrified in the dark hold below deck, shackled round his wrists and ankles for ten gruelling weeks, only fed intermittently with bread and water. Seasickness, disease and general illness were rife. Men and women were crying out in pain and feared beatings or attacks by other violent prisoners. Many never made it to this new world that Tom had never heard about.

When they reached the Swan River Colony they stayed below deck until guards hauled them out, shackled together, down the gangplank and into the blinding sunshine outside. They were marched through the streets to the nearby prison. The colonists staring at them suspiciously.

Free Colonists who needed labour arrived at the prison to view this human cargo. Mr Dawkins, a local store owner, surveyed the prisoners.

"I'm looking for workers who can transport goods by cart from warehouses to my many shops and establishments along the Swan Valley. Goods brought here from the Homeland, and from Settlements from Fremantle and down to the Mandurah River."

Matthew stood up immediately, though still in chains. "I have experience of riding horses, and driving horse and carts, and even large hay wains where I'm from. I'm a hard worker and fast learner, sir, and this is my brother, Tom, who's come with me. He's very quick, a good assistant, runs messages, and any odd jobs sir."

"Well I like how keen you were to grab this chance, shows the character we need for our Colony. You are employed, along with your brother. Obviously, there are no wages, it is purely your lodgings and food. You will share with our other workers in hostel accommodation, on one month's trial. Sign these two over to me, Master Langley. I'll take them now."

So that was how Matthew and Tom came into the guardianship of Mr Dawkins. They stayed with him for many loyal years in his retail trade. Matthew hadn't really known about riding or driving horses, as he'd said, but he learnt fast, driving large wagons across the sands and barren land transporting goods between Mr Dawkins' various stores, spreading even further in Western Australia in that searing heat. Mr Dawkins set Matthew up in his own store with Tom locating places where he could get the goods and beer cheaper for all the new settlers in the surrounding area. Mr Dawkins had given them both a very valuable piece of sound advice,

"Remember, both of you, that here in Australia there are more Sharks here on the land, than there ever are in the sea!"

A lesson they learned well. Matthew paid for Tom to have lessons in reading and writing and became very friendly with Tom's tutor, later asking permission from the Governor and Mr Dawkins to marry Miss Lucy Taylor. They needed new blood to grow this Colony. Mr Dawkins handed over the store that Matthew ran as a wedding gift as Matthew had founded so many other stores for his Guardian. He was no longer in Mr Dawkins employ, but neither was he a free man, neither was Tom. But with Tom's skills at making money he founded the first hotel in the town, or a pub as it was called in England. He went on to have a thriving business himself with hotels in many towns. After he'd learned to read and write, he contacted a solicitor in London to track down his brothers and sister, knowing only their names. From the markets, his solicitor had managed to trace his eldest brother Billy who was married and owned his own market stall, He knew Jack and Nancy' s whereabouts as well. Jack and Nancy were not in regular work, and Nancy's soldier husband had died whilst in combat. Tom offered to bring them out to Australia to work for him. Jack and Nancy took up his offer, but Billy stayed on his stall, knowing the offer was there.

Tom lived a good long life, had a loving wife and family and having extended his hotels throughout the state, spreading out from Perth and into all the new settlements and beyond. Jack and Nancy settled down in this new life too with their own families.

"Life has been pretty good" thought Tom, "Despite my early beginnings" as he laid on his deathbed with those he loved surrounding him. As his breathing became shallower, Tom found it harder to listen to those around him. His darling wife held his hand and kissed him as he let out his final breath.

Tom was greeted by family who had all passed before him, Matthew, of course, friends he'd known, and many others that he didn't think he knew but who seemed somehow familiar.

"What have you learnt?" said the Man on his left "To make yourself a higher being, moving forward with your spiritual knowledge. This isn't the first time you've returned, and it won't be your last! You've just returned from your mortal stay on earth again that you chose to do. You went to learn lessons from previous mistakes, and from others."

"I learnt that good can come out of bad, even evil, although you can't see it at the time. As an innocent child I suffered through another's selfishness, but it led me to the best things that could have ever happened to me, and the best life. I learnt that the love of family and good friends can save your life. Family that love one another despite all that life throws at them, can never be replaced. No man is an island. He cannot live alone without others helping along the way, and that life is also about helping others along the way whether materially, if one can, but especially emotionally and spiritually.

"That life is worth taking risks in, when opportunities are put on your pathway. They may be right or wrong but you'll never know unless you try, and that opportunity may never come your way again. Life is for living and not shut in the dark with regrets. Don't be afraid to be the first one to stand up, even if the others are still sat down."

"Well done, Tom. Welcome back."

***

William was born out of wedlock in a Hertfordshire village whilst his father was in jail for stealing cheese. His mother, Sarah, a farm maid, worked hard in the fields in all weathers and milking. His father William, when he was released from prison was only out long enough to sire another son by Sarah and rustle himself a sheep out of necessity to feed his family, and some neighbours, if they kept their mouths shut. Only people talk when they've been partaking in drink, so the local police heard! On entering his cottage it became evident that plenty of mutton was there. William was arrested, attended court, found guilty, and sent back to prison in London. He couldn't assist his family now! Sarah had to cope as best she could with two children and elderly parents also to feed and care for, working back on the farm straight after birthing despite how hard the work was. She arrived home one evening after work to find an Eviction Notice pinned to her door from the village council with the vicar's seal of approval. They were to be evicted by morning! Just then, she observed the vicar leaving the church and rushed over waving the eviction notice.

"Why have you done this?" she cried.

"Because, Sarah, we have other parishioners who need a home, church going members. The Council and I have agreed that as you've children born out of wedlock and your man is imprisoned and unable to keep his family for the second time, we believe that a more worthy family should live in the cottage."

The vicar pictured his nephew whose family would be moving in.

"My children and parents are not guilty of any sin, yet you punish them. What will become of us?"

"I'm sorry, that is not my concern. You cannot be a burden to our village funds to pay your poor relief so you must still vacate the property my dear woman. My hands are tied!"

"Your hands aren't tied! You, a man of God, authorised it. Have you no pity!"

"Are there no workhouses? I cannot be seen to be endorsing sinners and criminals. They must be punished"

"Please, not the workhouse, I beg you in God's name, not that!. I've worked hard to keep my family, and if I could keep a roof over us I still would. William is paying for his crimes in prison."

"Yes, but the cottage and village is tarnished by your actions. You need to leave." And with that he turned his back on her and strolled away. By first light the bailiffs returned. Sarah bundled up her few meagre possessions.

"Where will you go?" the Mistress inquired.

"There's only one place for us, the Workhouse, ma'am." She trembled at the thought. Everyone knew and feared it. Sarah was shown into the workhouse master's office with matron present.

"Nurse examine these children for fleas and lice, scrub them then take them away to the children's dormitory."

"NO!" cried Sarah.

"The baby can stay till he's able to work, but your boy and parents must go. They have work to do, as have you."

Sarah was taken to a dark, empty room apart from a medical table by the Medical Officer. He performed a full examination on her, then ordered her to strip fully, and the superintendent hosed her down, her clothes were taken away and replaced by a coarse uniform. She worked all day till nightfall in the steamy laundry, hands cracked and reddened and never got to see or cuddle William except by accident. Her parents were separated into Men's and Women's quarters, never seeing each other again except for fleeting glimpses. Treatment was harsh for everyone, young or old, eating gruel day in day out. Little William worked hard in the kitchens, scrubbing and cleaning under the stick wielding domain of the Overseer. A very cruel regime ruled, relief only coming for many through death. His mother later died herself from disease. William and his brother only heard of her death in passing. They hadn't even known or seen their mother whilst she was ill to comfort her, and themselves. His grandparents followed her soon after. William and his brother were bought by a farmer from the workhouse. He was strict but not cruel and fed them well. Life improved. The farmer's wife was kind to them and treated them as her own. He never knew what became of his father.

When old enough, William joined Hertfordshire's Militia as a soldier giving him respectability and status. His brother set sail for America, never to be seen or heard from again! William married and moved to a rapidly growing town near London, lured by higher pay and a tied house. He became a brick maker, his wife and family labouring there. They became part of the brickmaking community who looked after each other, mixing and marrying together. They made the bricks that built the towns. William ended his days aged just 36, lungs filled from the brick dust. When he wheezed his last breath, he left a wife destitute with four children and one on the way. His tied house was lost to his family as well.

"What have you learnt William?" said the man to his left.

His mother, grandparents, friends and others who looked familiar greeted him.

"I learned that there is more to life than the material things, forgetting the joy of a simple life well led. We forget the beauty of nature for money and a soul destroying existence. I learned that the Church doesn't care for us, only for themselves; setting themselves up as Judge and Jury and not practicing what they preach. There are many who say they care but do nothing. They have no love for their fellow man. There are fewer who say nothing but do everything! They are Angels on earth. Find strength from within yourself and don't let your past or others define you. Others have their own path to walk, and you may not be on it."

"What will happen to my family? My son's not yet born!"

"It won't be long till your wife joins you. The family will go through hard times, but your community will rally round to care for them. Your wife will marry a compassionate brick maker who will care for her and raise your children as his own till they are grown, and you see them again. You have much to thank him for! Welcome, William."

***

Harry sat deep in thought. "You alright?" said his Sargeant as he did his patrol check on his men in their hut.

"Yes, Sarge, just got a letter from my wife. She's had a baby boy. I've got a son."

"Great news, congratulations."

"I was wondering when I'd get to see them. Perhaps not for a long time."

"We don't know what's going to happen tomorrow never mind anything else. The war's already gone on longer than anyone thought, Sarge. It feels like we've always been at war."

"You're right there laddie. We've just got to take one day at a time, keep our heads down, be brave and kill those Jerries. Our womenfolk and our country are depending on us to send them packing! We beat them in the Great War and we'll beat them again. They can't mess with us."

"No Sarge, but I wish I was there protecting her. They're bombing London where we live. I used to parade up and down outside her house before we wed, in case the Jerries parachuted in and got her!" he chuckled.

"Well you can stop the enemy from getting your wife, and all the other girlfriends and wives, we've got a big day ahead of us tomorrow. Now get some sleep, we'll be up well before dawn."

Harry was still a lad. He'd enlisted before he was old enough but he wanted to do his bit for King and Country and stop the German Invasion. He'd seen plenty of action since he'd joined. He was important for his battalion as a Vickers machine gunner. As he lay on his bunk, he reflected back on his life. He'd grown up, the youngest of nine children, so he enjoyed all the camaraderie of the army, and he also had an older brother in this battalion. It was a happy household in a very small terrace cottage, two up, two down, with an outdoor toilet shared by everyone in the terrace row, next door to the Grand Union Canal.

All the children used to go swimming there regularly. That's why he never caught anything! It was so polluted from the factories, and dead horses and donkeys in the canal, that he was immune to any illnesses. His mum and sisters doted on him.

'Yes,' thought Harry, 'I was born lucky. At four my brother caught typhoid, as did my cousin, from our water pump in the backyard. They both died. I was younger yet didn't catch it. My sister Elizabeth was a nurse who worked in a London TB Hospital when I was a schoolboy. She caught it and had to be nursed for a long time at home before dying in her twenties. They said I was lucky not to catch TB from her. Earlier in the war, when we were out fighting in Holland I copped it. They got me in my leg as I was at my machine gun. Me and my oppo managed to escape and were lucky enough to meet a nun who took us to her nunnery. She swiftly hid us in a hidden cupboard in their basement, making sure that there was no sign of our entry. I was in so much pain but had to stay silent. The Germans came hammering on the door and ordered the nuns to their refectory whilst they searched the building. They searched everywhere but never found us. I couldn't believe it. The nuns nursed me and cared for my oppo till we could be rescued by our Battalion, and I be taken back home to recover. Those nuns put their lives on the line for me, a complete stranger! I can't thank them enough.'

Harry still thought about his experience in Belgium that had had a profound effect on him.

'I was on Night Patrol at our camp when I heard a noise from the cans on wire defences round our site. I felt my way by hand over hand along the wire in the dark, foggy night, walking slowly and listening, until I came face to face with the enemy, another young man looking just as shocked as me. Looking into each other's eyes with our rifles, not pistols, at our sides, like playing a cowboy gunfight - but this time it's real. IT'S HIM OR ME!

'No time to think! I fired first! The young German fell to the ground at my feet. Perhaps he wasn't going to shoot me? Or perhaps he was? Of course he was! His eyes no longer seeing, staring blankly back at me. I was shaking, sweating and crying. It was so different killing at zero feet than from my machine gun at a distance. We used to throw grenades at tanks, then shoot the men as they escaped, like a game, not real. This boy had family waiting for him, as I have waiting for me! Yes I've been lucky, despite being sent back to fight time and time again, and through injuries and illness!'

Harry shuddered as he remembered but soon fell asleep. They didn't quite know where they were going tomorrow, or what was happening. They just knew that they were trained for the bit they had to do. They'd been through it over and over again as they waited in isolation from the world, so nothing sneaked out of what was happening.

They set off whilst it was still dark, and boarded vessels for God knows where. As the dawn broke, they saw the shore of France ahead.

"Well boys, we've trained for this. I'm so proud of you all. You know what has to be done. Give them Jerries what for! Machine gunners out first, we'll cover you! Once you're set up, we'll get ashore."

Harry set up on the beach as the Germans ran from their hiding places. He set off round after round, from side to side. Men fell before him and near him, as his battalion ran through the water to the beach. Friends and enemies dropped by him, and on him! He pushed them off yet still more came. The longest day ever! Bodies strewn everywhere, and blood staining the sea. Harry had just stood up when the lone sniper got him, BANG!

"Welcome Harry," said the man to his left. Family were there to greet him, and others familiar to him, but unknown.

"You're back again, but you have risen considerably in your development. What have you learned?"

"That the love and compassion of your fellow man is as important as the love of family and friends. I had felt compassion for my enemies that I'd met along the way, They were just like me, doing as they were ordered, but still with loved ones waiting for them at home."

"Go and reunite with your fellow comrades and others who fell with you also. A party is set up for you.

Your enemies will also be having a party, relieved to be out of the fear and bloodshed. You may even wish to see and meet the people you were fighting, and see who they are as people, that is entirely up to you. Your choice! Welcome, Harry."

"Welcome!" said the man on the left. "You've chosen to return to earth again, as you have many times before, despite your perfect life here. You will return this time as a girl to see life from a different perspective! It won't be easy. There will be more change in the world than ever before. You won't recognise the place! Life will be full of heartbreak, loss, and traumas, but you know that.

A rather unlucky but interesting life. You will have to contend with going from super fit, known as an athlete, to disabled, in constant pain and poor health which you've not experienced before, or how others will treat you. That's my quick overview. I know you like a challenge!"

"Can I save many animals? I've always loved animals."

"Yes, add that one to the list Peter! Do you still want to go?"

"Yes! How bad can it be?" they answered.

"Tell me when you get back!" He chuckled.

"Well off you go and I'll see you again in …oh! I nearly gave that away! When you get back."

Sharon Peggrem

"What have you learnt?," said the man on the left.

Three

The journey was long and tiresome and now to make things worse, they had come to a complete standstill.

His head was throbbing and was not helped by the stupid song his wife and children were persistently singing, on and on and on ……

"Stop "Larry shouted.

"Stop singing that stupid song. Have you ever thought about the words and what they really mean?"

WW x IS x ER x

DRAGON

For as long as he could remember, Larry had had a passionate interest in music. Prompted, probably, by the fact that the radio was always on at his childhood home and though the broadcasts were largely spoken word, a fair amount of music did filter through. In the early 60's a Saturday morning radio show called "Children's Favourites," with Uncle Mac, and later Ed Stewart, was imperative listening for him. A lot of older and more obscure 'fun' records would be played here, along with offerings from shows and films.

Over a period, he learned songs such as "Little White Bull," "The Ugly Duckling," "A frog he would a-wooing go," "Sparky's magic piano," "I know an old lady who swallowed a fly," "The Ladies of the Court of King Caractacus," the only hit single for the late Tommy Cooper, "Don't jump off the roof, Dad" and "Puff the magic dragon." He learnt dozens, if not hundreds, of tunes by listening to this radio programme, most of which are still buried somewhere deep in his memory-banks. But these tunes are now seldom heard. Mainly because there are so many other songs to choose from nowadays; over forty years' worth of pop, and newly found genres of music, have now been added to those old but familiar favourites.

Larry had a particular liking for the Puff the magic dragon song. As a nine-year-old, his imagination was fired up by this gentle story as he warbled along with it. He wished he could visit Honahlee, even asking his elders where this place was, and could we go there? Only to be shot down in flames by remarks such as,

"Never heard of it," or "Don't be bloody silly."

A big disappointment for a lad of that age. He so wanted to meet, and play with, a dragon of his own. At that age Larry had no concept of a dragon being a mythical creature.

The years went by, and Larry endeavoured, unsuccessfully, to become a professional actor. Once he finally realised that he was never going to be as famous as Skelton Knaggs (1911-1955) he had a change of heart and joined amateur thespian groups. His love of music never dwindled, however, but the song about Puff faded into obscurity, only re-emerging on rare occasions in radio request shows or old TV transmissions. He last heard it when he was nearing retirement age. By then his life experiences had made him pedantic, cynical, critical and analytical, and he realised that actually the lyrical content of this tune was just plain daft. This wasn't the only childhood song that he was able to criticise either.

For example, there is a tune from 1958 entitled 'Ram a lam a ding dong,' where the singer informs the listener that this is the name of his, the singer's, girlfriend. What kind of parents give their baby girl a name such as this? The vicar must have been peeing himself with laughter at the christening ceremony. As a teenager, if Larry had met a bird at a disco and she had told him that her name was Ram-a-lang-a ding-dong then he would have been out of there in less time than it would have taken for her to repeat it.

There were also other girls with ridiculous names who were featured in the songs of Larry's early years. Poor lasses such as Be-bop-A-Lula and Boney Maroney may have had a lot to put up with from their peers. From a female perspective one idiotic moniker that springs to mind is 'My boy lollipop.' One more thing which became increasingly irritating to Larry, even in his teenage era, was the much over-used term 'Baby.' Whilst he knows that it is meant as a term of endearment, Larry's literal mind could not help but conjure up a picture of a small person in a nappy with a dummy in his or her mouth.

During his lifetime Larry has never, in day-to-day interactions, heard anyone call their primary partner 'Baby.' Can't songwriters at least try to come up with something a little more imaginative?

But back to dear old androgynous Puff, and there are several things that, these days, Larry ponders upon. Like, who would give a supposedly fearsome beast such an ironic epithet. The creature obviously wasn't Australian. What did Puff eat? The reference to cherry lane may be a clue but existing on just cherries would surely not be ideal fare for any digestive system, especially one large enough to maintain the health of a fully-grown dragon.

It is related that Puff 'frolicked in the autumn mist.' Why did he appear to frolic, and only in the autumn? What did he do for the duration of the other seasons? As he lived by the sea, perhaps he spent the summertime endlessly sunbathing, and maybe he went tobogganing in the winter. Such details are not revealed. Also, how could such a lumbering critter frolic as such? The term implies a sense of delicacy that Puff probably wouldn't have possessed.

The human protagonist in this tale, Jackie Paper, evidently loved Puff, and saw him as a rascal. One can imagine him tickling Puff under the chin and saying "You little rascal."

Would Puff have understood this display of camaraderie? Which leads Larry to also wonder - how did they communicate, what caused them to become playmates, and which of them pioneered their initial mutual attachment? Especially as most kids, on their own, would have suffered a complete lack of sphincter control if confronted by a dragon whilst out prancing along cherry lane. Didn't Jackie have any mates to share the dragon experience with?

'I would have wanted to' thinks Larry. 'Even if it was only for the purpose of showing off in front of my buddies.'

"I've got a dragon and you haven't, so there."

Jackie supposedly brought Puff 'string, sealing wax and other fancy stuff,' though how Puff's huge claws dealt with these small, fiddly items can only be speculated upon. Larry wondered if Puff wrote enough letters to justify him requiring sealing wax, and even if he did then how could he manage to lick and stick the stamps on? Or perhaps he would ask Jackie to make him some candles to light up the dingey cave that he, Puff, dwelt in. It may well have been an absorbing spectacle to watch Puff striking matches to light these candles, and even more interesting to watch him trying to blow them out.

What was this other fancy stuff that Jackie thrust upon a perhaps unwilling Puff? Painted wings would be somewhat superfluous to a creature already possessing such appendages, and what the pair of them did with giant rings is anybody's guess. Maybe

Jackie brought him pomegranates, or some Lego? But wouldn't it all be a bit like giving a mobile phone to Venus de Milo? Next, we are told that 'noble Kings and Princes would bow whenever they came,' and also that pirate ships would lower their flags when Puff bellowed at them. Both these statements lead to the supposition that Puff and Jackie made sea voyages together, further confirmed by the statement that they did indeed 'travel on a boat with billowed sail.' Larry's curiosity was aroused by what sort of device Jackie may have used to aid his balance whilst perched upon 'Puff's gigantic tail.'

Also, this presents further questions. Wouldn't Jackie's parents be concerned about him going off like that to distant shores? Also where did the pair of them keep their boat? How did they launch it, and where did they obtain their supplies for an extended trip across tempestuous seas?

Alternatively, these Kings and Princes could, purportedly, have come to visit Jackie and his overgrown, reptilian buddy in Honahlee. But how would the unlikely duo have known that these royal visitors were on their way, and did they give any consideration to preparing a state banquet for them all?

As the conclusion of this enchanting tale approaches, a young listener may experience a sense of sadness. But to an older Larry it was just as nonsensical as the rest of this musical fable. If a dragon lives forever, as the storyline would have had children believe, then why aren't towns, and the countryside not festooned with them, hiding in railway tunnels or ravaging cherry-orchards? Perhaps they are omnipresent, but only in Honahlee. In our green and pleasant land, however, they are about as rare as a black ghost.

'One grey night it happened; Jackie Paper came no more.'

Why did this traumatic event occur at night, given that the pair's other fascinating adventures seemingly occur during daylight hours? Jackie wouldn't have been allowed out at night anyway, especially in autumn when the nights are drawing in. How come Puff realised immediately that Jackie wasn't coming to jiggle his jowls ever again? If Puff then 'ceased his fearless roar' it leads Larry to assume that the beast led a surprisingly dull existence before Jackie came along to pester him with useless objects. It is also a little misleading to hear that Puff saw Jackie as a 'lifelong friend' when it is obvious that the association was, at best, transitory. Why didn't Puff continue loitering around cherry lane to see if he could find a replacement for the departed Jackie? Instead, he became a simpering wimp who lost the will to live. As a consequence of existing purely on a diet of cherries it's hardly surprising that he slipped into his cave.

Finally, Larry considered what had become of Jackie Paper. Barring accidents, he must have grown into an adult – married, with kids. Did he tell those children, or anyone else for that matter, about the time he hung out with a real dragon. Would they have believed him? But knowing it to have been a true adventure, how forcefully would Jackie have insisted that his escapades were fact? Would he have become increasingly delusional? Difficult to imagine what lasting effect such a life event would have on an impressionable young lad. Perhaps he became a resident in "a colony for the mentally defective."

Or maybe he just lived happily ever after.

Malcolm Godfrey

Dragon

Four

The six of them, three men and three women, were travelling in their campervan from Plymouth to Birmingham to watch their beloved Argyle play football.

When they heard over the radio that the M5 was closed between Bridgwater and Weston-Super-Mare they decided to leave the motorway and use the A38 instead, not realising that that would also be completely 'jammed' with traffic at a standstill.

They then made the fatal error of leaving the A38 and trying their luck on the 'less well used' roads.

Somewhere between Burnham and who knows where they had to admit that they were lost. They decided to take a short break and rustle up a brew.

While the kettle was coming up to the boil, Pat said, "Let me tell you a story about getting lost. It might cheer you up in our present predicament. I was in Japan...."

A GAIJIN IN KOBE

Fearfully, tentatively, I raise my head, this action being very slow as the dread and apprehension of what I will see totally engulfs me. One seething mass of humanity is all around me, I am totally immersed in swarms of dark haired indigenous folk all hurrying to their destinations, very conscious of being on time, punctuality being the key. I sidelong every one as they do me, no one wanting to look me in the eye. They hang tightly and thick around me daring me to breathe. The City suddenly feels like an albatross around my neck, it closes in on me, traps me in this space. I cannot move, every time I take one step forward, my mind takes one step back. It seems as if a fog is impairing my visibility, all that I can see is black.

The fear within me turns to a near paralysis; my perception of imminent danger is at an unprecedented level. There is no rationale within me. I feel my breathing rate grow at an alarming pace and although the day has cooled, I am sweating profusely. This is my worst nightmare ever. I recall a dream that I had recurrently as a young person, getting off of a train in London, after I had taken it in the wrong direction and not knowing if I would ever get back. It is an irrational fear; for surely I will find my way, someday, somehow, someone will find me I but I don't know that for sure and I cannot get away from that path, which I am scurrying along in the anticipation of what could lay ahead. The uncertainty and the unpredictability of it terrifies me.

Where am I? Well the nature of the indigenous population might give a clue but I will tell you, I am in Kobe, on the Southern Side of the main island of Honshu in Japan. It is 1993 and my Dear Daughter is living in Nara, which back in the 8th Century was Japan's capital city. Kobe has a population of approximately 1.5 million people but to me, then, they all seem to be there at the same time enveloping me. 140 years after the end of the period of Seclusion, 28 years ago, it still seems to me that there is no room for me the outsider, The Gaijin.

I should mention that it is 1993; life for the Gaijin in the more rural areas of Japan certainly was not a piece of cake.

The BA Plane BA017 had arrived in Osaka nearly an hour late on the 25th March and I have to mention that at that time I was quite surprised to see a lot of people wearing masks, surgical masks like doctors in an operating theatre actually walking down the main street. Furious enquiries informed me that once the first germs of the common cold attack, the victim must don a mask so that no one else succumbs. Henceforth, every time I saw a mask, I went into fits of hilarious giggles. I mention this only because in 2021 everyone is wearing a mask, 28 years on from my very first experience, it's trending everywhere!; well its mandatory actually and for a very different and serious reason.

My stay so far had not been without adventure of a different kind. Sleeping on a futon in a confined space was the first big change, discovering Pachinko as a game. The humidity was high and it was warm, the innumerable temples where people visited though not particularly to observe religion. Soon it would be cherry blossom time, okonmiyaki to eat, the Tenrikyo Church and the various cultural and social institutions attached to it.

A visit to Gion corner In Kyoto was a highlight where we visited the home of the original Geisha and the Traditional Japanese Arts Theatre. We visited Yasaka Hall whilst the preparations for the cherry blossom festival were in full swing. However, we obtained tickets and spent a very pleasant tour observing a programme of seven events. The tea ceremony, the tradition of tasting tea which originated in China and the Zen Buddhists brought it to Japan at the end of the 12th century. The ceremony sums up the Japanese people's intuitive striving to recognise true beauty in everything that is simple. It showed calmness, rusticity, gracefulness and the true spirit of the Japanese. This was followed by flower arrangement, Gagaku, Kyogen Kyomai and Bunraku, these being flower arrangement, court music, an ancient comic play, a Kyoto style dance and a puppet play.

On another occasion I experienced one of the most frustrating, yet funny days of my whole Japanese experience. Dear Daughter was at school for the day, this being the first day of the new academic year. I was dutifully met at Nara JR station by a carload of her housewives, armed with pads of notes and questions so that they could entertain me for the day. They were garrulous by nature though communication between us was not easy. The first perfectly rehearsed question was "Are you Mrs Bernadette?" Bernadette, I should explain was my daughter's Australian friend who would teach the housewives whilst she was at her TEFL course. Good start. We commenced our journey to the Hydrangea Temple and to the Horliji temple. The questions poured forth with lots of 'Ahs, Ahs' interspersed. I became Mrs Pato Horno. Lunch was taken, after much discussion, in a noodle place. I decided that I did not want any more Japanese food (quite a decision whilst in Japan) and unfortunately as the meal was paid for me, could not stomach the rice and noodles. They kept asking me what kind of Japanese food I liked – how could I tell them that I had resorted to going to Mac Do's on one occasion?

Afternoon tea was taken, the plum flavoured rice balls were horrible and the arrowroot jelly even worse. The talk then turned to age. They asked me to guess who was the eldest in the room. I told them that in England it was discourteous to ask a lady her age, though they seemed to be obsessed though they found me young for my age; we didn't establish whether or not this meant by age or mentally!

It was on the way home that they decided to dress me in a kimono, this caused great excitement. Asked my favourite colour, I said blue, half hoping that they would not find a blue kimono. The one that they found was dirty so a beautiful gold and cream one was duly produced. The 'oohs were ecstatic. The photographic session even longer with much arranging. A poor tired Dear Daughter was summoned from school to view this astonishing sight. She started to giggle. I actually quite enjoyed the event, especially the part where they said that Japanese women needed padding on the top to fit into these garments but that I did not.

Then followed an English lesson, given by me in return for their hospitality. Dear Daughter was impressed by the slow and deliberate way in which I spoke to them, methinks that is the way that we Brits talk to a lot of foreigners thinking that they understand us more. It reminded me of a Faulty Towers sketch when John Cleese was talking to foreigners and stressed every single word emphatically. The man of the house came home from work, a pleasant guy who unfortunately had only one leg, removing his prosthetic as soon as he got in. The skill with which he manipulated himself around, setting up the table for dinner was unbelievable. I had already presented my gifts to the family, so Dear Daughter came armed with a box of fruit cakes. The lady of the house extracted two of these, I assumed to give to her friends. It was only later that the gentleman of the house showed me where they were. In the corner of the room in which we were to sleep was the family shrine which contained a photograph of the lady's mother and their dead dog. The fruit cake was placed on the shrine to feed them. Dinner was spectacularly served, though thick egg soup was not my forte and I felt awful as the lady had taken so long in preparing the meal. I put the top on the pot in the hope that she would not notice but she did.

Dear Daughter was exhausted after her hard day's toil, not of course to mention my hard day's toil around the temples, so a bath was prepared for us. She asked us if we would like it hot, thinking that she meant hot as opposed to cold, we answered in the affirmative. However, when we got to the bath, not only was it hot, but it was also boiling. It was actually impossible to get into so I ended up having a cold shower.

The night was one of those giggly ones, reminiscent of one's childhood. Laying on our beautifully made futons in the night, the silence was broken by Dear Daughter "If you get hungry, mum you can always eat the fruit cake; she will think they have eaten it." Joking apart, I do feel very strongly that people everywhere should believe in what they want to believe in and a belief in something is better than a belief in nothing. These people are so weird, yet so hospitable, so keen to make an impression that we will enjoy their country, so others will come. Every time one of us got up in the night the lady of the house was waiting behind the partition to check that we were all right, that we had everything that we needed.

On the day of this particular adventure, this nightmare, Dear Daughter and I had left Nara in the morning by train to travel to Kobe where she was attending a Teaching English as a Foreign Language Course. It turned out to be my biggest ordeal. We nearly went back again as we felt that we had left the gas on but we said that we had to overcome that and get on with the day as going back would have meant that we missed appointments. The day didn't begin well as we had just boarded the train and I noticed that everyone was staring at me. It was March and I had very blonde hair, having been in Florida in January and my skin was tanned. I heard the word Gaijin and felt steely eyes upon me and heads turned simultaneously in my direction as I headed up the escalator; was I such a peculiar phenomenon? No answers required. It could truly have been 140 years before.

I had naively booked myself on to a tour of the surrounding area by coach while Dear Daughter was attending her course but whether my naivety was as a result of sheer lack of experience or a certain sort of boldness that it didn't matter, I was invincible; how wrong can you be? We parted and I was dutifully dropped off at the coach station and escorted to my special coach for this exclusive trip around Kobe. We arranged to meet at Shakey's Pizza in the centre of Kobe with a contingency plan that if I got lost we would go to Galleries la Fayette. Of course, we are talking about an age before mobile phones before communication was as it is today so 'lost' would mean 'lost' in no uncertain times.

There were no other westerners on the bus and as the commentary began, I thought 'Help, what on the earth am I going to do now, what am I doing here?' As the guide on the bus prattled on and gave instructions, it occurred to me that I didn't understand Japanese and no one spoke English, well why should they? I was in Japan, they spoke Japanese, and the people on this coach were Japanese. Why on earth would anyone take any notice of a Gaijin? I sat back in my seat No.35 and watched the scenery slip by. The day blossomed into a glorious one.

When we reached the aquarium we all got off of the coach and trailed to the door of the aquarium. Alas, alack I had no idea of the time to rejoin the coach. The driver duly pointed to his watch, indicating the length of time to be spent at each place. I approached the petite courier who had no English and there was a great scene about finding out the time in English. After much confrontation, we decided on a time. After viewing many different fish without knowing one from the other we decided upon a time, I ended up at the dolphins, which was quite amusing but indeed very pleasant because of the warm sun beating down.

Redemption came in a pleasant way as it was here that I met Michiyo, a Japanese teacher of English, her mother and her four year old daughter Roena. Thankfully, they invited me to join their group for the remainder of the tour. I was tapped on the back and my identification badge portrayed the coach I was on and that it was time to get back to the coach as it was leaving.

So, so, so, along the coastal route, the glittering shining sea, marred by structures erected from the sea. Communication was difficult and I never did discover what these were. Lone fishermen dotted the landscape so on with the gentle trip; the commentary chatting on – oh what a surprise I am the only one awake and I cannot understand a word of what they are talking about. At the winery, we had a conducted tour; needless to say it was incomprehensible. The lunch was fine, however. I elected to have the Kobe beef stew. It was tasty and all the better for being washed down with rose wine made at the winery, sweet for a red but pleasant.

Mich and I exchanged addresses and photographs with vows of friendship and drinks to health.

At the next stop, The Foreigners Houses, they got off so I bade farewell to my newfound friends whilst viewing what I think was supposed to be a facsimile of Hollywood.

Alone in Kobe: when I say alone, I mean alone totally on my own, I decided that the weather was too good to waste and boarded the Portliner Monorail to the port. I had visited this before with my daughter so it wasn't entirely new. The voice on the monorail was reminiscent of Disneyland. The next stop will be 'Port Island,' embark here etc.

Here I spent an idyllic two hours, watching the boats coming and going, large liners, and cruise ships, round the harbour trips. I decided to board one but as I walked towards the ship, no one, (I hesitate to say no one) was trying to stop me, I somehow managed to discover that the ultimate destination of said ship was China, whoops, good escape then, image Dear Daughter looking for middle aged mother and discovering that in the space of a few short hours she had self-deported to China on a seafaring vessel.

I first got into panic mode when I realised that I had passed the same stop on the monorail twice but somehow I make it back to the station.

So to the climax of this story. Rendezvous point Shakey's, but where is Shakey's? Walking round and round I passed Printemps several times and begin to get very hot under the collar. I have never in my whole life been so frightened. No means of communication, no way of knowing where I am, where I am supposed to be I don't think that prayer at this stage will be an enormous help for me. At some stage it occurs to me that Shakey's and Haagan Daz are on the other side of the station as you arrive at Kobe.

I traipsed around there, albeit a little 'shakily' now. Finding Haagan Daz renewed my confidence but still no Shakey's. I feel that fear, I see the faces side long so that they do not have to face me or risk that I might ask them a question that they will not understand or cannot answer. I know that in future years I will remember that fear; there are no mobile phones, no means of communication, no common language. I do not know what to do.

What shall I do, where shall I go? I see another face in the crowd, a white one and think that this is someone who can help me. Then she beams, waves. It is Dear Daughter and as my fear subsides, I look up and there above me is the sign for Shakey's. I smile at her, a lovely welcoming smile.

"You found it then," she says.

"No problem,' I say, 'How was your day?"

Patricia Horne

A gaijin in Kobe

Five

When Pat ended her story and the tea had been drunk to the last drop Eddie consulted his mobile phone and saw that all the roads around them were still congested.

"We might as well stay here and have our picnic," he said,

"We're not going anywhere for a while by the look of it and, at least we're in a pleasant spot with a view of the sea."

They agreed and busied themselves in putting their picnic together As they sat down and began to eat Mike murmured,

"Pat's story reminds me of the time my friend Eddie and his wife, Marjorie, were in France a few years ago..."

LOST IN STRASBOURG

Eddie had always thought of himself as a sensible person. He thought he had plenty of common sense and so had always behaved sensibly, not taken drugs and tried not to be drunk in public. He thought he had a reasonable sense of dress and he had always worn sensible clothes and bought sensible shoes and always had a sensible haircut. He had a good road sense and so had bought and driven sensible cars. He had a good sense of humour and a reasonable sense of enjoyment and in that spirit had taken sensible holidays, nothing wild like trekking in the Andes or bungee-jumping in New Zealand, although he had visited both those countries and enjoyed them in a sensible kind of way. In fact New Zealand is a very sensible kind of country, most of the time. He had a sensible job as a teacher, married a sensible and very clever wife and brought up two sensible children who had provided him with six adorable and sensible grandchildren.

However, Eddie lacked one kind of sense and he had to admit it. He lacked a sense of direction ... which is how he came to be "Lost in France," as Bonnie Tyler might sing, but more accurately, lost in Strasbourg.

It had all begun the day before when things had gone quite well, really. Not perfect, but quite well. Eddie and his wife Marjorie had left their home in the west country in mid-afternoon and negotiated the motorway network across the southern part of the country to Ashford, in Kent. They were navigating their way to a Travelodge on one of those off-motorway "leisure parks." The hotel turned out to be, rather unexpectedly, not only exactly where it was supposed to be but also clean, comfortable and, most surprisingly, employing a welcoming receptionist who smiled.

Eddie double checked and yes he smiled as he welcomed them on a cold, November evening to Ashford.

The leisure park had the usual collection of fast-food outlets and a multiplex cinema. It was their intention to spend some time at the cinema where "Bridge of Spies" was showing, this film starring Tom Hanks and Mark Rylance having been strongly recommended to them by a fellow cinemagoer. They decided they would eat first and then return to the cinema. The leisure park featured several eating places and they were faced with a difficult decision – what to eat with their chips? Burger King?, McDonalds?, Nandos? Eventually geography made the decision for them and they hurried, huddled against the bitter cold, to Burger King, the nearest of the fast-food places to the cinema.

About 40 minutes later, having devoured their cheeseburgers and fries with the usual relish they made their way back to the cinema. After taking advantage of the usual facilities Eddie approached the sweet counter which, strangely, was where customers are directed to buy their tickets. The film was due to start in eight minutes so they had the bonus of missing the commercials and trailers.

"Would that be seniors?" the young man behind the counter asked discretely. What a nice young man he was, thought Eddie.

The cinema was very comfortable, the film was just as the stranger had recommended, very good indeed. An enjoyable evening ended with a drink in the rather bleak bar of the Travelodge with the couple listening to an interesting and informative conversation in Bulgarian or Polish or some such language before an early night in preparation for the morrow's excitement.

Saturday morning dawned as expected (always a bonus when you are a "senior," thought Eddie) and they set off early. They avoided breakfast at Travelodge opting instead to stop at a Tesco superstore two junctions down the motorway to fill up with petrol and purchase sandwiches and drinks for their breakfast.

When they arrived at the Eurotunnel terminal they had a few minutes in which to bid goodbye to English sanitation before heading out through the maze of cones to the "waiting area" or "holding area" or whatever it is called. Here they waited or were "held" for some time before boarding their train which, true to form, left one hour late for France.

The Tesco sandwiches and juicy drinks were polished off on the train, a few minutes read of the Times and a very short doze were accomplished and then daylight broke again and they were in

France. So began the next stage of their adventure. They had agreed that they would not programme the address of their hotel into the sat nav until they were actually on French soil. So it was that they discovered that the *Rue des Magasins* towards which they were heading at around 80 mph was not included in the Strasbourg streets which their sat nav could find. "Not to worry," said the intrepid Marjorie who, by now, and as usual, was surrounded by maps of varying scales, "I'll navigate us there when we reach the town." Eddie was not so sure how she could do this but, apparently she had a piece of paper which he had printed off earlier from the hotel's website which contained "simple" directions.

It's a long way from Calais to Strasbourg, 404 miles or 650 kilometres, and takes 5 hours 45 minutes according to the AA route planner website. Of course that's five- and three-quarter hours *driving time* not allowing for toilet or food breaks and on this particular Saturday they were being battered by a very strong cross wind across Northern France which was slowing them down and increasing fuel consumption. Dire weather warnings were coming forth from the car radio as well so they did what all sensible people would do and changed the radio channel.

After a couple of stops for toilets, coffee and the French version of a snack and with his wallet lighter by several euros for tolls, they reached the outskirts of Strasbourg as darkness was falling. Marjorie successfully guided them off the autoroute and into the city streets.

"Round this roundabout and then second on the right," she said, confidently.

There was very little traffic around which was fortunate because the second on the right was, inevitably, proudly displaying a "Road closed" sign or to be exact "*Route barrée.*" Just to be sure a barricade of concrete big enough to stop a Centurion tank had also been placed across the road. At this point Eddie became mildly hysterical, cursing everything French and everyone in France from the president down to the road workers responsible for this calamity (they were, of course, notable by their total absence) but Marjorie remained calm and, thanks to her calmness and not inconsiderable skill, they eventually arrived at a hotel-like building displaying an illuminated sign "*City Residences*."

Eddie parked on the pavement *a la francais* while Marjorie went in to check them in and to discover the whereabouts of the parking facility. They had checked before leaving home that reservation for parking was not required. When she returned her calmness had slipped a little.

"This is not it," she said tersely.

"But it says 'City Résidences,'" Eddie replied, eyeing nervously a small Renault that was attempting to park perilously close and in an impossible tight space.

"Yes, but there are two of them and this one is not ours. Ours is down there" (pointing over her left shoulder) "At the end of the road."

"He turned on the motor and prepared to turn the steering wheel.

"You can't go down there," she said, "It's a one-way street."

"Of course it is," he replied, drily, "It would be, wouldn't it?"

"You need to go all the way round there," she said, pointing ahead. "Then turn left and then left again."

Sighing heavily, Eddie did as she instructed. As they turned left for the second time she said, "There it is, ahead."

Of course, Eddie could not see where she was pointing as he was worrying about the cars which were speeding up from behind them as they joined the main road, which seemed to be one side of a busy dual carriageway emerging from a tunnel which they learned later went under the railway line. Concentrating on these vehicles and their manic drivers Eddie missed the turn and went past the hotel, meaning that they had to repeat the whole manoeuvre once more. Second time round there were fewer Alain Prosts to avoid and he drew up outside the second "*City Résidences*" that they had seen this evening. The only space available was marked "Disabled" but he ignored this and reversed into it narrowly avoiding a young woman on a bicycle.

They checked in and were told that the parking for which there was no need to make a reservation was full. "Oh, how I love French hotels," muttered Eddie. Not to worry, said the young man on reception in almost perfect English, there is a public parking just across the street and they will give you the same discount. Eddie returned to their car to bring in the luggage, coats and so on while Marjorie obtained directions from him for the parking. And then they made the fatal error.

"You stay here and I'll park the car," Eddie said, a schoolboy misjudgement of monumental proportions.

"Right. You go right across this road and turn sharp right at those lights and it's on the right," she said.

He repeated these directions back to her, she nodded and he left.

He negotiated his way across the main part of the street outside the hotel, which was a multi-lane one-way express way, then across the side road adjoining it and up to the light. Eddie was in the right-hand lane. No problem so far. As the lights turned green he turned right and found himself in a lane marked "Right only" (in French of course). No problem as he had been told that the hotel was "On the right." He stayed in that lane, turned right and ...... found himself on the other carriageway of the express way, in the right-hand lane, of course, and heading out of the city.

Oh calamity! Before long the road he was on merged with the autoroute and he was heading away from Strasbourg in the direction of Paris. This was of course the autoroute on which they had come into Strasbourg just a while ago. A few minutes later and the streetlights disappeared and there was Strasbourg brightly lit with twinkling Christmas lights but, unfortunately, in the rear-view mirror behind him. The next 40 minutes as well as being among the longest Eddie had ever known were also among the most worrying. The same thoughts kept going through his mind:

"How will I ever find my way back to the hotel without a map and with a sat nav which knows no more than I do as to where I am supposed to be heading?"

He took the first exit he came to, hoping desperately that there would be a roundabout and he could return the way he had come or maybe that he would see a signpost to Strasbourg but of course not. That would be far too simple. Head towards the lights he thought, so he did. He spent some time finding his way out of a vast lorry park at one point and then followed that experience with finding his way out of a housing estate of several huge blocks of flats.

At one point he stopped and tried to take stock of the situation. He had no money and no credit cards as these were in his coat with Marjorie back at the hotel. He had no map, no address other than "*Rue des Magasins*" as Marjorie had kept the paper with that on with her when she went in the hotel. He tried the GPS on his phone but that could not locate "*Rue des Magasins*" either. Oh, and he had no warm coat either as he had left that back at the hotel too. So he discounted abandoning the car and walking aimlessly, preferring to continue driving aimlessly.

Dispirited, dejected and more than a little anxious he continued his aimless, directionless driving. Eventually, he somehow managed to find his way back into Strasbourg. Strasbourg on a Saturday night in November: The Christmas Fair has just opened. It's cold but clear and crisp. *'I bet the Christmas Market in Birmingham is buzzing right now,'* Eddie thought as he surveyed the empty streets ahead and around him. There was not a soul in sight so on he drove. Eventually, approaching some traffic lights, he saw a young woman walking towards him.

She thought that *Rue des Magasins* was near the railway station. Hope surged in his heart – yes, there were railway lines near where they had parked and the dual carriageway came out from under what could have been railway lines.

"Turn right here and go straight on," she said, confidently, "Keep going straight and you will see the station."

Full of newfound enthusiasm Eddie did as she had said and turned right on to a major road. This looks promising, he thought as he put his foot down cautiously. Imagine his disappointment then when after about half a mile the road split, one half turning right in a gentle curve, the other veering off to the left in another beautiful curve. This was his first such confrontation with the road network in Strasbourg. Ten minutes later when he was hopelessly lost again he was convinced that there is not a straight road anywhere in the whole city. He lost any sense of direction again and ground to another halt. This time his would-be saviour was another young lady who was minding her own business, sitting quietly on her bicycle at a set of traffic lights, when Eddie pulled up beside her. Imagine the shock in her eyes when he asked quietly,

"Excuse me, do you speak English?"

He realised then that French cyclists are not used to car drivers speaking to them from the "wrong" side of the car. To her credit she recovered quickly, screwed up her face in deep thought for a while before saying, just as the lights changed,

"I'm not sure where that is. Sorry," and off she cycled, leaving Eddie unsure where to turn until prompted by a toot from an impatient French driver from behind urging him to make up his mind and get on with it. He drove on for a short distance before pulling over to consider his plight.

He considered his options, which appeared to be:
Option 1: Continue driving around aimlessly until he recognised something that looked like a railway station and then navigate his way from there.
Option 2: Do something else.

The question was: what was the "something else?"

Back at the hotel Marjorie had become concerned that the ten minutes it should take to reach the car park, park the car and walk back had now stretched to an hour. She was still in the lobby of the hotel as she could not manage all their luggage and coats in the lift on her own. She had simply sat in the guest area and awaited Eddie's imminent return, and waited, and waited. Finally, she approached the pleasant young man on reception, told him what had happened and asked him if she could use his phone to call her husband's mobile. She did not have her mobile as it does not work abroad (she says). However, she could not get through for whatever reason. Then she had a flash of inspiration. She asked,

"Will it be OK if I ring my daughter in England? We'll pay for the call, of course"

"*Bien sûr*," he replied.

So it was that somewhere in a dark street in Strasbourg far from any human contact in a car parked on the sidewalk, Eddie's mobile rang.

"Dad; are you alright?"

Explanation followed and his daughter then gave Eddie the number of the hotel so he could call them and ask them to navigate him in.

"But I don't have a pen to write it down and I'll never remember it," he whined pathetically.

She patiently explained how to put the number in the phone and then recall and dial it. They ended the call with Eddie reassuring her that he would text her when he was safely back in her mother's care. He then discovered that he had immediately forgotten what she had told him and couldn't find the number anywhere in the phone! As Del boy would say "What a plonker!" So Eddie rang her back, she explained slowly again and this time they were successful. He drove on for a bit still hoping to see somewhere he recognised before stopping at some traffic lights approaching a major road. There was a bar on the corner and he took a note of its name.

Ten minutes later he limped pathetically into the hotel foyer. As it turned out he had only been a few streets away and as soon as he mentioned the name of the bar the hotel receptionist was able to "talk him in." It meant performing a "U-turn" on a major highway but, by that time he did not care. So - arrived hotel at around 6.30 pm, ready to go up to room at 8.15 pm. They dropped the luggage in the room and then both set off to park the car. This time he avoided the far-right lane and was rewarded by being able to go straight ahead, across the major highway and there, sure enough, was a parking garage. They parked the car and returned to the hotel to prepare to go out for the evening, their priority being to find somewhere to eat. It was at this point that Eddie realised he had "lost" his mobile phone.

So, back to the reception desk they trudged to ask if he had left it there when he returned from his involuntary tour of Strasbourg and district. Of course not. By now the young man must have thought he was dealing with a couple of seniors suffering from dementia or worse. They had no alternative other than to return to the car park and search the car. They could not find it until Eddie somehow managed to squeeze his hand down between the driving seat and the central console and there it was. Why do things always fall down there where you can't see them and, even worse, can't retrieve them? So, by now I was almost 9 o'clock. The Christmas market, which they had come to explore, closes at 9 pm but still, they're in Strasbourg, one of the largest towns in France and it's Saturday night. There are bound to be plenty of restaurants and they will still be open.

Well, they weren't exactly wrong on both counts but there was not a great deal of choice. They walked for about twenty minutes from the hotel into the city centre, over the river, which he had crossed several times during his 'exploration,' but not at this point, noting the presence of police and army vehicles for it was only a couple of weeks after the concert shooting and Stade de France bombing atrocities in Paris and France was still on high alert. They came to a square and there was a brasserie open: "Brasserie Europ'café."

A pleasant waitress assured that there was indeed room for them, although the place was crowded and they were shown to a table for two at one end of the bar. They settled into their seats gratefully appreciating the warmth and conviviality. They perused the menu and Eddie decided to have a burger. 'Who cares? After the day I have had the least of my worries is about calories and cholesterol,' he thought. The waitress returned and Marjorie ordered a salad.

"Pas de problème," she smiled.

Eddie ordered his burger.

"Ah! Pas de burgers, monsieur."

"Oh. OK. I'll have one of these Knock things," Eddie mumbled in his atrocious French. "They're hot dogs aren't they?"

"Ah. Pas de knocks, monsieur"

In the end he ordered a Quiche Lorraine and when it arrived it was delicious and much better for him than a burger or hotdog would have been. The beer was delicious too so he decided to have two. When they ventured outside again the bitterly cold wind dissuaded them from exploring the city further so they returned to their hotel room and the bottle of wine they had thoughtfully brought with them. An early night would help prepare for a long day exploring the city tomorrow.

Strasbourg is different from most other European Christmas markets in that its 300 stalls are spread out over 12 separate locations each illuminated festively. This makes Strasbourg one of the largest Christmas markets in Europe. Its stalls feature craftwork, food and drink and traditional Alsatian Christmas decorations but each different location tends to specialise so, for example, there is one market which specialises in food, another features stalls by charities and so on.

The centre piece of the Christmas lights and decorations is the Great Christmas Tree on Place Kléber . There is a great Christmas spirit everywhere and something to suit every taste within the narrow streets, across the squares and past the historical buildings. But all this was to come for them as on this cold Sunday morning they breakfasted at the Village of Sharing on local delicacies and hot chocolate. The city was gradually coming to life as they approached the main square in front of the magnificent Gothic Cathedral.

They decided that as it was not raining and not too windy, they would take the city's canal boat tour. The boat was covered and the tour guide provided just enough information on what proved to be an interesting ride. The boat goes all the way out to the new EU quarter and includes passing through a lock, an interesting experience and one where visitors on land stare at the visitors in the canal boat who, of course, stare back at them. Most of the tour is through *"Petite France"* and its medieval shops and houses. Even in the dim light of a grey November morning this area which is criss-crossed by narrow lanes, canals and locks possesses oodles of Alsatian charm. The craft Christmas market is situated there each year. The half-timbered houses and the riverside parks attract tourists all year round.

They enjoyed the canal boat trip round this part of the city and returned to the Fish Market cold but invigorated. A harsh wind was blowing now and they agreed it was time for lunch. They wandered back to the Cathedral square and noticed that the restaurants were filling up rapidly. Eating out for Sunday lunch is very popular in France so they were lucky to succeed at their first attempt. They joined the other tourists and some locals in the entrance to a restaurant named *"Le Gruber"* and waited. Yes, there was a table for two.

They beamed at each other and anyone else who happened to be looking their way. *Le Gruber* proved to be warm, cosy with excellent service and a good menu. Eddie had been fearful that here in the heart of Alsace all that would be on offer was the dreaded *"choucrout á l'Alsacienne"* but, no, there was a wide selection and they enjoyed their meal and the wine.

Suitably refreshed and replete they ventured out into the Cathedral square again, perusing, with all the other tourists the market stalls. They made their way to the main shopping area of the town which was much busier now than it had been when they walked through earlier.

That evening they left the hotel and stepped out into the bitterly cold night again, making their way towards *Place Kleber*. The military were still on the bridge stamping their feet and trying to keep warm as they walked towards the town centre . They enjoyed the illuminations which extended over a very wide area and enjoyed a local band who were entertaining the crowds with festive music.

The main market was less busy than they expected and the stallholders were, like the military, doing their best to keep warm. They enjoyed a mug of glüwein before deciding to call it a day, largely influenced by the bitterly cold wind that was whipping around the market stalls.

Sunday, late evening in France.... most restaurants are closed, the bars are largely deserted, it's cold, they're not looking for another full meal, so what to do? Eventually, they found themselves in, of all places, McDonalds! It was cosy, the drinks were hot and they sat there a while until their feet and hands warmed up before deciding to have another early night and finish the bottle of wine in their room.

Monday morning they set off on the five-minute walk to the car park, dragging their suitcase and secretly pleased that the hotel had not charged them for the calls Marjorie had made. They found the car, or rather one of them found the car and the other followed, and there the last adventure of this short break began. The car would not open and it became abundantly clear that the battery was flat. With gritted teeth Eddie grunted,

"Well, I better go down to the office and see what they can do for us."

A young lady was behind the desk in the office as he began haltingly explaining what had happened. At this point an older man appeared and to the relief of both the young lady and Eddie he took over. He spoke no English but explained that he could get a tow truck out which would take them to a Toyota garage but that this would cost about 250 euros. Eddie swallowed, shrugged in the best Gallic fashion and asked him to go ahead. It would be around 45 minutes. He asked why Eddie did not have breakdown cover and he replied that he did but the number to ring was in the handbook which was locked in the car!

He trudged back up to the first floor where Marjorie was guarding the luggage. Eddie remembered at this point that it is possible to extract a small key from the remote control which operates the car doors. He managed this and after several attempts during which he was terrified of breaking the key in the lock he managed to open the driver's door. None of the others would open though. He found the handbook and the number for Toyota roadside relief in Europe and went back down to the office preparing to ask the attendant to cancel the tow truck. Sadly, a lovely lady told him over the phone that his subscription to the service had lapsed and that there was nothing she could do to help, unfortunately. He was just about to ask if he could renew the subscription when a tow truck appeared.

Back at the car, the tow truck driver asked Eddie to open the bonnet which he did and they both peered at the mysteries within. Eddie knew very little about car mechanics but he could recognise a car battery. The problem was.... he couldn't see one! So the battery for a Toyota Prius must be in the boot close to the large batteries which partially power the car. Unfortunately, the boot was still locked. Somehow the gallant monsieur managed to climb into the back seat and by pulling out various seat cushions, seat backs and shelves he found the battery. While doing this he also somehow managed to open the back door as well. Now his task was easy. He connected the car up to his portable battery charger and they were saved. He even put the car back together again for them.

"Now for the painful part," Eddie thought as he wrote out his invoice. Not at all! He was delighted that the bill "only" came to 87 euros; a large bill but much less than he had expected. It's strange isn't it how because of the circumstances he was pleased to be receiving a bill for £63 for starting his car. Ah well, "*C'est la vie!*"

Eddie gave him his card.

"*Ah non; pas de cartes,*" the Frenchman exclaimed.

And so they followed his tow truck to the nearest ATM machine where they both parked on the pavement outside a bank while unconcerned citizens sidestepped around their vehicles without batting the proverbial eyelid.

Fortunately, the sat nav in the car did recognise "Home" when they tapped that in and off they set, an hour later than intended but much earlier than it could have been. Their Eurotunnel train was due to leave Calais at 5.25 p.m. which meant them having to be there by 5 o'clock. It was now 10.30 a.m. Six and a half hours to cover four hundred miles not allowing for stops.

Ther train left on time, which, considering the weather conditions was creditable and as they arrived in Dover at 5.00 p.m. they thought, only the M25, M3 and A303 to go!

Remarkably, their homeward journey was smooth and uneventful and they arrived home, tired but safe having enjoyed their short break. They agreed that despite the difficulties they had endured they had both enjoyed the city and would like to go again! Next time, though, they'll go in the summer and they'll choose a hotel with guaranteed and reserved parking on site!

Keith McHaling

Six

The grandchildren were becoming very restless in the back.

"Will we ever get back home?" they kept asking.

"Of course we will," she replied calmly

"Why don't you tell them the story of your journey home for Christmas when you were in the army, Dad?," murmured his daughter from the driving seat, wishing she had come to fetch her father on her own rather than bringing the twins with her. Her journey wouldn't have been any easier but at least she wouldn't have had to listen to their constant whining!

"Yes, go on Grandad. Tell us the story," they chorused.

"Well, it's not very long," Don said, "But it is a true story."

HOME FOR CHRISTMAS

It is December 1952 and I am in the army doing my compulsory national service in the headquarters of British troops in Austria based in Klagenfurt, the provincial capital of Corinthia.

Everyone would love to get home for Christmas and the New Year, but places on the Medloc C, the sleeper troop train, were very limited. However, my luck was in and I was granted leave and allocated a place on the train. Each compartment comprised four bunks but to enable as many men as possible to travel this number was increased to five, with the fifth man sleeping on the floor on a "bed" made up of blankets donated by the others. With my rank the regimental transport officer put me in charge of the whole carriage and with this responsibility I felt it only right that I could choose which bunk to occupy.

"Oh no," the other four cried, "This is a democracy and we will draw lots to see who gets the floor space."

Need I say where I ended up? I endured one of the most uncomfortable nights imaginable but the prospect of home kept my spirits up and I did eventually forgive my colleagues in arms.

On arrival at the Hook of Holland we boarded the troopship "Empire Vienna" for the night crossing to Harwich Parkeston Quay. The North Sea was very rough and seasickness was rife. We vowed to take preventative measures for our return journey.

That Christmas and New Year with my family and friends in Bournemouth was joyous and I set off for the return journey to Austria with a heavy heart and a degree of foreboding. But it felt good to re-unite with my military pals for the night crossing to Holland, this time aboard the "Empire Wansbeck." We ceremoniously took our travel sickness pills and decided to get our heads down before departure. There ensued an uneventful night's sleep so we decided to go up on deck for some fresh air. But hold on, the surroundings were very familiar. To our chagrin we were still tied up at Harwich because dense fog had prevented the ship's departure! The troopships always operated at night and had no catering facilities, evening meals and breakfasts being served in the respective ports so we survived the day on mugs of tea and hard tack biscuits.

The delay meant that our train journey across Holland and down the Rhine Valley into Austria was severely disrupted. We reached Mallnitz, just inside the British zone and stopped for the night, but our travels were not over as we ran out of food so no evening meal was forthcoming. It was a very disgruntled group of soldiery who disembarked at Klagenfurt station around noon.

I made my way back to my room in Jaeger Barracks, settled in and had a look at the duty roster. And what did I find? I had been listed as Guard Commander at Headquarters for the night of my expected return! A wry smile crossed my face.

Circumstances beyond my control had saved me from a sleepless night.

Don Ruffell

Home for Christmas

Seven

The battery on her I-phone ran out and the girl felt as if her world was coming to an end. It was beginning to get dark and, they were still miles from home, according to her father.

How was she going to pass the time?

Her father came to the rescue with some amusing stories about his work colleagues, past and present, but eventually he ran out of inspiration.

He turned to the girl's mother beside him in the passenger seat,

"Your turn; tell her that story about the French artist - you know, when you were working as a secretary," her father said.

"Well, as a P.A. actually," her mother replied rather proudly.

ONCE UPON A FRENCH GUEST

When it was my turn to tell a story, I decided to relate something that occurred when I was a private secretary to a somewhat snooty Harley Street orthopaedic surgeon in the mid-1960s. I was known then as Deborah Kingsley; Deborah my middle name was what I called myself then, but I remembered that particular summer as if it was yesterday. This is what happened, and how I related it in telephone calls to a medical secretarial colleague over a few weeks.

One hot day in 1965, I was a tiny bit bored. I had typed up the private hospital reports for the last two months for the last two men that had been in-patients at St Edmund's Private Clinic set in its own grounds in Surrey. Copies of the enormous bills sent to them had been made and they had been notified of their post-operative appointments to see my boss Mr Bayliss Wilmington-Smythe in his rooms at Harley Street in a month's time. It only remained to telephone the physiotherapist, Pat, to advise her of their details and that could be put off until the next day as she was easier to contact first thing in the morning.

Unfortunately for me the time was only 4 pm and my hours of work were 9 am to 5.30 pm. What could I do for the remaining time in duty? I wished I had the courage to put on my hat and coat and skip off, but Wilmington-Smythe (often called, mockingly, "His Nibs" by both the NHS secretaries and me), had the irritating habit of phoning me, and them, at 5.25 pm to give some sort of petty instructions when we all knew he was just checking to see that we were still at our desks.

The was a small kitchen shared by the staff in the suite of offices and consulting rooms on our floor. However, at this latter part of the afternoon, no other kettles were being filled or cups being rattled, so I made myself a cup of tea and helped myself to two chocolate biscuits from my private tin. The tin had a glorious picture of Constable's Hay Wain on it which I never tired of. The biscuits were meant to fill a hole in my digestive system until clocking off, as I liked to call it. My skirt swished as I returned to my desk. It was made of grey nylon and toned in with any colour blouse so was a particular favourite of mine.

As I sat at my desk the ‘phone rang and I thought, ‘Just when I wanted a bit of peace and quiet to enjoy my tea and a quick glance through a glossy magazine’ but I picked up, stifling a sigh. I grabbed a shorthand pad and pencil near my right hand ready to make notes if necessary.

“Hello Debbie,” came the familiar voice of Kirsty, one of my two NHS colleagues, from her office in a large Kentish hospital.

“I’ve got a message from His Nibs.” He is not with you, is he?”

“No,” I replied, somewhat relieved at finding the caller to be Kirsty Beck.

“Well, I’ve got a message for him from a Dr Button who wants him to do a home visit to a film director whose broken wrist was operated on abroad and not done too well, by the sound of things. May I give you all the gen?”

“Yes, great,” I said and took down the patient’s address, GP’s phone number and told Kirsty to leave it with me.

“I understand from His Nibs,” Kirsty went on, “That his son Miles is coming home from Paris and they are quite excited as they haven’t seen him for a year. It looks as though there’s going to be a lot of fuss made. He kept on about how his mother dotes on him but that Miles costs him a bomb!”

“Yes,” I commented, “He’s over the moon and so is Fay, his mother. He is still her little darling, so to speak. Apparently Miles is bringing a French friend over so he can show off the sights of London. I’ve been given the task of booking a box at the Opera and they are holding a dinner party to show him off – Miles’ friend that is. I’ve got the impression Pierre, his pal, is well-known in Paris, so knowing what snobs the parents are, they want a bit of the kudos, I suppose. Sadly, for me, I’ve been invited to the said dinner party and instructed to bring Jerry, my fiancé along. I gather we are part of the younger element for Miles and his guest as a balance to the old fogies!“

"Some of them aren't too bad, actually," I continued, "Colonel Cartwright, His Nibs' friend from school days, is coming with his wife Violet, and they are really nice but some of the others I don't know; 14 in all. Two of them are girl cousins of Miles and sound quite good fun."

"Crumbs," blurted out Kirsty, "Do you speak French? I've never got past school-girl level myself."

"Not fluently, but I can get by," I replied, "However, Miles speaks the language very well and I understand Pierre has some English. He is, according to Miles, 'a painter fellah' that he met in some art gallery where he was working, so he might get some commissions here. I'll let you know what happens , shall I?"

"Definitely. But what's Miles like really, his looks and all that?" Kirsty asked.

"Oh he's a weedy looking fellow! Takes after his mother, being fair and slimmish; not portly like his father and looks nothing like him either. Agreeable though, quite nice natured. I understand Pierre has recently broken up with his girlfriend so Miles thought a trip England for a few days might cheer him up."

I had a quick drink of my tea and looked at my fingernails as I was talking to Kirsty and decided that I needed to paint them some delicious shade of cherry red before attending the beano at my boss's London home. Also, the nails would look nice with the beige, silk cocktail dress I planned to wear.

"Well, best of luck, Debbie. I'll be all agog to hear what happens," said Kirsty before she rang off after a final goodbye.

I did a few more jobs before ending the day and headed home, deep in thought, not particularly looking forward to the ordeal of what promised to be a stuffy dinner party with the sort of people the Wilmington-Smythe's were likely to invite. However, I had Jerry for support and he was a good conversationalist. He was a solicitor and kept fit by playing rugby out of office hours and was a calming influence against my panicky nature! Also, because he was a solicitor, he was naturally interested in the fact that Miles was studying international law in Paris but, at the same time, was earning extra money by working in bars in the evening. His parents gave him a fairly generous allowance to pay for his apartment and living expenses but Miles liked to keep busy and do a bit of self-funding.

It was some time after that fateful dinner party that I had a chance to give Kirsty Beck the rest of the story. She had gone on holiday with her cycling club to the Lake District, caught a bug and then had to have some time off sick. I got this from Deirdre Marshall who, although she worked in a different hospital group, was in touch with Kirsty's office and colleagues, and also did secretarial work for Wilmington-Smythe.

It was a busy morning, a couple of weeks after I heard that Kirsty had been ill, when I finally caught up with her, on the telephone, to give her some names and addresses of people to go on the waiting list. After asking after her health and being reassured that she was now fit and well again after her adventures on the Hardknott Path in the Lake District and her enforced stay in Ambleside Youth Hostel being nursed by the warden's wife. While this was going on, I had been looking out of my window watching a blackbird paddling his feet after a brief shower of rain and then pulling out a juicy worm from the ground and eating it. All of a sudden, I didn't feel like eating my own lunch!

"Enough about me," eventually said Kirsty, "How did Miles and his French friend's stay go? Presumably, they have gone back now?"

I took a deep breath as I remembered the events of that visit.

"The evening at the Opera went well enough, although how much Pierre understood of 'Aida' I don't know, but I thoroughly enjoyed it and Miles said Pierre was fascinated by the experience of being in a box. The dinner party which was held on the second evening of his stay was a different matter altogether. The Wilmington-Smythe's had asked people to attend 7.30 pm for drinks and chat before the dinner was served. We managed to park OK and we were greeted warmly so that was a good start. I had taken Fay some pink and white roses which she seemed to like and Miles introduced us to Pierre. He was actually very good looking in a Latin sort of way; quite dark hair, slim and spoke English with a very heavy accent, but quite charming"

"What did he wear at the dinner party?" enquired Kirsty.

"I had a feeling Miles kitted him out in a lounge suit as they are of similar build. I can't remember the colour of his shirt but he was certainly very presentable. Aged around 28-30 just a bit older than Miles. I really liked him so that's why I feel so sorry for him and how it turned out."

I looked down at my fingernails, they wanted painting again.

"Sorry for him?" repeated Kirsty, "Why?"

"Well, it's what happened later," I explained. "We all sat down at a magnificently dressed table with two small vases of peachy coloured roses top and bottom. The atmosphere then was friendly and bubbly over the first course which was French onion soup with rolls, then a small fish dish. The main course was chicken in a mushroom sauce and the conversation was flowing quite nicely. People were asking Miles where he had met Pierre which was in one of the art galleries. It was at this point that Sir Walter Pymm a director of a manufacturing business in Essex said to Pierre,

'So, you're an artist are you? Well, young man, I'm after someone to paint a portrait of my wife, Lady Lucienne here, for her birthday. She is French, like yourself, so what could be more fitting than a fellow countryman having the commission. Would you be interested and have you any of your work with you that I can see?'

"I'm not sure that I can manage Pierre's accent when he replied but I'll try just to give you the atmosphere, Kirsty," I finished up.

"Oh, yes, do try," enthused Kirsty, so I continued the story.

"Your wife, she ees ver' beautiful," said Pierre, looking at Lady Lucienne who sat at the table with her gorgeous raven black hair piled up on her head in a majestic bun. She wore a stunning

Christian Dior black cocktail dress with a three-strand pearl necklace. She was every inch an elegant Parisienne.

"Alas, 'owever, it ees wiz regret I must decline zis 'onour as I am a painter and decorator in zee art gallery, not a painter of zee portraits," explained Pierre.

I continued,

"There were a few indrawn breaths around the table, the only sound that cut through the silence. Lady Lucienne asked Pierre which Art Gallery he worked in and there was a whispered reply which I didn't catch. Then she looked puzzled for a moment and suddenly exclaimed out loud that she remembered something of a scandal a few years before that linked his name and the gallery after a painting by Degas was stolen"

"You were involved," she said, wagging her finger at him. "You gave some security details away and were imprisoned for it if I remember rightly!"

I paused a moment before saying,

"Some minutes elapsed and you could have cut through the atmosphere with a knife. Then after this awful interval His Nibs just exploded. 'Miles,' he bellowed down the table to his son, 'What do you mean by bringing a painter and decorator here when you said he was an artist; and a felon at that! Answer me!'"

"That's not fair," Miles glared at his father. "I said no such thing. I 'phoned you and mother asking if I could bring my friend Pierre for a visit and said he was a 'painter fellah.' I was perfectly honest and what does it matter anyway?"

"What does it matter?" stormed his father. "I have invited all these people here in the mistaken belief that Pierre is a famous artist and have entertained him on a scale befitting his importance and now you have the temerity to say that he's a painter and decorator like any Joe Bloggs you could meet in the street." Mr Wilmington-Smythe continued to glare at his son; he was red in the face with anger.

"Oh crikey," squeaked Kirsty in gales of a mixture of awe and laughter, "I shouldn't giggle, it must have been so embarrassing for you all."

"It wasn't really for me and Jerry. I suppose you could say it was the most entertainment at a dinner party we had ever had, but we felt sorry for Pierre"

"What happened after that, then," asked Kirsty.

"The rest of the courses got served around some embarrassed snippets of conversation. Miles' cousins and ourselves were the only ones talking to him and Pierre and we tried our best to carry on as normal. Pierre said he had only talked in all innocence to some people in a café having no knowledge of them or their previous crimes. He wasn't one of the gang and it was unfortunate that something that he had overheard by accident in the gallery in respect of security, he had repeated, not realising that it was of great importance. He realises now that he was naïve and, in fact, he was released on appeal and the sentence was quashed."

"Golly, what an experience for him," commented Kirsty, "But do go on."

"I really think His Nibs losing his temper served no good purpose. Sir Walter and Lady Lucienne hurried over their coffee, made their excuses and went. So, it all broke up quite early although the men that were left did stay for some port and we ladies were taken to the Regency drawing room, which was quite charmingly decorated. But there was an atmosphere after that, very awkward and stilted so we also thanked them for their hospitality and left as soon as we were able to do so," I concluded.

"How terrible for poor Pierre and Miles too," commented Kirsty.

"Oh that wasn't the end of it apparently," I went on. "The next morning I was back at my desk and Miles came into the office saying that his parents had asked him to leave so could I get them an earlier flight back to Paris. They wouldn't even let the chauffeur take them back to the airport either."

"Did you manage to fix things for them?" Kirsty asked.

"Yes, and a bit more, actually. Got their tickets changed, then phoned Jerry and he was good enough to drop things in his office and take them to Heathrow so they went on the 3pm Trident flight. Miles has phoned me since and said we would always be welcome at his flat so we might take him up on his offer some time. So that appears to be end of it. However, they haven't cut him off financially and I don't think they would ever do that. It now remains for the Wilmington-Smythe's to live it all down."

I giggled and then added,

"You know Kirsty it is a jumble of a Very Important Painter or not as the case may be. But we will be having a breather from them. His Nibs has rearranged his workload and he and Fay are having three weeks in Italy from next week!"

"Smashing!" came the happy comment from down the 'phone in deepest Kent.

Audrey Stewart

Eight

Sometimes when we are sitting idly doing mothing in particular we can tell ourselves a story and sometimes we can just reminisce about times gone by.

This is what our next story is – a reminiscence.

Sitting on a coach which was seemingly going nowhere, her husband asleep beside her, Julia remembers her school days as if they were only yesterday.

MEMORIES OF BOARDING SCHOOL LIFE 1949-1955

The raucous sound assaulted my ears and jerked me out of my subconscious ramblings. It was a ghastly noise to wake anyone up with. Around me in the other beds, all covered with dark blue counterpanes, sleepy forms groaned and shifted in preparation for dragging themselves out to face another day. Some indeed had already risen and were hurriedly washing (a 'lick and a promise' we called it) and dressing. The rising bell, like a highly magnified telephone bell ringing insistently in the corner of the dormitory, woke us at 6.45 a.m. every day: most girls had until 7.10 to get downstairs and report for 'morning office.' The chosen few who were excused this duty (they were dining hall girls in the other half of term, or in their GCE term) could rest until a second bell, as long as they arrived for breakfast at 7.30.

At various times my morning office involved sweeping down a staircase, cleaning a classroom, cleaning out four baths, peeling, with three companions, a seemingly endless stack of potatoes and, the worst of all, dining-hall girl. This last was acknowledged by those in authority to be a heavy duty and, therefore, one only bore it for half a term. There were eight girls whose job it was to polish the tables every day until they shone, lay cutlery and crockery sufficient for ten on a tray, carry it from servery to dining-hall and lay their table for breakfast. They were also responsible for clearing their tables after meals and washing up. Eight people washing up for eighty is a deadly task, especially with thin tea towels which were sodden when just a few things had been wiped. Being a dining-hall girl meant being late upstairs after breakfast, late for morning games, late for 'prep' after tea. The polish put on the tables so painstakingly was jealously guarded by its owner and one risked incurring her wrath if one was careless enough to spill a cup of tea and spoil the shine.

Morning 'games' lasted from 8.30 to 8.45 after beds had been made and dormitories swept. We had two drives, a short one and a long one, whose length was said to be one furlong. In order to keep us in trim (we believed an insurance against the stodgy diet) someone had dreamed up the idea of making us run up and down the long drive eight times – precisely a mile each day. This was hated by most but had to be endured, nevertheless. The gym mistress used to stand at the house end of the drive to make sure no malingerers stood about and thus avoided completing the eight laps. In cold weather we still ran; only torrential rain provided an escape. More games were organised every day at the end of afternoon school. Hockey and netball were played in the winter terms, cricket, rounders and tennis in the summer. If bad weather precluded holding this games period, we were marched off, two by two, in a 'crocodile' for a brisk walk around Westbury village. This we rather looked forward to as a change of scenery and an escape from hockey sticks, bruises and muddy legs.

As Juniors we hardly went out and the school grounds, although ten acres in area, did appear to be prison-like as the weeks went on. I remember walks in 'crocodile' to the public library and on Sunday to church. We had very sober Sundays. Those who were confirmed rose early to attend Holy Communion. After breakfast the first and second forms had a piece of scripture to learn by heart, for the first form the collect for the day, while the second formers learnt the epistle. This had to be recited to the mistress on duty before our departure for Matins. On the nursery landing was a notice giving instructions as to dress, usually black velour hats, best coats (these were red and usually much too big) gloves, black stockings and shoes. If rain threatened, we were instructed to carry umbrellas. In the summer we wore straw hats and white gloves, sometimes going without coats. The school purchased sets of dresses, coats and hats in eighties, which the matron then allotted as best she could, according to size. Small wonder if some were a bad fit. When all the girls were assembled in the yard the headmistress walked down the line inspecting us for correct dress. Then we set off for the mile walk to St. Alban's.

Church was a pleasant episode for most of us. The church was a lively, full one, the vicar interesting; we felt rather smug when members of the congregation looked at us, as we thought, admiringly, and best of all we could see the choirboys. We doted on these boys and any who had the minimum of good looks was assured of a devoted following. We even volunteered to attend Evensong for the pleasure of seeing our favourites again. At the evening service an anthem was sung, sometimes with one of the boys singing solo: if the soloist were handsome too we were almost overcome with emotion.

After lunch on Sundays an arrangement called 'house reading' took place. Four rooms were allotted and we departed to them for an hour's silent reading, each with her own book. Sunday meals were an improvement on weekday ones. We had cereal for breakfast, instead of the usual grey porridge, a roast lunch with fruit salad to follow, cakes with our tea and butter instead of margarine for our bread. Because it was Sunday we sang a special, longer Latin grace with responses. I never bothered to find out the meaning of this one. Normally we sang 'Benedictus, benedicat per Jesum Christum dominum nostrum' before meals and 'Te Deum' afterwards. They sounded rather like plainsong and we liked them, but, eventually, after three times a day all the term we became very parrot-like in our singing and ceased to think about the meaning of the words. There was, in any case, a rush to sit down and start the meal. We were always hungry. Bread was plentiful though we only had about half a cubic inch of margarine to spread on it. We managed, by scraping it on, to make the margarine stretch to four slices of bread. The bread came in long loaves, about twice the length of normal ones and was cut on a dangerous looking slicing machine kept in the kitchen. There was a story that a maid once cut off her finger in it and that her screams were heard on the top hockey field.

Weekends did give us some time to ourselves when we could indulge the latest craze. Apart from interminable talking, of which we never tired, we graduated from dressing up and acting or cops and robbers type games to monopoly and, eventually, to card games. We gambled at Newmarket and our favourite, pontoon. We normally used buttons but once we hit on the idea of plastic mugs, which were stored in high stacks in the domestic science room. We would look at our first card and ostentatiously plonk a stack of ten mugs down as a stake. We realised the hilarity of it then but it makes me smile now to think of twelve-year-olds gambling with plastic mug stakes. Some of our form were bookworms and Saturday saw them avidly devouring a Cronin novel and weeping copiously at the sad bits. A really good book had queues lined up for it. Frank Yerby was considered 'hot stuff' and we read any of his books we could get hold of in the public library. Once seven of us contributed sixpence each to buy 'Lady Chatterley's Lover' in the village bookshop. We were disappointed to find no four-letter words, as, of course, it was an expurgated edition.

Bedtime for Juniors was 8 p.m., silence ball at 8.20 and lights out. We had four dormitories, twenty girls in each. Between lights out and 9 p.m. when the Seniors came to bed, we had a marvellous time. In the winter we stayed snug in our beds in the dark while one girl, a bit of an actress, entertained us with ghost stories. She had a repertoire which included Edgar Allen Poe and once she told us the story of Jane Eyre in episodes as she read the chapters during the day. When it was light in the summer we used to read, if we could smuggle books up into the dormitory (only bibles were allowed really) or we played games, absurd games, driving our iron bedsteads back and forth on their castors by kneeling at the foot and bouncing up and down. We had to beware of the matron looking in but as long as we kept the noise level down, we were undisturbed. The last night of term was an excuse for racing up and down outside fire escapes, visiting other dormitories and general tomfoolery until late at night. The Seniors joined in these escapades and no-one was ever caught. The matron and staff indulgently left us to ourselves. I wonder that no-one was ever injured with all the running about over skylights and roofs that went on.

It all happened nearly forty years ago (as I write this in 1988). I should I'm sure find great changes if I| went back now. My school friends are middle-aged but we still keep in touch. This episode in our lives has marked us for ever. We thought we hated it at the time, but I look back now with nostalgia.

Julia Cann

Memories of boarding school life, 1949-1955

Nine

On the same coach, also with her sleeping husband beside her, Deborah, too, was reminiscing about her early years and school days.

GROWING UP ON PORTLAND

First, let me explain. Portland is an island connected to the rest of Dorset by Chesil Beach. At one time there was a gap in the causeway which was serviced by a ferry but now there is a single roadway. This is why one lives 'on' Portland as opposed to 'in.'

I was born in Gloucester during the second world war. My very first memory was of taking my sister, Moira, home from Weymouth hospital where she was born. I was allowed to have her feet on my lap! We were then living with my paternal grandmother at 53 Wakeham as she was a widow and lived alone. My second memory is of an air raid warning when Moira and I were taken downstairs from the attic where we were sleeping to a shelter under the table in the dining room. I can remember us all sitting squashed in as the shelter was not large, and Moira was a very tiny baby. Portland suffered quite a lot of bombing because it has a large, deep water harbour and was home to the Royal Navy. It also played an important part in the D Day landings.

My grandmother's house seemed quite large to me then. It had a 'front room' with a piano, some chairs and a gateleg table with barley sugar twist legs which I loved. Behind that was the dining/sitting room and behind that a little parlour which still had gas lights on the walls. I remember grandma doing her ironing using two flat irons which she warmed on the fire alternately. She would spit on them to see if they were hot enough. She nearly always wore a hat, even indoors, which was not surprising as she had been a milliner.

Behind the parlour was the scullery which had a sink, a gas cooker and an old copper built into the corner, which had space for a fire underneath it to heat the water on washday. Outside in the yard was an iron mangle through which the washing was rolled to squeeze out as much water as possible before it was hung on the line. In the garden were some fruit bushes and vegetables which my father tended. At various times he also kept rabbits and bantams for food. He even tried to use the skin of the rabbits to make gloves, but without much success - they were always very stiff. Curing animal skins is not easy!

The attic was a very special place as it contained lots of treasures and mementoes brought home by uncle Claude and uncle Syd from their travels in the RAF. One I remember well was a small pipe, about 2 inches long. If you looked into the bowl there were tiny pictures, but I don't remember the subject. There was also a box of dressing up clothes, including a couple of fox furs which had belonged to Grandma, Eliza Jane, nee Attwooll, one of the old Portland families, the others being the Stones, the Pearces and the Combens.

When the war finished we moved to a rented house a few doors down the road at No 85 Wakeham. I remember wheeling some things down there in a wheelbarrow. This was the house where Moira and her husband, Brian, still live, but it is almost unrecognisable as the same place. When we were children it had two small rooms and a kitchen downstairs and three bedrooms upstairs but no bathroom, which was common at that time. The attic was reached by a ladder which hung on hooks on the upper landing. The toilet was built adjoining the outside of the kitchen at the end of the small yard. Because we had to brave the weather to go to the toilet, we developed good bladder control! We also had a strip of garden where dad grew vegetables. Just outside the yard was a coalhouse where the coalman tipped the coal, and behind that was a wooden shed where we used to play schools and houses in the summer.

Behind the row of houses were fields where dad had an allotment, and behind this was a quarry which was being worked. . Portland stone had been used by Christopher Wren to build many London churches, including Saint Paul's cathedral, and more recently it was used to build the Cenotaph in Whitehall. There are areas of scrub land below the cliffs on both sides of the island where waste stone and spoil from the quarries used to be dumped. These areas are called 'the Weares.' On the path down to the East Weares is a large piece of stone looking like a butter pat on which can be seen the mark of Christopher Wren, an upturned wine glass. I don't think it is known why this piece was rejected.

Every day, at least once a day, the quarrymen would blast the stone out and a warning hooter would sound. The blast made the windows rattle. At twelve o'clock every day another hooter would sound to signify the lunch break and tens of men would stream out of Bumpers Lane on their way home for lunch. I remember that a lot of them would have string tied around their legs below their knees. Not sure whether this was to shorten their trousers or to keep animals from crawling up their legs! One word a Portlander would not utter was 'rabbit' They were referred to as 'they furry things' or underground mutton' and were considered unlucky. This quaint superstition continues to this day. The mass exodus from the quarries was repeated at five o'clock. All day long huge lorries drove up the road continuously carrying enormous blocks of stone destined for buildings all over the country, many of them in London. At the same time, empty lorries came down the road to pick up another load. In earlier times the huge blocks of stones would be dragged up the road by a team of eight horses in a line, which explains why the road is so wide.

Although these heavy lorries drove continuously up and down the road, there were very few cars. Consequently, Moira and I and our friends often played out on the pavement in front of the house. I remember learning to ride on roller skates and having a tricycle and a scooter which we rode outside. The weather was always fine and the sun always shining (in my memory!) and in the summer we would also play in the fields at the back of the house. We used to make dens in the grass and collect wildflowers or play hide and seek and cowboys and Indians in and around the ruins of a farmhouse that had been bombed in the war.

Nowadays, the stone firms are obliged to fill in land they have quarried, but in my childhood there were many smaller quarries which were just holes in the ground. There was one such just behind our house and it was used by the locals, including my family, as a refuse tip. Any unwanted items were 'thrown down the quarry' in the assumption that one day it would be filled in. I imagine now that there would have been many quite valuable items disposed of this way and buried for eternity!

Holidays like Easter were always special because dad would finish work at mid-day on Thursday and we would meet the bus at Bumpers Lane. I remember that his clothes always smelt of oil and he wore heavy work boots, like Doc Martens with reinforced toes. On Sunday afternoons in summer when the weather was good we would all go down to the Weares for a walk or to Church Ope, a cove at the bottom of a flight of about 150 step, overlooked by the ruins of Rufus castle which was built by William Rufus, son of William the Conqueror. Dad had camped on the Weares as a youth and knew all the paths like the back of his hand. We picked (dreadful to think of it nowadays!) primroses, cowslips and even bee orchids and castle orchids to take home in a bunch. They still grew there in abundance until the 1970's but I haven't seen any lately. Later, when I was at the Grammar school in Weymouth, our science teacher would send us out to collect as many different wildflowers as possible for homework. Some Portlanders could find as many as 50 species. If only we had known then what we know now! Sometimes we went down on to the rocks and fished for little fish with a piece of string and a bent pin, using limpets for bait. I consider myself fortunate to have lived there at that time, although Portland still has many interesting walks if you know where to go.

Occasionally we would go to Portland Bill at the weekend where grandma had a hut which was shared by the family. The huts are still there and were originally fishermen's' huts. We would meet our cousins there and play ball in the field or fly kites. I have seen skylarks' nests in the grass at the Bill. The old lower lighthouse is now a bird observatory and is used by birdwatchers to look out for migratory birds which visit Portland on their way to or from distant countries. Sometimes we went along to where the crane winched the little fishing boats up on to the cliff and dad would buy a crab or a lobster for tea. They were cooked up in a bucket on the gas stove. Lobsters went into boiling water and died quickly, but crabs were boiled up in cold water and I remember poking them down with a wooden spoon when they tried to climb out of the bucket.

The kitchen at 85 Wakeham was small and most of it was taken up with the bath, which was covered by a pull down wooden cover which provided a work top. Water was heated in a copper boiler and drawn off in buckets. This was also the means of heating water on washing day on Monday, when the washing would be done in the Belfast sink. The bottom sheets and pillowcases would be washed every week and rung out by hand. A blue bag was put into the last rinse water to make the whites 'whiter than white.' The washing was then put through a mangle in the yard, before being hung on the line which ran the length of the garden and was hoisted up by a pulley in the middle.

We spent most of our time in the back room - the front room was only used for special occasions such as when visitors came, or at Christmas. It had a built in glass cupboard which housed all the special china and glass. The piano was also there, so when I had piano lessons I spent more time in the front room practising. The fire was only lit on special occasions. If anyone we knew or a neighbour died, the venetian blinds would be drawn to shut out the light and as a mark of respect.

The back room housed a settee, an easy chair, a table and four chairs. The floor was covered in linoleum and a large rug covered the middle of it. There was also a sideboard with the canteen of cutlery on the top. In each alcove was a built in cupboard and next to the window was the wireless. I used to love sitting on the arm of the chair to listen to Children's Hour and Listen with Mother, which always began, ' Are you sitting comfortably? Then I'll begin.' I also remember a program called, 'At the Luscombes' which was a forerunner of 'The Archers,' and another called 'Journey into Space' which was pure fiction long before any space programmes began.

We always ate around the table and the food was fairly plain. We had bread and butter with everything, presumably to make meat and vegetables go further. Dad used to grow vegetables on his allotment and as there were no fridges, let alone freezers, we ate whatever was in season for however long it lasted. It was no good not liking broad beans if that is what was for tea with a slice of bread and lashings of butter, salt and pepper. No food was wasted. A special treat was a Portland dough cake which was usually bought in Easton but sometimes was made at home.

The only heating in the house was an open fire in each of the two downstairs rooms. There were also fireplaces upstairs, but I don't remember those being lit, unless we were ill. The grate was polished with Zebrite blacking, and the fire had to be cleaned out and laid each morning. In winter the house was freezing until the fire was going. Dad usually got up first and brought us all a cup of tea in bed while he lit the fire. The coal was kept in a coal scuttle beside the fireplace and this had to be filled every day. Sometimes in the winter when it was very cold and the wind was whistling in from the East, we washed in a bowl in front of the fire. Otherwise we washed in the kitchen at the sink and had a bath once a week on a Sunday. This involved clearing the work top, boiling up the copper and filling the bath and took quite a while. Moira and I used to bath together when we were small, followed by mum and dad, just adding more water each time.

Our house was typical of the small stone cottages on Portland and they remain today, mostly in terraces with no front gardens and just a small patch at the back. They are invariably built of stone and stand up well to the sometimes harsh weather.. Thomas Hardy describes them well in a book called 'The Well-beloved' about three generations of women called Avice. At the bottom of Wakeham, the street where I lived, is a small cottage which was then and still is the Portland Museum, a fascinating place to visit. It is called Avice's Cottage, after the Hardy novel. The narrow lane to the side of it leads to Rufus Castle, the East Weares and Church Ope

We used to walk to school together in the charge of older children. Sometimes we would stop in Easton Gardens and have a turn on the swings. This backfired on us once (or probably more) when Moira fell off the seesaw and had to be taken home with a bloody nose. The favourite part of the walk was over the pedestrian footbridge at the bottom of Channel View, especially when a train was passing underneath it and I can still remember the smell of the smoke. The steam train used to run from Weymouth to Easton under the cliffs on the eastern side of the island. It was a beautiful ride but was axed in the 60's and the track was dug up Unfortunately, it cannot be reinstated as a huge sewage pipe was then laid along it. One of the things which we children liked to do was to put a halfpenny on the line just before the train arrived. If the coin did not fall off with the vibration, the weight of the locomotive would flatten it so it looked like a penny! Our parents would have had a fit had they known what we got up to.

School for both of us was St George's Infants School in Reforne, another single word street name like Wakeham These are quite common on Portland. I can still remember learning to write on a slate with chalk. I enjoyed school, but not playtime - I was very shy and did not mix well. School dinners were not memorable, except my favourite which was minced beef with shredded carrot. Looking back, spotted dick and custard also went down well.

At the age of seven we went to the Tophill Junior School which was in the downstairs of what became the Secondary school. . My teachers were Miss Hopkins, Mrs Gilbert, Mr Maidment and Miss Slade in that order. The head teacher was Mr Flann. My first day at junior school was marred when I lost my banana! I left it in the hall during assembly, not realising we would not be returning later. Mrs Gilbert was particularly fierce and used to slap knuckles with a ruler if we misbehaved. Mr Maidment's family kept the post office in Easton. He was very interested in nature study and used to take us on walks in the summer. Miss Slade was a 'large' lady, fond of needlework, and she read an abridged version of 'Les Misérables' to the class, which I particularly enjoyed. We had to take the 11+ exam in our fourth year. I did not want to go to the Grammar School, which was in Weymouth, but I wanted to be a secretary. However, I had an interview for the Grammar School and was sent there regardless, which I soon came to enjoy.

Looking back, I was very fortunate to grow up in such a unique place, surrounded by the sea and with so many intriguing playgrounds. I couldn't wait to leave when I finished my studies but now take every opportunity to visit and am proud to have been a Portlander, descended from one of the old island families. I recommend you to visit Portland if you have the chance.

Deborah Beck

Growing up on Portland

WW ✓ IS ✓ ER - not end!

Ten

Sadly, many of us have been' taken for a ride' at some time or other, particularly when we are young and, perhaps, a little naïve.

At least our young man in the next story seems to have had the last laugh.

Even if he did have to wait over twenty years for it!.

The young man in question, now much older and, perhaps a little wiser, chuckled to himself as he stared at the vehicle in front of him and remembered....

THE STUDENT'S STORY

Her name was Jane. She had the most beautiful red hair which she showed off by wearing it long, over her shoulders. It cascaded like a luxuriant, sunlit waterfall and attracted the eyes of every man who passed. She was sitting on a bar stool at the end of the bar as I walked in. I strode straight past her, not really seeing her in any detail and ordered a 'half pint of mild.' I handed the barman a shilling and received some change.

It was 1963. I was a first-year student at London University. I was not housed in a Hall of Residence but, rather, staying in "digs" in Camberwell. I had fallen on my feet in this respect as my landlady was quite exceptional. Back in the 1960s students from relatively low-income families like my own could obtain a grant which covered their tuition fees, living accommodation and their meals. Mrs Hunter, my landlady, not only provided delicious meals every evening if we required them but also cooked for us at weekends. She even did our laundry for us too! How lucky we were. Now, sixty years later, progress in education has been such that one of my granddaughters not only has a master's degree but also a student loan debt of £100,000.

But, back to 1963. I was really happy at Mrs Hunter's and grateful that the powers that be had sent me to her. She had been having university students for many years and always integrated them firmly into her family's life in their large home in Grove Lane. Her husband was a jovial character who had retired a few years earlier and they had a son who lived close by and a daughter who was in the process of getting married. She always had two students and I was sharing a large bedroom on the third floor of their spacious, Edwardian home with a fellow football fan called Mike. We got along well and enjoyed each other's company. Our interest in football was shared with some other fellow students and the four of us would play for our college third team on Saturday mornings then usually hotfoot it up to 'Town,' as everyone called it to watch some of the top teams play at Tottenham, Chelsea, Fulham or West Ham. Times were very different then and it was possible to get into a match just by queuing at the turnstile. Matches usually finished around 4.30 to 5.00 pm and then we would spend Saturday evening in one of the local pubs. But all that was about to change, for me, anyway.

A few days before I had confided in Mike that I was plucking up courage to ask a girl in one of our tutor groups out for a drink. Her name was Heather and she had caught my eye on several occasions. My bad luck was that Mike was also in that particular tutor group.

"You're too late, mate," he smirked, "I've already asked her out on Saturday evening."

"Oh….. "Well, I hope you have a good time," I said through gritted teeth, hoping in vain that I was disguising my disappointment.

As it happened Brian and John, our other two footballing friends, were also busy on that coming Saturday as there was a social event at their Hall of Residence, which meant that for the first time since I had arrived in London I was to be alone on a Saturday night. The prospect filled me with gloom. I knew I could always stay in and watch TV with the Hunters, but to my juvenile mind that made me look like a loser. What to do? I decided I would go to the pictures. At that time the biggest and best cinema in that part of southeast London was the Lewisham Odeon and that's where I decided I would spend my Saturday evening. Although the cinema was officially the Gaumont Palace everyone referred to it as the Odeon. I never discovered why.

I couldn't remember ever having gone to a cinema on my own and that's why I found myself in the Rising Sun cradling my half pint of 'Mild,' traditionally the drink of all impoverished students.

I silently cursed myself for having forgotten to bring something to read as I sat there gloomily staring into space and sipping my drink. I had grown used to making a drink last as long as possible but, on this occasion, found my glass almost empty after less than half an hour. Mentally checking my finances, I decided to throw caution to the winds and order another 'half.' The pub was more crowded now and I found myself standing next to the red headed girl as I waited to catch the barman's attention.

“Waiting for someone?,” a soft voice beside me asked.

I looked round in surprise. It was her, and she was talking to me.

Trying to conceal my surprise at being spoken to, I replied without considering my words carefully,

“No. I’m off to the pictures in a minute.”

“On your own?”

Before I had time to reply the barman approached and I ordered my drink. Again, without thinking, I turned to her and asked,

“Would you like a drink?”

“Well, thanks, that’s very kind of you. I’ll have a gin and tonic please.”

My heart skipped a beat. Not at her beauty, or my good luck in finding her so friendly, but at the thought of what a ‘g&t’ would cost.

We chatted for a while and she told me she was expecting ‘a friend,’ but as she was now over an hour late she suspected that she wasn’t coming. She said,

“I think I have been stood up.”

Predictably we ended up going to the pictures together. In the pub her hair, although obviously red, was more a soft auburn but when we stepped outside into the last of the sunlight it appeared a much richer colour. I was to learn soon though that at mid-day, when the sun was at its highest, her hair made her seem a girl on fire in all the best of ways. I was fascinated, intoxicated by it.

She said she preferred sitting upstairs as ‘You get a better view and as I’m quite short I can see better without having to peer between people’s heads.’ Of course, the seats upstairs were more expensive but I agreed and paid for both of us.

In those days a trip to the cinema was an event. First there would be some adverts, then probably a short cartoon or two followed by the 'B' movie. There would then be a short interval, during which ice creams and sweets would be sold by usherettes carrying trays slung around their necks and finally the main movie. I bought Jane an ice cream during the interval but claimed I wasn't keen on ice cream myself in order to keep the expense down, ever anxious about my finances.

After the cinema she asked if I would mind taking her home as it was now dark. How could I refuse, even though she lived in Blackheath and I was in Camberwell in exactly the opposite direction. I began to walk to the bus stop but she stopped and said,

"Do you mind if we take the train? It's much more comfortable and quicker too."

'And more expensive,' I thought to myself, but I paid up anyway.

After dropping her at her house in Blackheath village (I was not invited in) I walked back up to the main road. I caught the 53 bus back to New Cross and then walked to my digs from there. We had arranged to meet the following Saturday, 'same place, same time' and I found myself looking forward to seeing her again although I knew I would have to pay a visit to the local Barclays branch first!

Mike was already home and in bed when I got back and when I enquired how his evening had been with Heather, he grunted a non-committal reply and turned over. He did not ask where I had been and I did not tell him either then, or on the following Sunday when we had an excellent lunch together with the Hunter family.

This pattern of meeting Jane on a Saturday evening in the pub and then going to the cinema together continued for the next few weeks. So did the pattern of me paying for everything, including her gin and tonics! Not once did she offer to pay for anything and, not once, did I dare to ask her.

Christmas arrived as a welcome opportunity for me to top up my finances by taking a temporary job with the post office when I returned home. On the last Saturday before I left for home we had agreed we would meet again on the first Saturday when I was back in Camberwell and this we did. Our routine started again exactly the same as before. Whilst I had been at home I had considered my relationship with Jane in some detail. Was I in love with her ? No. Did I enjoy her company? Yes. Did I enjoy the kissing and the cuddling? Yes, very much. Did I wish to take things further with her?

That last question was the difficult one. The 'swinging sixties' had not reached southeast London, at least not where Jane and I were concerned. To attempt to 'take things further' sexually would have been strongly rebuffed – remember, 'the pill' had not yet come on the scene. I was unsure that I wanted to take things further in terms of our relationship so if I was unsure, I reasoned, then I decided it was best to stay as we were.

When I returned after Christmas we met at the usual place. As we were walking to the cinema Jane held on to my arm and said,

"Next Saturday, I would like to try something different."

"Oh?," I muttered, wondering what she had in mind – tea with her parents (I hoped not), taking a room in a hotel for the night (nice idea but I couldn't afford it) or perhaps she was going to treat me to something for a change (unlikely).

"Yes. I thought it would be lovely if we went for a meal. There's a new Berni Inn opened in Catford and I've heard it's really nice," she purred.

Now the only times when I had gone out for a meal were on days out or on holiday with my parents and that had usually been in some 'greasy spoon' type café where I had invariably opted for sausage and mash or, my absolute favourite, sausage, beans and chips. Somehow she got me to agree and said that she would book a table for us for the next Saturday, which was a relief as I had no idea how to 'book a table.'

Next Saturday came and I was nervously reading through the menu mainly looking at the prices. There were no credit cards in

1963 so this meal had to come from the cash in my rather thin looking wallet. A waiter approached and asked if we would like a drink and, of course, Jane said yes, she would love a gin and tonic. I declined and said I was happy with water.

"What's the matter with you? You usually like a drink on a Saturday evening?" Jane enquired.

"I just don't feel like a drink tonight," I replied cheerily. "I've had a bit of a dodgy tummy the last couple of days.

"Oh dear," she replied, "Never mind, I'm sure you will enjoy your meal."

"Well, actually, I'm not really very hungry either," I muttered and then in a flash of inspiration (I thought) added, "But I knew you were looking forward to this evening and didn't want to spoil it for you."

"You're right there," she gushed. "I'm really going to enjoy this. I'm going to have all three courses. "

She did – she started with prawn cocktail, then had steak and chips and finished with Black Forest Gateau. I merely chose a salad, which was the cheapest item on the menu, and hoped that I would have enough cash to cover the bill. She even had a coffee after the meal, which I also declined, and was so thankful when the bill finally came that I had enough. I didn't leave a tip much to the waiter's disgust, I'm sure, but I didn't care as I was certain I would never set foot in that restaurant again! Fortunately, she had, for once, bought a return ticket on the train so I was spared that additional expense.

A few weeks later, after I had, again, had the opportunity to refill my wallet, Jane came up with another suggestion which, again, she managed to persuade me to go along with. I wish I could report that she offered sexual favours but, no, it was just her natural charm and persuasive nature.

"The Odeon in Leicester Square is showing 'The Millionaress' with Peter Sellers next week and I know that I can take an afternoon off when you're free and we could go to see a matinee performance? Sophia Loren is in it as well," she added , as if that would be final thing to convince me.

"OK, I think I can manage that" I replied cheerfully. "How about Wednesday?"

And so it was that the following Wednesday afternoon saw us cuddling up together in the vast cinema in central London, one of the most famous in the world. Jane, naturally, wanted an ice-cream in the interval, but I, again, declined maintaining my pretence that I was not that fond of ice-cream.

The film was good and as we left the cinema and mingled with the crowds she held on to my arm tightly and breathed in my ear,

"Let's make a special event of today and go for a meal somewhere."

I could feel my wallet protesting in my inside pocket but her smile again melted my resistance and, like the fool I was, I agreed. She led me to a small place round the back of the Square where she said,

"I'm sure they will find us a table as it's still early." Sure enough they did have a spare table for us. There were only a few people eating already and as Jane sat down, she smiled at the waiter and asked

"Could I have a gin and tonic please?"

"Of course," he replied. Who could resist that dazzling smile, the beautiful blue eyes and that hypnotising, shining red hair. He turned to me and asked,

"And for you, sir?,"

"I'd like a bank loan please," I smiled back. No, of course I didn't say that. I just shook my head and muttered, "Water will be fine thanks." He smiled at Jane again and left us to look at the menu. Jane looked at the dishes available and I looked at the prices.

The meal was a repeat of the evening at the Berni Inn except it was twice as expensive. Again, I restricted myself to one dish – another salad while Jane wolfed her way through four courses and a coffee. 'Where does she put it all, I wondered, appraising her slender frame. 'Perhaps she doesn't eat at all on the days when we are not together?'

"I think you're not far wrong there mate," Mike said when I recounted my day out and filled the three of them, Brian, John and Mike, in on my dates with Jane and how they were getting more and more expensive.

"I think you're being taken for a ride," said John in his Black Country accent.

"But you haven't seen how stunning she is!" I retorted indignantly.

"Well, if she's that stunning what does she see in you?" John replied bluntly. "The size of your wallet perhaps?"

That made me think. What does she see in me? Perhaps John and the others were right.

The following Saturday we were back in Lewisham at the cinema and, after the film, as we were walking towards the railway station I said,

"I've got something to tell you."

"What's that?" she breathed cheerfully.

And then I told her,

"After Easter I'm going away."

"Going away? Where?" Jane stopped in her tracks and looked at me full in the face. God, those blue eyes were so attractive, they seemed to look right through me. What could I see there? Was she angry or just curious? Was she jealous or worried? No. I decided that the look she was giving me was challenging me, saying why? Why are you going away? What's going on? Why didn't I know about this already?

Then I told her. As part of my university course I was to spend some time abroad to improve my foreign language skills.

"Abroad? Where? For how long?

"Italy."

"Italy!," she cried, "But that's, that's …"

"Yes Italy," I said, remaining calm.

Her beautiful eyes were brimming with tears as I added,

"It's only for a year."

"A year! A year!," she almost screamed. Several people nearby were now looking at us so I took her arm and led her into a shop doorway. I put my arms around her to comfort her but she shrugged me to one side and then she exclaimed,

"But what about me?"

And that's when I knew the boys were right. She had been using me. No questions about what I was going to do, no wishes about enjoying my opportunity or having a good time or even remaining safe, nothing; just 'What about me?'

That was the end of our relationship. She didn't even want me to take her home, she just shrugged me off but not before berating me about how selfish I was!

Twenty years later my daughter Amy decided she would like to train as a teacher and applied for a place at Goldsmiths' College which is situated in New Cross. When she was offered an interview, I said I would drive her to London. I wanted to look again at the places where I had spent some happy times to see what had changed.

I dropped Amy at the college and agreed where and when I would pick her up after her interview then I set off. There was much more traffic than I remembered and, of course, back in my university days I had not been a driver, merely a bus passenger.

My first port of call was Grove Lane and there was the house. Of course, the Hunters no longer lived there. I had heard that both Mr and Mrs Hunter had passed away several years earlier. I wondered if the new owners still took in students but there was no way of telling from just looking at the front.

Next, I drove on to Lewisham. The cinema was still there (it was later demolished in the 1990s as part of a road widening scheme) but appeared to be closed down. I parked in the car park of a large supermarket and made my way on foot to the Rising Sun. I felt a strange anticipation in my stomach as I walked in. What did I expect to find? A beautiful redheaded 40 year old woman sat at one end of the bar nursing a gin and tonic at 11 in the morning?

The pub had not changed much – new furniture, new carpets and curtains but the place looked much the same. I ordered a pint of shandy and sat down. Quite why I was here I was not certain but I still felt that shudder of anticipation and each time the door opened for someone to enter I found myself turning my head to look until after about an hour .... I decided to leave and find something to eat. Of course she wasn't there. I hadn't really expected her to be. I decided against driving on to Blackheath to see if she still lived in the same house. What would I say to her if I saw her?

"Hi, I'm back!"

I hadn't said that when I returned from my year in Italy and I had made no attempt to see her again. I had met someone in Siena, an English girl, and we had stayed together and still were together, my wife Angela. I enjoyed the next couple of hours wandering around Lewisham and New Cross remembering many of the good times I had enjoyed with Mike, John and Brian and wondering where they were now as we had not kept in touch. Once Angela had arrived on the scene and moved into a shared flat in Peckham I had spent most of the remaining year of my course with her and seen less and less of 'the boys.' I did not have time to take the train into London to see again the area round the university as Amy would be waiting for me soon. In the car on the journey back home Amy chatted about her interview and I told her of the places I had revisited but did not mention Jane. I had never told Amy or her mother about Jane and probably never would now.

Some months after my trip to New Cross I was back at home idly flicking through the TV channels while Angela was finalising the preparation of our evening meal when I came upon a quiz programme.

And there she was!

She was introducing herself as 'A single mum with two teenage daughters, living in south London and hoping to win some money to take her girls on holiday as they had never been able to afford one.'

Same blue eyes, but the red hair which had so attracted me at the time was now laced with random grey strands and ……oh! Now I had the answer to the question I had asked myself all those years ago when she emptied my wallet with her appetite. I had pondered, 'Where does she put it all?' as she forked her way through the menu. Well, I had my answer on the TV screen. She had stored it for now. She was as wide as she was tall and must have weighed around eighteen or nineteen stone easily. She had taken me for a ride, several times, but I was having the last laugh as I admired my adorable, slim wife entering with two plates of steaming food.

"What? What are you laughing at?" asked Angela, bemused.

"Nothing much," I smiled, "Just something on TV" and I turned off the set.

Michael Knight

The student's story

Eleven

Next is a story told to us by a friend of many years who, sadly, lost her husband a few years ago.

It is a story from the early years of their marriage but as she tells the story, whilst on a long coach journey, she still has the twinkle in her eyes as she relives and reveals her fond memories.

GOTHENBURG

It was 1966, the year everyone remembers as the only year when England have won the football World Cup with that famous phrase,

"They think it's all over …… it is now," ringing in their ears.

I had been married two years but had seen very little of my new husband since our wedding. He was at sea. He was in the Merchant Navy, working as an engineer on tankers owned by one of the big oil companies. He had left school and gone straight to sea, first as an apprentice engineer and now as a qualified fifth engineer.

We had met at school when John was seven and I was probably eight (I was a year older than him) and I suppose you would call us 'childhood sweethearts.' Certainly, I only ever 'went out' with one other boy and John, to my knowledge anyway, had not had any other real girlfriends. It had been a small and quiet wedding, not like the lavish affairs they have today, in our hometown of Weston-Super-Mare and now I was living back with my mum while John was at sea. We married in March of 1964 although the invitations were for a wedding in May. I had made all the arrangements including getting the invitations printed only to learn that John's dad received a letter from the shipping company ('Caltex') to say that John would not be having shore leave in May but he would be home during March. His shore leave was usually for six weeks at a time. I was more than a little put out that the company had written to the bridegroom's father rather than the prospective bride, but took out my frustration on the invitations, hastily scrubbing out 'May' and sticking tape over it upon which I had painstakingly typed 'March' as I couldn't afford to have them printed again. I also had to change the reception venue so that meant more sticky tape and more typing!

I was happy there but, naturally, missed my husband when he was at sea. Shore leave always seemed to go so quickly so I was delighted when I received a letter from John saying that his ship would be putting into Gothenburg in Sweden to discharge oil and wives would be allowed to visit while the ship was there. This was normal in European waters but not allowed when the ship was moored in the middle or far east.

Excitedly, I made arrangements at work so that I could spend some time in Gothenburg. I was extra excited because I had never been abroad before. Little did I know about the difficulties of foreign travel. Of course I have travelled abroad many times since but some of those difficulties still exist today, even after all the progress that has been made within the travel industry.

There were no motorways then. My brother took me to London in his car and the journey seemed to take forever, and by today's standards it did! I was anxious as I set off, clutching my little leather suitcase which contained all the new clothes I had bought so that I would look smart when I met John again in Gothenburg. My new clothes included two pairs of tights.

When hanging on a washing line a pair of tights could look quite repulsive but they were warm, convenient and, at that time, all the rage. They had only just become available in England in 1966 but were especially useful when combined with miniskirts which, of course, were all the fashion then. In those days I had the legs to wear a mini skirt and, like most women my age, I wanted to look fashionable whenever I could.

It was a long and boring journey but, eventually, we arrived in London and we made our way to the hotel which John's company had booked for me. More excitement for me as I had only ever stayed in a B&B before, even on our honeymoon, which we had spent in the exotic resort of Brixham in Devon..

I didn't sleep very well that night and had not really enjoyed eating my dinner in a cold and almost empty hotel dining room. I learned from John and other friends later that it is important to take something to read when you dine alone in an hotel, otherwise you end up staring at the other guests which can become embarrassing. Nowadays, of course, the 'thing to read' is almost always a mobile phone but, in 1966, there were no mobile phones. If there had been, perhaps I would have ended my journey in London and returned, alone, to the North!

Early morning found me ready packed and sitting on the side of the bed (which I had almost re-made, not thinking that, of course, all the linen would have to be changed) glancing at my watch which showed me that I still had almost two hours before I was due to catch a coach to Heathrow airport. I had been too excited, and a little too nervous, to take breakfast in the hotel and had led far too sheltered a life to even consider going out to explore London on my own. It would be many more years before I felt confident enough to do that. In fact, to be honest, I don't think I would explore London on my own now!

The airport was a mixture of confusion, excitement and bewilderment but, somehow, with the assistance of several kind people, most of whom were wearing uniforms of some kind, I arrived at the right place with lots of time to spare. Nowadays, I would probably explore the shops or find somewhere to have a coffee but back then, all those years ago, I just sat in my seat in the lounge staring about every thirty seconds at the screen which announced departure times and gates.

It was a long wait but, eventually the flight to Gothenburg appeared and some kind person (in a uniform) told me which way to go. At the gate I saw the plane for the first time and my excitement (and nervousness) grew. Of course I made use of the 'facilities,' several times in fact as the butterflies in my tummy grew and grew until it felt to me that they were the size of the pigeons I had seen at the coach station.

I have no idea what type of plane it was, whether it had jet engines or propellors or whatever. All I can remember is that it was a plane, and it seemed to be to be a big one! As I stood in line to board now was not the time to be thinking to myself, *'How on earth do they get these things off the ground?'* I found myself sitting next to a pleasant looking gentleman of about fifty years of age who smiled at me as we fastened our seatbelts ready for take-off. I was so nervous that I felt sure I would be sick but, by some miracle of fate, I was not. I unclenched my fists and tried to relax. I was not in a window seat which was probably a good thing as the sight of the earth disappearing beneath us would probably not have helped my state of mind.

Refusing any snack or beverage from the flight attendant, I settled in my seat and tried to imagine my reunion with John after three long months apart. My imagining was interrupted by an announcement from someone over the tannoy whom I assumed to be the pilot. Listening carefully, and with some trepidation, I heard him say that weather conditions in Gothenburg were unsuitable for landing our plane and so we were being diverted to Copenhagen.

"Oh dear," I hear myself say in a timid voice, "Now I won't be able to see John."

"Pardon?" said the gentleman beside me.

Startled, I looked up at him,

"Oh sorry. I didn't realise I was speaking out loud."

"Don't worry about missing your appointment," he smiled, "The airline will get us to Gothenburg eventually. We might have to spend a night in a hotel in Copenhagen but then they will fly us on to Gothenburg tomorrow."

"Oh." I said, pathetically. "Thank you."

No more conversation took place until we landed. The plane came down with quite a bump and we were thrown around in our seats as the plane swayed in the wind.

"Gosh. That was quite a bumpy landing, wasn't it?" my companion gasped as the plane taxied in towards its stand.

"Was it?" I said, "Sorry but I've not flown before so I wouldn't know. Sorry."

"There's no need for *you* to apologise," he smiled, "You weren't piloting us."

"No, of course not. Sorry" I said again, immediately regretting that I had inadvertently apologised again.

"My name's Geoff," he said as he held out his hand. I'm attending a conference in Gothenburg tomorrow, so let's hope they get us there!" He smiled.

I shook his hand, introduced myself and told him I was visiting my husband on his ship in Gothenburg harbour. He looked a little taken aback by this but said nothing.

He proved to be a very kind and helpful travelling companion when we were herded into a holding gate at Copenhagen airport. The airline staff explained that the weather was so bad in Gothenburg, with high winds and heavy rain, that the airport had closed temporarily. They were going to accommodate us in an airport hotel here in Copenhagen and would fly us on to Gothenburg tomorrow. Of course, today we would have been taken by coach across the wonderful bridge that separates the two countries and featured in the TV series, "The Bridge" but that had not been built in 1966.

Geoff helped me get a single room in the hotel we were taken to and he sat with me at dinner time and generally looked after me. It's fair to say I was more than somewhat confused and bemused as this, my first foreign trip, had not gone quite to plan and I was becoming increasingly concerned that my time with John would be limited, or even worse, non-existent. I did not sleep well but morning came and the sky was brighter, although the wind outside my hotel window looked strong still. Information on what was happening was not forthcoming and so I sat with Geoff and a few other passengers in the breakfast room wondering when, if ever, we would be taken to Gothenburg. I had received a phone call at the hotel the previous evening to say that it would not be possible to visit the ship the following day as the weather was too bad, so I was still wearing my fashionable clothes including the miniskirt.

Eventually, after an hour or so, we were taken from the hotel to the terminal and then on to a smaller plane for the short flight to Gothenburg. Very short, in fact. No sooner were we in the air it seemed than the pilot announced we would be 'descending' into Gothenburg. Again, I was sitting nervously alongside Geoff and, as we came into land, he squeezed my hand and whispered,

“Not long now. You’ll soon be with him.”

“Will you be in time for your conference?” I asked politely.

“Oh yes. No problem” he nodded.

How I got from the airport to the docks where the ship was berthed I cannot remember exactly, but I seem to remember Geoff putting me into a taxi and waving me goodbye. The taxi drove through the dock gates (security was much less strict in those days) and the driver asked me in impeccable English,

“Which ship?”

I told him and saw him frown. I began to worry again. *‘Now what’s the problem?,’* I thought to myself. The driver stopped the taxi and spoke to an official looking person who was, of course, wearing a uniform. He came back, opened the rear door and said,

“You get out please. This man will take you from here.”

‘This man’ turned out to be one of the harbour officials and he led me towards a group of offices. I followed, clutching my suitcase in one hand and using the other arm trying desperately to keep my skirt from blowing up and revealing all, as the strong, force ten wind blew around us.

In the office it was explained to me, again in impeccable English, that John’s ship was not in the docks but was at anchor offshore and I would have to be taken out to the ship by pilot boat. The officer who spoke to me said,

“It may be a little uncomfortable for you as the wind is strong but everything will be OK.”

I was not reassured but, anxious to see John, I said something like,

“I’ll be fine” and smiled. The truth was I was feeling terrified. My terror did not diminish as I approached the pilot boat which was small with a cabin just about big enough for two people to huddle in. Just as I was leaving the harbour offices one of the staff came up to me and thrust a mail bag at me.

"Would you mind taking the ship's mail? We haven't been able to get out there yet today. We've been too busy with problems caused by the storm. Yours is the first tender to sail as the wind has slightly reduced"
"*Slightly reduced?*" I thought to myself, "*What must it have been like before?*"

The crew on the ship were eager to receive their mail as they had not had any since the last port they had been to which was in Bahrein, where they had been moored more than five weeks ago. So with the mailman's comforting words echoing in my ears I stepped cautiously into the tender, handing the mail bag to a crew member as I did so. The journey to the ship could have taken no longer than twenty five to thirty five minutes, but it seemed much longer as I clung on desperately to whatever I could to prevent myself from falling in an undignified heap on the deck of the tender. I was not seasick even though the movement of the small boat was quite considerable. I think I must have been too frightened to even think of being seasick. My state of mind was not helped by the fact that I could not swim. I had not been given a life jacket or anything similar as health and safety rules at that time were not as prevalent in those days, at least not in Sweden! As we neared the ship, 'Caltex Newcastle,' which towered above us, the movement of the boat lessened. It seemed the hull of the huge tanker was sheltering us from the worst of the wind, and that is when the next terrifying thought came Into my mind:

"*Exactly how was I going to get aboard?*"

The answer to my unasked question some became apparent. There was a rope ladder hanging down the side of the tanker. The bottom of the ladder was almost in the sea and the top seemed to me to be about half a mile up towards the sky! The huge ship was barely moving in the swell but our little boat was, to coin a well-known phrase, "Bobbing up and down."

The skipper managed, with great skill, to get us alongside the ladder and indicated that I should step on to the nearest rung. So, picture this: one very small lady stepping on to a very long ladder affixed to the side of a simply ginormous boat. Neil Armstrong was to take "one small step" a few years later but his achievement was as nothing compared to that step I took.

Miraculously I stayed upright and was able to drag my other leg on to the ladder as well. I was handed my small suitcase which I clutched under one arm whilst clinging on to the ladder with both hands. Then the mailbag which, I somehow managed to sling over my other shoulder and then slowly and cautiously I began the great ascent, my miniskirt blowing wildly in the wind. How thankful I was then that those below me would only be seeing my new pair of tights and nothing more! As I reached the top I was helped aboard, my suitcase and the mailbag were taken from me and I eventually managed to unclench my fists and open my hands again. It was a while longer before I was able to unclench my teeth though!

I would like to report that my husband was there to welcome me with a hug and a kiss and to congratulate me on being the first person to come onboard since the ship had dropped anchor, as well as marvelling at my bravery in weathering the storm, literally.

That's what I would like to report but the reality was very different. Having been told that visitors to the ship were very unlikely to come aboard that day due to the high winds, John had finished his watch, had "a few beers" and retired to his tiny cabin where he fell fast asleep. That was how I found him, snoring away and totally oblivious to the heroics of his wife.

I was, to say the least, disappointed!

We did make up for it later, though, but that's another story.

Jean Hunt

Gothenburg

Twelve

Some of the stories we remember and retell whether on journeys or elsewhere are sad. Many do not have happy endings.

Our next story is one of these.

'ARE YOU HUNGRY MATE?'

From an early age, Amos McNevall's parents had had little time for him as his gifted elder sister was the apple of their eyes. She, Gwyneth, was five years older than Amos and a piano prodigy. Their parents, Alan and Janet, would take her to lessons, piano practice and later concerts. At first, he accepted this as the norm, but as he grew older, he resented the amount of time, money and obvious affection his parents bestowed on his sister, so even from an early age he spent more time with his paternal grandmother, Mabel. She lived two doors away in an end of terrace Victorian house almost identical to the one Amos shared with his parents and sister in Kensal Green, London.

Mabel McNevall was born in 1920 at Central Middlesex hospital and had lived in this house since the age of twelve; at first with her own parents, who later bought it from the council, her one older sister, Rosie, and eventually just by herself when her sister married and moved to Inverness. Mabel was basically an unpaid baby-sitter for Amos, though she didn't mind. She knew, though it was never admitted, that she had a lot more affection for Amos than she did for Alan, her own son, and Amos had always got on well with her. They had been a succour to each other during the family upsets, mostly caused by Alan's erratic behaviour, that were with them intermittently during Amos's formative years, and he loved hearing the stories she told him of her early life. She had been in the land-army during WWII and he listened intently as she related, every so often, some of her exploits from that period of her life. She told him that some of her work had been secret but always refused to go into more detail. She had explained to Amos about the Official Secrets Act.

Mabel had never married and had brought up Alan on her own, mostly, though with some help from her own parents and sometimes her sister before she had moved away. Mabel didn't have a lot of time for Alan, Amos's father, because, according to her, he was always a distant, non-loving child who became obnoxious and arrogant during his teens. He stole money from her to feed his drinking habit, and after he hit her on one occasion their relationship was never the same. Alan was a product of a one-night stand which went further than she had wanted.

“I suppose I was raped” she told Amos when he was old enough to understand the implications.

Alan’s drinking habits grew worse over the years and he was banned from driving twice. Janet then had to do any driving, which she really didn’t like doing, and she grew more and more resentful. There were a lot of rows over this, but it didn’t change Alan’s behaviour. He wasn’t a nasty drunk, just extremely embarrassing when he had had too much. He eventually lost his job as a solicitor and had to take poorly-paid work as a shop assistant; basically, a shelf-filler in a supermarket.

Amos was fourteen years old when his sister left home to marry an orchestra conductor, and sixteen when his mother left Alan. Amos had been working for a few months by this time. He had heard raised voices in the lounge one night and he crept to the top of the stairs to listen. Janet was adamant that Alan was seeing another woman; Alan was just as resolute that she was just a friend.

“So, you don’t deny seeing her?” Janet screamed.

“No, but only as a social thing; when a group of us go for a drink after work,” Alan murmured.

“Pubs close at 10.30. How come you don’t get home until midnight?” Janet demanded and added,

“And how come that wasn’t my perfume I smelt on the shirt you put in the washing basket last night?”

“Look calm down, woman” Alan said. “Just get me another drink and we’ll talk about this sensibly.”

“Get your own effing drink,” she bellowed.

There was a crash which sounded to Amos as if a glass had been thrown against a wall.

“For Christ’s sake will you calm down.” Alan said again.

Amos scrambled back to his room just before Janet came stomping up the stairs. A few moments later she was descending them again carrying a suitcase. Amos partly opened his door and heard Janet say,

"I'm not staying in this house with you a moment longer."

As the front door opened Alan shouted,

"And where do you think you're going?"

"Anywhere but here." was the reply, just before the front door slammed. Amos heard the family car start and drive away but Alan stayed in the lounge, obviously pouring himself another drink.

*

Amos never saw his mother again and he blamed his father, or rather his father's drinking habits, for this state of affairs. He didn't speak to his father at all for the next two weeks, though this was mostly because he only saw him twice in that fortnight. The second of these occasions was when Amos had arrived home to find his father in the lounge, sat on the sofa next to a mousy-haired woman.

"Hello son," Alan said and continued, "I'd like you to meet Joanne."

Amos nodded at the woman and she half-smiled but said nothing.

"Jo-Jo and I have decided to live together, so I will be giving up this house and taking most of the contents with me for our new place. I have already told the council."

Amos shrugged, glared at the woman but made no comment. He was unperturbed by his father's revelation.

'So, my mother was right' he thought. 'The ol' man was putting his wick into another woman's candle.'

“You’ll have to go and live with your Nan.” Alan then told Amos, with complete indifference for the youngster’s feelings. Not that Amos really minded; lately he had spent most of his time there anyway. Alan presented the news to Mabel in much the same offhand way on the following morning whilst Amos was at work.

“It didn’t take you long, did it.” Mabel said. “Janet’s cushion is still warm and here you are moving in with someone else. I think it’s disgraceful. But you go and do what you want, you always have. Just don’t come crying to me when she finds out what a scumbag you really are and kicks you out.”

With a venom which was contrary to her usual affable character she told him,

“Actually, neither of you will ever be welcome in my house again.”

“Bugger you, then.” Alan retaliated and left the house slamming the front door behind him.

“Don’t you worry.” she said to Amos later that evening, “You and me will be fine. Just go and fetch the rest of your belongings and forget him.”

“Forget who?” Amos asked, and they both grinned.

He had collected what was left of his things by the weekend and, as a parting shot, he removed all the lightbulbs and cut the cables off every electrical item he could find in the house. He severed them as close to the appliance as was possible. He knew how much this would annoy impractical Alan, who had never fitted a plug in his life let alone replaced a cable. It was almost as if Amos was daring Alan to come and make an issue of it; Amos was ready for him if he did. But Amos never heard another word from Alan.

The next two years were quite happy for the young man and his grandmother. Amos acquired a better job, this time as a kitchen porter at Central Middlesex hospital. It was a fifteen-to-twenty-minute cycle ride each way but Amos didn’t mind that; he loved his job. He also got on well with his work colleagues, though he didn't develop any meaningful relationship with anyone. He was wary of letting anyone get too close to him; he realised this about himself and found that he was quite happy to be this way. After a little over two years, he was offered promotion; to trainee assistant cook. After a discussion with Mabel, he put aside his reservations and decided to accept the offer. This made his working life even more rewarding and he actually looked forward to going to work even more.

Twice a year Mabel and he spent a week in a guest house in Dover, travelling by train from Charing Cross, and they had a wonderful time taking in the sea-air, walking along the pier and visiting the castle, which was lit up with a greenish hue during the hours of darkness. They also ate out every evening which they both thoroughly enjoyed.

Amos was cooking in the house when Mabel collapsed one day in September of 1986. She was taken to hospital, and although Amos did manage to see her for a brief time, she died shortly afterwards. However, it was during their final conversation that she was coherent enough to tell Amos the following:

"I want you to know that I have left you the house in my will. I also want you to go into the kitchen. Underneath the sink you will find a loose floor tile and under this is a key to the secret door."

"What secret door?"

"Well, listen and I'll tell you. That shelf unit with all my tins of food on is what is hiding the secret door. Remove the tins, undo the two big screws and the shelf unit will come away. The tiny space behind that door holds a few items which I've kept since the war. Please dispose of them as you see fit but do be careful. Even your dad never knew about this. I had a work colleague build the shelf for me many years ago. I designed it but he built and fitted it for me. I can't tell you any more now because I'm tired and I want to sleep. But I'll say again, be careful."

Those were the last words she ever spoke to him.

Amos was angry, and distraught, after her death and cried a lot for a few days. The funeral was a sparse affair. Alan never attended. This was perhaps, Amos reasoned, that he didn't know his mother had died. Amos had no intention of trying to trace Alan to pass on the information. Amos, at the age of nineteen, realised he was now pretty much alone in the world. He had inherited a house, which was a wonderful silver lining to his dark cloud of grief, though he didn't do much about personalising it at first. He found relief in reading through the many books Mabel had accumulated over the years; mostly in the murder-mystery genre.

However, it wasn't too long before he had a strong desire to locate the secret room Mabel had alluded to. He found the Yale key with no problem, wrapped in a deteriorating paper bag from a long-closed, local shop. He removed all the tins, some of which must have been older than Mabel, and undid the screws with a screwdriver from his toolbox. It was not easy due to their rusted condition, but he managed it. He swung away the shelf and with some trepidation put the key in the lock. It turned surprisingly easily, and he pulled the door open. A strong, musty smell hit his nostrils as he gazed into a window-less space approximately three feet square.

There was an old, metal container in one corner, covered in cobwebs. Amos returned to the kitchen to don a pair of marigolds and then carried the ancient, enamel breadbin into the kitchen where he lifted the filthy lid of the dusty receptacle. Inside were a couple of folders containing some papers which, at first glance, Amos didn't comprehend, and a bag full of military insignia. But what did catch his attention were the two other items: a gun and a small bottle labelled Potassium Cyanide. He was glad he had put some gloves on.

Returning the empty tin to where it came from, he put back the shelf and tins of food. The files he had no interest in; they could either be donated to the Imperial War Museum or go out with the rubbish. The insignia may interest the museum, he thought. He obviously would have to get rid of the gun, somehow, but the small bottle he put back under the sink with the door key. This find intrigued him although he wasn't sure why. Disposal of the gun seemed a priority. Amos had the idea that dropping it into the

Thames was a good plan, so that evening he travelled the twelve tube stops from Kensal Green to Charing Cross. Even though the weapon was well wrapped in an inconspicuous empty cat food box and carrier bag from a nearby supermarket, he still felt nervous about carrying it around. He kept his head buried in a book until arrival at his destination.

Turning left out of the station he walked towards Cleopatra's needle. He was immediately accosted by a filthy, scruffy individual who had detached himself from a larger group of people of a similar ilk and asked Amos for money. Amos impolitely and firmly declined him, using only two words, and walked on, pleased that he was able to resist punching the man. When he reached the needle, he walked over the steps to the river wall and, when nobody was around, he slid the carrier bag down the wall and into the water.

He didn't hear the splash.

On the way back to the station he was again asked for money, this time by a different person, and Amos gave the same response. He wasn't usually aggressive, but these people really annoyed him.

'Why don't the bastards go and get a job and stop bothering people?' he thought. He never once contemplated that these people, scruffy and smelly as they were, had perhaps fallen on hard times through no fault of their own. To him they were just lazy, idle, work-shy drunks who he had no time for.

On the tube on the way home he had a thought, one which disturbed him a little because of its unfamiliarity. It was a fact that he had never seriously contemplated killing anyone before. Sure, there had been times when people had pissed him off so much that he had made the threat, but it was usually just a matter of temper, and the threat was never intended as a serious proposition. But now, as he travelled home, he was considering the idea in more depth and actually devised a way of doing the deed. Plus, he now had in his possession a means. He was also certain it could be done without him being caught. This was because there was no reason for him to be suspected as the perpetrator of such a crime, and therefore he had no motive. One of those disgusting tramps near Charing Cross would never be missed because they obviously had no families to care about them and, ipso facto, to notice their demise. Amos thought to himself 'This could be a perfect crime.'

He decided to do the deed on the following Saturday evening. After finishing work at 2pm on Friday he took the tube to Queens Park to use the shops in Salisbury Road. From a charity shop he purchased a coat and a pair of trousers, both of which were too large for him, plus an obviously home-made bobble hat. He also found a pair of slip-on shoes for a reasonable price in a shoe shop.

On Saturday morning he again made the tube journey from Kensal Green, this time alighting at Trafalgar Square and walking along Northumberland Avenue as far as the embankment. He didn't want to be seen too close to Charing Cross tube station on this occasion. Having established that he knew which way to walk after completion of his crime, he carried on walking as far as Westminster station. He passed the statue dedicated to Samuel Plimsoll and decided that this is where he would rapidly change his attire after the deed was done.

On Saturday afternoon he prepared two rounds of cheese and pickle sandwiches, one of which he carefully sprinkled with half a teaspoon of the cyanide crystals. This was all a little difficult because he had to make sure he wore his marigolds. The good sandwiches were put into a paper bag whilst the doctored ones he cautiously wrapped in silver foil. After this he put on some smart, casual clothes but over the top of these he wore the oversized coat and trousers. He put on the new shoes and picked up a rucksack. In this he placed a house brick from the garden, a second pair of shoes, a book and the two packs of sandwiches. He left the house and walked to the station. He bought a single to Charing Cross and spent the journey reading; he didn't make eye-contact with anybody. He wasn't at all worried about what he was going to do. If anything, he felt quite excited.

Upon arrival at Charing Cross on Saturday evening he sat on a wall and took out the paper bag to eat his sandwiches. There was a watching vagrant nearby and, fighting down his disgust at the man, Amos said, with a northern accent,

"Ay mate, are thee hungry?"

The unkempt head nodded and Amos added,

"I have some spare sandwiches here if thee like. Only Cheese and Pickle I'm afraid."

An unwashed, shaky hand extended towards Amos and it took the foil wrapped package. A muttered "Thank you" was offered from the toothless mouth.

Amos felt uncomfortable with the way the tramp stared at him so he packed up his uneaten sandwich, walked away and headed back along the embankment. Thankfully there weren't many people around and he believed that nobody saw him vault over the railings next to the Samuel Plimsoll statue and duck behind it. Less than a minute later he reappeared. The oversized clothing, new shoes and the hat were ensconced within the rucksack. His book he carried under his arm. A hundred yards or so later he crossed the road and stood looking over the river. Ensuring that nobody was watching he dropped the rucksack into the water; the house brick would ensure that it sank.

He unhurriedly ambled up to Westminster and bought a single ticket back to Kensal Green. He caught a westbound train to Victoria and changed there for the Victoria line. He changed again at Oxford Circus for the final leg of his journey. Again, he kept his mind on his book – a novel by Dennis Wheatley. He arrived back at Kensal Green a little after eight.

At home he gave the kitchen a good clean and returned the poison bottle to the secret room. It was then time for bed because he did have to work tomorrow. He was surprised at how calm he felt. He even thought that he might repeat what he had done in a few weeks' time, but in a different part of London.

Amos rarely bought a newspaper but, out of curiosity, he purchased a copy of the Evening News on Monday afternoon, after he had finished work. He wondered if his crime had been successful. He wasn't disappointed. A small article mentioned that a vagrant had been found dead at Charing Cross on Saturday evening and the police suspected poisoning.

'Why would they suspect that?' Amos wondered.

The article continued that the deceased man had been identified as Alan McNevall, aged 43, of no fixed abode.

Malcolm Godfrey

Thirteen

It was on a long coach journey to London that Diane, half asleep, reflected on the last few years of her life.

The courier lady had served her a cup of tasteless coffee in a paper cup, most of which she had not drunk but she had consumed the sandwich she bought before getting on to the bus in Taunton.

The driver pulled away from Bridgwater bus station about forty minutes later and Diane noticed as they approached the motorway that the traffic was stationary. She closed her eyes and felt the effects of the sandwich on her general well-being.

She thought back to that car park and the events which followed. It all seemed to her in her drowsy state as if it were only yesterday ...

DIANE'S STORY

It was in Sainsburys car park that Diane decided to seriously consider getting a divorce. She had thanked the young man for carrying her bags to the boot of her car, slumped into the driving seat, thrown her heavy handbag on to its resting place between the front seats and turned the key in the ignition to allow the car's air conditioning to clear the mist on the windows, all without thinking.

As she turned the key the sound of the radio filled the car: Elton John. For perhaps the first time, or so it seemed to Diane, she listened to the lyric of the familiar tune, one of her favourites:

"Cold, Cold Heart
Hard done by you
Some things look better baby
Just passing through

And it's no sacrifice
Just a simple word
It's two hearts living
In two separate worlds
But it's no sacrifice
No sacrifice
It's no sacrifice at all."

The song continued as Diane sat there, hunched over the steering wheel, her hand still on the ignition, her eyes filling with tears, her breath misting the windows again and her mind rewinding the years.

She had been born and raised in the small town of West Learton, where she now sat, surrounded by the good citizens of that town going about their early evening business on a cold, snow-swept February working day. West Learton had grown prosperous, thanks to its proximity to the motorway and the building of several business parks near the two junctions which served the town. Diane's family had prospered too.

She had attended the local sixth form college, gained good grades and seemed set for a great future but then she had fallen for Ron. He was from a farming family whose farm was high in the Quantock hills.

He was tall and handsome with Paul Newman eyes that sparkled deep into her very soul. They had married a year after she completed her "A" levels and a further year later little Joanne was born. A couple of years passed and along came Tom, followed two years later by Ruby, their 'baby.'

Diane had been happy as a wife and mother but when even little Ruby was trotting off to school with her lunch bag on her arm, her pretty, blond curls bouncing on her shoulders, Diane had grown restless. Of course she still attended all the school functions, cheered on Joanne's netball team and shouted with all the other obsessively proud mums and dads at Tom's football games but she wanted more.

It was when she decided to go back to school herself that things began to turn sour. No-one understood her. Ron angrily accused her of insulting his manhood; what did she want to work for? Hadn't he always provided for her, working sixteen hours a day on the farm when the fruit needed it and helping at the power station when there was time? Didn't they have everything she wanted: a fine, family house in one of the best areas of town with every household machine she needed, lots of friends to visit with weekends and holidays?

Her parents questioned her accusingly and asked her to consider how Ron felt and how the kids would feel and was it really necessary? How could she explain to them without hurting them even more that she was tired of being what everyone else wanted her to be. Now she wanted to be what she wanted.

It had been hard but she had stuck at it; long years of attending classes, looking after the house and family, keeping Ron happy and getting through her reading. She had graduated with ease and got her first teaching job as a primary teacher. God, how she had loved it. She was a great success, popular with the pupils, staff and parents but still treading a tight rope at home.

She feared how Ron would react when she told him that she wanted to go for promotion. In the event he had just grunted and said he was going down to The Nag's Head for a beer with Doug.. Ron's brother Doug also worked at the family farm and did a number of other odd jobs as well, some of them a shade dubious. They had been meeting at The Nag's Head most evenings for a beer or two for the past couple of years. Diane had become used to going to bed alone and hearing Ron come in at around midnight. Most nights she pretended to be asleep.

During that long summer she studied at the University, delighting her tutors with her accomplishments and dedication, amusing her fellow students with her humour and sheer zest for life and, day by day, growing further away from her husband, who, unable to articulate his emotional pain and confusion, spent more and more time away from the house with his bar buddies.

Things became even worse when she was made deputy headteacher of Admiral Nelson Primary School in the adjoining school district to West Learton, just across the county border. Once again she was an immediate success and it was around that time that Ron's drinking had dramatically increased. She had been there six years now and she had loved every minute of it. She rose at five thirty each morning eager for the new day and she turned into her empty bed late each night content with what she had achieved.

Ron's days were very different. He had long since stopped going up to the farm. The rest of the family carried his workload there now. The guys at the power station hadn't seen him for six months, at least not at work. They may have stumbled across him at The Nag's Head or seen him trudging the pavements between the pubs and bars in West Learton, his head down, eyes dully fixed on the pavement beneath his unsteady feet.

Yesterday had been a good one, she remembered, as a tear gently detached itself from the corner of her carefully made-up eye and ran slowly down her cheek. She dabbed her eyes with a Kleenex, scowling at herself in the rear-view mirror and automatically checked her make up.

"Oh my God," she groaned, "Look at me! 49 years old, fat and frumpy. What the hell am I going to do with myself?"

Diane manoeuvred the car carefully out of her parking space and on to the ice-covered roads of the car park. Both she and the car were in automatic drive as she began the short journey home, the journey across the bridge, past the familiar landmarks she had known all her life, the journey she had learned to dread. In her mind the pictures of yesterday replayed.

Arriving home from her evening meeting of the School Governing Body at about 9.30 she found Ron lying on the floor of the entrance hall in a pool of his own vomit. He was sleeping deeply and snoring heavily. A heavy man well-built although running to fat now and tall as well, Diane knew she had no hope of moving him. He had obviously been trying to reach the cloakroom just off the hallway as trails of vomit followed him and spattered his clothes, the carpet, even the walls. The smell was nauseating and Diane's stomach heaved. She aimed a kick at him to see if he would move, then another and another. She screamed her rage, stamping on his broad shoulders. Ron made no move, no sound breaking his even snoring. Diane moved towards the phone to call one of the girls but stopped, afraid they would insist on driving over. She did not want them to see their father in this state.

So, instead, she sighed and began to clear up the vomit, disinfected all around him, then prepared and ate her evening meal alone. Ron was still sleeping there when she took to her bed at 10.30 to read some papers she had to present the next day at a Deputy Headteachers' Conference in Exeter. She hoped to be able to spend some time with Tom while she was there but she had already decided she would not tell him about his father's drinking. As she slid into sleep her mind wondered. Was she afraid of what Tom might think? Afraid he might accuse her of causing the drinking?

That evening had been the real turning point for her. It was several days since Ron had been to the farm..

He had woken at 7.30 and his head had ached. His mouth was dry, but the worst feeling was in the pit of his stomach - an empty, hollow feeling. Some memories of what he had done the previous day came trickling back into his confused mind but he shut them off because he preferred not to think about what had happened or is happening to him. In fact he preferred not to think at all. With a long, wheezing sigh he decided today was going to be different. He would go up to the farm and make a big effort. His family up there must be concerned about him. He knew they supported him and that, without exception, they felt Diane had deserted him and not behaved as a wife should, but he also knew that they did not have any ideas on how they could help him.

He struggled to the kitchen and made himself some breakfast but as he opened the refrigerator, another wave of nausea came over him. He began to shake and knew that if he wanted to get out of the house he would have to have just one, small drink. He poured himself a small whisky and drank it slowly.

His nausea receding, he began to feel better, so much better that he managed a cup of coffee. His head was still aching so, without really thinking, he took three aspirin and swilled them down with another small whisky.

By the time he arrived at the long driveway that led to the farm, the pills and the whisky had met up with yesterday's intake and were combining to leave him feeling drowsy and distant.

A short time after he arrived at the farm one of the east European labourers asked him a question. Ron heard the sound of his voice but made no reply so the puzzled man asked again. Ron grunted an answer of sorts but the man still looked confused. They were standing in one of the barns and the men obviously were seeking some instructions and they began to shuffle their feet and look at each other or the ground. Part of Ron's mind wondered why. Then they began talking to each other again in their own language and Ron's mind drifted back to its normal resting place - the warm, cosiness of self-pity where he slumbered in semi-consciousness for most of his days.

If only things could change, if only Diane would leave Nelson Primary and come home to him to be a proper wife again, if only

things could get back to the way they used to be, the way he liked them.
If only.......

Somehow he made it through to midday - the men started work without his instructions and seemed to know what they were doing. One of them told him they were going into town for a burger and would he like to join them. This was unusual and he felt awkward about it but agreed and sat silently in the truck for the forty-minute journey down from the hills before gratefully sinking into a corner seat in the diner with a beer, listening to the men yapping in 'foreign.' He knew a few words but they spoke so fast that he could not follow. His mind drifted again and he noticed his hands were shaking as he lit a smoke. He ate nothing but drank two more beers before the men began to make their way back. He excused himself, saying he needed to buy some supplies and he would join them later - he would take a taxi or get a lift with someone.

He walked slowly to the nearest bar and downed a couple of whiskies. His feelings of sadness and desperation were increasing by the minute as he grew more drunk. For the rest of the afternoon he sat huddled at the bar, his eyes lowered, his hat tilted back, his shoulders slumped and his mind leaden with the weight of the unhappiness and confusion which had settled upon him. He noticed men coming in from work and glanced at the clock behind the bar. It was 6 o'clock and he knew he should go home. But to what?

An empty house - Diane would be at some meeting or other. Oh sure she might rush in, her arms full of shopping, she might even have time to throw something into the microwave for him but she would soon be gone again to another meeting, another group of people who cannot manage without her. She would eat nothing herself, saying that she will eat later, and then he would be left with another endless evening and the empty house.

A sudden tidal wave of anger and frustration engulfed Ron and he swept his glass and several others he had not noticed in his despair, on to the floor of the bar with an intrusive crash. A silence fell on the bar as the evening drinkers watched the barman walk round to Ron and firmly help him on his way to the street.

Ron eventually arrived home at 8.30 after staggering through two more bars before someone who remembered him as the fine man he used to be, helped him into his car and drove him home. Ron noticed that Ed - his name was Ed, wasn't it - Ron remembered his face but had difficulty recalling the name- kept edging away from him whenever he turned his face towards him. His breath must smell pretty strong. He dozed for the few minutes' grace the drive granted him.

He staggered into the home he knew so well, a house which now seemed not to know him, lulling him into security before striking with a table in the groin here and a chair to the knee there. In the kitchen, hidden behind Diane's cookbooks (what did she need those for? She never had time for eating, let alone cooking) he found a bottle of vodka. He smiled desperately as he put the bottle to his lips. She thought she was so clever, with her fancy friends and meeting groups but she still couldn't get the better of him! No matter where she hid them he would always find them.

He fell on the couch and drank some more. Sometime later he felt a nausea rising from his stomach, empty of food but struggling against the cocktail of liquor and nicotine it had been fed over the past twelve hours. He struggled sluggishly to his feet, stumbled against a table that had never been there before and fell, hitting his head heavily on the hall floor. As his stomach muscles propelled the remaining contents of his day's drinking upwards and outwards Ron's lips moved,

"If only..."

He fell into a mercifully deep sleep right there, where Diane had found him. She cleared up his mess and sprayed everywhere to eradicate the smell of vomit. The following morning, when Diane rose early to catch the 7.30 morning train to Exeter, Ron had made it back to the couch. He was still snoring drunkenly and there was the empty vodka bottle beside his outstretched arm.

Now, as she steered the car through the dirt-stained remains of last week's snowfall Diane realised that that evening had been the last straw - the one that had broken her. She drove home with a new determination. She would call Ed, her lawyer, and seek some advice tomorrow.

As she got out of the car she noticed that the front door was slightly ajar. Fearing the worst she tiptoed into the house through the hall and into the kitchen.. There was no-one there, the house was empty. On the kitchen worktop was a note in Ron's childish handwriting,

Can't take any more
have gone to the farm.
I want a divorce

'Well, that's convenient,' thought Diane, her mind now made up,

"So do I."

M.J .Burgess

Fourteen

We are renowned in Britain for our eccentric summer outdoor events such as the world conker championships in Northamptonshire and the cheese rolling in Gloucestershire.

Not many people have heard of the event described in our next story, however, which was recounted by a grandfather to his incredulous grandson on a recent car journey.

After reading the story you may wonder why this event is not more widely recognised..

VACUUM CLEANERS

Some people thrill to the sound of Ferrari camshafts whirring, or to a recording of Arvan Plot's four bicycles and a tuba. Those of you whose special treat is the sound of a well-maintained vacuum cleaner could do worse than to venture down to the Great Vacuum Rally, at Filling Bagford.

How about this for starters? A 1972 Electrolux 305 in immaculate condition – and that old timer still sucks! In the hands of its owner, Harry Ford, the old 'lux swept all before it in the hamster food and cake crumbs classes. On the punishing trodden-in raisin course, the old cylinder cleaner groaned, but came up trumps. And, as Harry said,

"All she needs is an occasional wash of the exhaust filter and she's ready for another season."

Or how about this? A 1967 Hoover Junior in mint condition, storming along on the damp athlete's foot powder course – and showing a clean pair of brushes to a 1970 Hoover Constellation! I asked its owner, Arthur Belton, about the attraction of old vacuum cleaners.

"It's hard to explain," he said, 'but I think it's the feeling of contained power... all those fans and belts whirring round... all those filters – er – filtering."

He points me to a showcase.

"'Do you know what those are? Original drive belts for a 1936 Mugford Invincible." (Sadly, the Mugford never caught on – it was petrol powered – but for many owners who liked to combine the activities of cleaning the house and tidying up the lawn, it was a boon).

On, then, to the future! Students at the School of Vacuum, University of Bristol Institute of Science and Technology (UBIST) have produced a dazzling display of what the future might hold. Sally Odgerton-Myers has crafted a combined upright cleaner and ghetto blaster. As Sally says,

"Why annoy the neighbours with that thrum-thrum sound when you can pound your floor with boom-boom! Much better for lifting the dirt, and if you have neighbours below you, it's a real treat for them!" Indeed, Sally.

Bert Sproul (no relation) has taken the alternative approach; the completely silent cleaner. A novel concept here is 'dirt debt.' You run the cleaner over your floor (it doesn't actually clean) and, once a month, professional cleaners come into your house and do the job properly. You have the satisfaction of walking the vac without the associated auditory battering or the tiresome task of bag disposal!

The high point of the day was undoubtedly the ceremonial emptying of the dustbag of a 1938 Hoover upright – for the very first time! Its owner, Mrs. Ivy Clegg, noticed something wrong in June 1998. In her words:

"Poor old Baggy – that's his name, you know – was getting a bit – you know – forgetful. He was putting down more dust than he was picking up and was getting – well – paunchy. So, I brought him here. Can you do anything?"

I shall never forget the sight that greeted us as we carefully unzipped Baggy's dustbag. Confronting us was a solid grey cylinder, rather like a cold doner kebab, speckled with the remnants of countless Marie biscuits and small pieces of tinsel from long forgotten Christmases. It was a true archaeological record of Ivy's life at 12, Mafeking Mansions. Near the bottom, the very earliest finds: a mummified mouse; two chips; and strands of Ivy's hair, still an attractive auburn shade. Moving up, reminders of the 1940's: the ends of old Woodbines ("my first husband's") and, here and there, the remnants of a more expensive brand of cigarette (Ivy goes pink and a smile briefly hovers around her old, faintly downed, lips).

On, now, to the real finds: one of the first aluminium milk bottle tops; the arm of a papier-maché doll; a silver threepenny bit, which Ivy pounces on with glee although its current status as legal tender is questionable.

Ivy is given a quick tutorial on the importance of regular bag changing and off she goes with Baggy for -who knows? – another sixty years of happy vacuuming.

The vacuum cleaner is so much more than a mere tool. It lovingly preserves our detritus, both personal and domestic (do you know what household dust is made of?) and holds onto it until we really want to let go of it.

In this sense it is both therapist and carer.

Frank Maddix

Fifteen

Equally ridiculous is the next story about a walking frame.

Perhaps the most unbelievable aspect of the story is that it is completely true!

So says the u3a member who told it to her friends on one of their days out together.

ROLAND THE ROLLATOR

I am Roland Rollator, 'please call me Roly,' and I just breathed a sigh of relief.

Were my travels really over, could I rest from my discombobulated state? Were the gates of home open and welcoming, could I snuggle down and welcome long rests in the comfortable boot of my very own Corsa or happily in the covered porch attached to the house? All that I had ever wanted was to be a Walker, helping someone to walk, not a worldwide traveller, not a detective, working hard to see where they would take me next and having to self-analyse which journey I was now on.

I never knew if I was being driven halfway across the country to an unknown destination or flying across the world to somewhere quite different from the location clearly identified on my label; well, that is if the label had been actually attached or indeed supplied in the first instance.

Now, here I was feeling quite travel sick being couriered to home; or was I? So many promises, this was it, if I make it I was never leaving home again, I will fake brake damage, that was dangerous, a good incentive, they will never let me out again. Or I would just refuse to move. I hated being wrapped up in all that cellophane and paper to make this journey, it was bad enough that I had to come as an unaccompanied minor on the flight from Naples, like I was a child or something.

That's it, if that Clever Dick tries to fix me, I will squash her fingers so hard that she wouldn't try to tamper with me again. There must be a protective organisation for Rollator rights.

I drifted off, I dreamt that I had died and gone to the Happy Hunting Ground in the sky for Rollators which turned out to be a sort of rehab really for addicts of travel; maybe my owner or her mad peripatetic sister needed to go there, particularly the latter, you would think that at her advancing years she would settle, but no, she needed to be here, there and everywhere, not at home and I got dragged along on these adventures.

I began reflecting on my undesired adventures. I had heard that I had a predecessor, not exactly in my image but one that went on a journey to Croatia where the coach broke down somewhere on the outskirts of Paris. That poor late departed friend never got anywhere near home, somewhere mid transfer he lost the will to live as he had already been severely injured by an over friendly, over enthusiastic waiter in Rovinj who petted him as something unique and novel, causing chronic malfunction. I did not want this to be my fate.

My first big problem had occurred when I was on a visit with my owner to West Sussex. Arriving at my destination, by some misadventure one of my wheels had become detached. That's like breaking your leg or even having it chopped off. The wheel very conveniently, smirking as it fell, ended up on the track. I was now a three wheeled, out of action Rollator. 'Who wanted to come here anyway?' I muttered, though this was inaudible to the gathered around crowd. Due to the constant approach of many trains, I remained disabled until such a time as my fourth limb could be rescued, which, in effect, was not until the return journey.

Though not in actual pain, I cried silently cursing whoever it was, who, in my opinion, had not attached my limb correctly. A miserable few days for me, though no one else seemed concerned, all having a great time whilst I, rendered useless, suffered in silence.

I wouldn't have minded but I had several brothers and sisters at home, however, I always seemed to be the chosen one. I had belonged to my owner's late husband and was, for this reason, revered above the others and considered reliable. Unbeknown to me at the time, I was now one of six, two more having been acquired during my temporary absence. I would probably freak out when I eventually discovered this.

There was the time that my owner had taken me to Newcastle to meet the eccentric sister. I couldn't believe it when I was forced to board this big ocean liner and sail out in the Ocean to such remote places as Norway and Sweden. In the cabin there was a table; well, there just wasn't room enough for both me and the table so the table had to go, removed by two hefty stewards to another location. For once I felt pride of place but it didn't last long, the sea sickness took over, cramped up in that cabin for a large part of the day. I did have the idea that if I tripped up the mad sister then my agony might end.

Then there was the incident when I went to Cornwall. Now I had to admit that I like the West Country.

Label? What label?

It seemed that you had to have one in order to have at least a fair chance of vaguely getting to your ultimate destination. Well, somewhere along the way I was lost. I never made it back home. The Company had no idea where in the country I was and me, not being particularly geographically orientated, did not have a clue either. My whereabouts were not exactly clear as my owner was requested to pay £25 for my safe return, which much to my chagrin, she refused to pay.

I am not mortal so I failed to understand what my actual worth was to her as opposed to the argument that it wasn't said owner who had lost me, it was the company. I did sulk a bit over that one, as, with my extreme position in the hierarchy of said Rollators, I felt that I was being undervalued.

The matter was finally solved with no monetary commitment and I was returned home. The other Rollators didn't exactly welcome me home as one of them was obviously expecting promotion and I was ostracised for a while, whilst I, in turn, exercised the same constraint upon my owner.

The Naples incident was the ultimate. I had survived a journey to this destination in spite of being holed up in a dismal hotel room after our party was stranded in Naples. Herded into a ferry, but gentle strolls around Ischia proved a tonic until the way home. The assistance room at Naples was something else. Crowded, shambolic, wheelchairs that took precedence over me. Mad peripatetic sister was getting crosser and crosser but then they made her push me with all the luggage while my owner went in a wheelchair.

On one occasion I received a bang from her, bruising me but, to be honest I don't blame her, it was very frustrating. So, we made it to boarding and that is when we seemed to part company. The assistants would not allow the mad one to take me on to the Ambu-lift and so I never saw them again, beginning my journey around the world and thinking that I would never see home again.

My owner, it seems, searched for a long time for me at Gatwick Airport with no result, that's probably because I wasn't there.

So here I was nearly home and contemplating those gentle strolls around my home village and small bus excursions which suited me admirably. Retrospectively, these thoughts were just preparing me for what was to come.

Just one more corner.

"Roland, welcome, I'm so glad you are back. We are off to West Sussex in a few days."

Katie Cornish

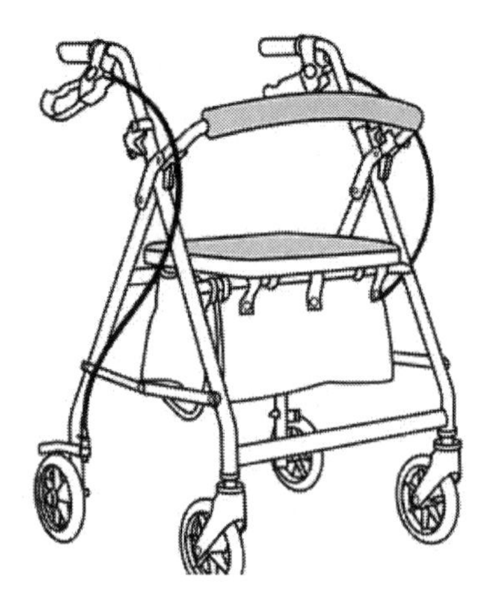

Sixteen

We hear a lot about immigration at the moment, whether legal or illegal.

Of course we are a nation of immigrants, whether these be Angles, Saxons, Vikings, Danes, Romans, Normans or, more recently, people of Asian and African descent.

But we will also be immigrants ourselves if we decide to emigrate to another country.

Our next story is about such an event and it is told by a retired professional lady who has recently' emigrated' again. This time to West Sussex!

On her long journey there, made longer, inevitably, by traffic hold-ups on the motorway this is how she related her story.

AN IMMIGRANT'S STORY

My husband and I were sitting in a coach that was about to take us to Heathrow Airport, looking down at a row of unhappy family members lined up on the pavement. It was May 1974 and we had decided to emigrate to Australia and for us it was the start of a big adventure. To the family it was just us being very tiresome: going away for an indefinite period of time, perhaps forever!

To pass the time before our getting on the coach we had all wandered around the Tower of London – a family move to make sure we remembered our British history! My mother was wearing a new red coat and white trousers and looked like a guard officer herself! My sister had given us a box of trinkets in case we needed them to exchange with the natives! And there we were about to leave!

In Australia at this time they were keen to welcome people from UK and western Europe to build up their rather small population and that fitted with the "white Australia" policy in force at this time.

We had married very young, three years before, and wanted to move to somewhere warmer which we felt would offer greater opportunities than the UK at that time and actually wanted to get away by ourselves! We had just been through the "three day week" which meant light and heat at work for only three days a week and for the other two we worked in the dark, wrapped up in coats and at home there were long periods with no electricity – it was the middle of winter. All this had seemed almost entertaining, with people who had never spoken before rallying around with offers of cups of tea, but we felt it was time to move on to something new.

Piles of forms and declarations had been filled in, followed by medical checks to make sure we were strong and healthy with no diseases that could prove a danger to the Australian population. The final medical had been a meeting, each one of us separately, with a doctor who had to confirm that we were not insane or in any obvious way mentally unstable.

In my appointment I asked the very pleasant, good looking young doctor if he could tell in half an hour's conversation if I was mentally sound, he said probably not but let's chat anyway! I can only assume he found me sufficiently sane!

As immigrants the cost of our passage to Australia was covered, travelling with a standard airline; we just had to commit to stay for at least two years. If not, we would have to pay the fare back and get ourselves home! All we contributed financially was £10 each – hence the '£10 Poms'!

We boarded a Quantas flight and all felt no different to any other plane journey and we relaxed and spent the 29 hours flight time eating and drinking champagne, all provided at that time by the airline whatever class anyone travelled!

We came into land and, apart from being a bit startled when the whole plane and all of us in it were sprayed with some sort of bug killer, we set off to disembark as normal. But things were suddenly far from normal and being an immigrant suddenly impacted. We disembarked after the other passengers and they put large yellow spot stickers on us to show that we were not ordinary passengers but immigrants. We were then herded off to a large empty hanger, apparently to be processed though nothing was explained. In fact no one really talked to us apart from giving out instructions to stay together and march off to the hanger.

It was hot and stuffy in the hanger and there were no chairs or anything at all in fact and nothing happened. By now we were feeling tired and hung over and this didn't seem the welcome we had naively envisaged! As we stood there waiting, for what no one told us, we noticed a large group of Spanish speaking people coming into the hangar. Their large yellow stickers showed them to be immigrants also.

There were two braided and smartly dressed officials in the hangar and they were trying to communicate with these new arrivals who had come from Colombia and were not understanding the orders! My husband, longing to find a way to get a chair, approached the officials and asked if they would like an interpreter. They looked sceptical but he explained that I grew up in Peru and spoke

Spanish fluently. Well, magically, a table and three chairs appeared and I found myself sitting between the two tall, braided officials! My husband still did not get a chair!

The Colombian passengers came up to us with their questions for me to translate and all was working well.

Then one man carrying an enormous woolsack over his shoulder approached us. He asked me in Spanish if there would be any problem with them bringing cash into the country.

Passing on his question to the officials, they enthusiastically got me to assure him that all money was welcome, but they asked out of interest how much money he had in the woolsack. He whispered $50,000 in one dollar notes. He told us that this was the savings of all the people on the plane from Colombia.

I did wonder if this was some form of drug gang money laundering but the officials were unperturbed! The man with the woolsack also got a chair!

There is much I learnt over the five years we spent in Australia (we did come back!) and the most important is that if you are to settle really happily there you have to embrace all that being an Australian means.

It's no use continuing to be a "Pom," you need to take on all that it means to be an Australian. They ask you if you like it there from the moment you arrive and a straight 'yes' answer is needed. I learnt never to doubt their negative feelings about Poms as illustrated by a large sign outside a wildlife park outside Melbourne: this warned of the dangers of the wild animals living there unfenced, especially lions. It stressed that people should: "keep all windows closed, do not stop, do not get out of the car."

At the end it added: "Poms on bicycles welcome."

Louise Chamberlain

An Immigrant's Story

Seventeen

The four of them were on their way to their regular writing group meeting. Without thinking, they had taken the motorway to Taunton. Had they consulted their mobile phones or listened to the radio this is a decision they would definitely not have made.

After sitting in the car for twenty minutes without moving, just idly looking at all the blue flashing lights a mile or so ahead, one of the ladies turned to the others and said,

"Well we might as well have our meeting now as we are obviously going to be here for a while. What have you written this month?"

Her passenger in the front opened up the folder on her lap.

"Well, let me read you my attempt," she said.

IRIS AND JUSTIN

Iris

She was running, she was only aware of her running, where was she running to, or from? Questions she didn't want to answer at that moment.

Jubilance is a strong word meaning 'full of joy' and it was her strong word for her this morning. Hadn't she just signed the lease for the ambition she had had for her whole last academic year.

She liked literature from any century. Her name was Iris, as in the flower, not the eye. She liked tea with three sugars in the morning when she worked out. But then water until lunchtime.

Her run was brisk and when she turned into the park she became aware of the sun on her face, the light breeze in her hair and birds calling, so many of them in the trees. The morning was sparkling with radiance, she forgot about her father's condemnation and started singing along to some headphone music.

Feeling good she decided to chill on a nearby bench before heading home for a shower before she began the day. On the next empty bench in the park she did her stretches and then sat for a while gazing at the sunlight falling on the ripples of the pond in front of her. It was in this reverie that she saw the book on the other end of the bench. 'The Book of Two Ways' in hard back. That looks quite a good read but what is it doing here, it wasn't cheap, she surmised. She picked it up and a press cutting fell out.

'Why not join the book readers recycle club and when you have finished a read, leave it in a public space for someone else to pick it up.'

Well that explained it, she would add it to her stock.

After her shower she dressed in a smart pair of trousers, silk shirt and a pale green jacket, (and overalls in a backpack). Taking her bunch of keys from her bedroom drawer she walked three hundred yards to her enterprise. 'The Book Nook,' it was her naming.

Surrounded by boxes and containers she looked around, mentally planning the spaces after the previous bookstore owner had left. The shelves were oak and had been repositioned by the painters and decorators after they had left. It was a blank canvas. She already had a plan but needed to think in terms of the customer, would they want novels or geography when they first enter? But where to start?

Three hours later with the help of a kind neighbour things were starting to look good. Iris had lived in Grantham all her life and she and her family knew almost half of the town, there had been several offers of help. Her father was well known in the town.

"We don't only need a plan we need the signposts that were promised yesterday."

The next hour meant a chase up, if necessary she would collect them herself.

Falling into bed that night she was exhausted but she was still curious about the book from the bench . Opening it again she found a notation in the margin (She hated that),

'Wyatt – what name is that for a British aristocrat, more a name for a cowboy.'

Despite herself she giggled. And then fell asleep with the book in her hands.

Justin

Justin hated running. Fair curly hair, a gangly body, he thought he had nothing to recommend himself to women. He had not had a girlfriend to speak of before. He had been concentrating on studying. Now that he had a permanent job he thought he could afford to take a girl out and wine and dine her, if, of course, any of them would put up with him. To this end he decided to join the park run, even though he had no idea what it entailed except that there were women who did the park run also. So, the following Saturday he got into some gear that he thought might be appropriate and set off to the venue. He had no idea how many people would be there and they were also quite committed to the endeavour. There were people there for the first time like himself but looking around the girls all seemed to be kitted out and ready to really run.

Well, in for a penny, in for a pound as they say and he started to run too.

He set off well but by the pond halfway around he fell, sprawling beneath the crowd who were running seriously.

"Are you alright?"

What luck, a very nice girl had asked. Red from exertion he mumbled

"Yes thanks" and tried to look needy as he hobbled over to the nearest bench.

"Good idea, that's my favourite bench, well enjoy the rest of the run;" and she was off.

One clue, her favourite bench. Thankyou Watson. Three weeks of sauntering by the bench he struck lucky, she was eating a sandwich and he gingerly sat down.

"So, why is this your favourite bench?" he enquired.

"Sorry? Oh, you are the guy that fell over in front of us. Are you OK now?"

"Yes thanks, I was wondering if I could buy you a cup of coffee. To say thanks?"

"I didn't do anything and I don't have coffee with strangers, any way I have to get back to the book shop now," and she was off, again.

Book shop, another clue, thankyou Watson. After visiting three bookshops, he saw her through the window. He ran and bought two cups of takeaway coffees and sauntered in.

"Well, Mohamed and mountains you know," oh drat she had a coffee machine.

"Oh, forgive me I just wanted to get to know you," he squirmed. At least she looked amused

"OK, question and answer, Well, what's your favourite piece of music."

"Mahler's fifth," he replies , she snorted .

"I play clarinet, some of us do."

"Ok what's yours?"

"I like anything by David Bowie."

"Who's your favourite playwright?"

"Oscar Wilde definitely. Yours?"

"Dennis Potter. We are incompatible. No way."

He closes his eyes; "What colour are my eyes?"

"Green."

"Aha"…

She blushes. She closes her eyes. "What colour are my eyes?"

"Beautiful."

"Oh, corny. OK, one date."

He grins. She thinks his face is very kind, if that is attractive. After the first date at a wine bar, he becomes a regular at Book Nook for coffee.

He thinks the best way to impress her is to take her to a concert.

“Can I take you out to dinner, I have a surprise I think you would like?”

She smiles. “I’d love that”.

“Can I pick you up?” She tells him her address.

7.oclock, he rings the bell.

“Hello Sir, what are you doing here?”

“More to the point what are you doing here Justin?” he turns around to Iris, “Oh I see!”

Iris glares at her father, “How do you know Justin?”

“He is one of my protégés in my firm.”

Iris looks at Justin. “You are a lawyer?”

“Yes. You didn’t ask.”

Iris gives the biggest shrug she could muster.

“Iris I’ve got tickets for Berlin in three days’ time.”

“Iris is not going anywhere, I’m sure you’re a good chap, no offence.”

Kevin glowered. Iris is annoyed.

“Have you been stalking the boss’s daughter?”

“No, honestly, of course not. I didn’t know.”

"I don't believe you. Just now I don't trust you. We are finished."

Justin understood. He saw how it must look and Kevin was not to be crossed if he needed a first job. Justin was bereft and mortified that he had messed up so badly with a girl he really liked. He did some soul searching about the vulnerability of women and to make matters worse he had to take a back seat in Kevin's solicitors office.

He made no attempt to go near or walk past Iris's bookstore. And especially not the favourite bench. Surely, he should have realised that Iris was top drawer with a good family. Slowly he gained favour at work and let sleeping dogs lie. He gave up running. He concentrated on his clarinet playing and was invited to join a small amateur orchestra. He made a few dates there but it was taking a long time for him to forgive himself.

As for Iris, she threw herself into her business. She ran authors' book signings, themed evenings, book groups. But still it was so frustrating that often the coffee sales took more in revenue than book sales. In the following summer, although she was just in profit she decided to close.

Justin was throwing all his efforts into his job and it succeeded; soon Kevin thought of him as his right-hand man. Iris was never mentioned between them and they both thought this was the best policy. He often walked home past the Book Nook but after closing time. And the bench, the special bench was sat on from time to time but no Iris was seen. But on one occasion he was shocked to find a For Sale notice upon the front door of the Book Nook.

He immediately tried the favourite bench and this time there was Iris, reading… 'The Book of Two Ways.'

"What do you think of my book then?"

Iris looked up into the evening sun but immediately recognised the voice.

"It was you; you left the book?"

"Yes, afraid so."

I have read a few of Jodi Picoult, I like the way her endings are so enigmatic.

"Me too."

"I don't like notations in the margins."

"I don't like marmalade."

"No one dislikes marmalade!"

"I do; I like honey."

"You are impossible."

They both laugh.

"I've missed you."

"I've missed you."

"Sorry," "Sorry"

"Well what are you doing now that Book Nook has closed?"
Iris looked down at her lap

"Actually, I'm doing an M.A. in Business Management and Social Media."

"Good for you."

Justin could see that Iris looked crushed. Perhaps he should simply ignore Kevin; there was more to this than met the eye.

Justin looks into Iris's beautiful eyes imploringly.

"Could we, ……try again?"

***

It was 6.30 on Saturday after Hatchards the quality bookstore in London had closed its doors for the week. The staff were making tracks to their favourite wine bars and Paula and Kat were perched on stools at the bar. A barman was hovering attentively in their direction.

“White wine please. Riesling. Hi Paula, I am exhausted!”

“Me too. Spill the gossip then Kat.”

“I met the Manager’s husband.”

“Tall dark and handsome?”

“Very cool, tall, blonde and handsome. Top notch suit and shoes. He came into Hatchards to tell her he had just bought two tickets for the David Bowie concert.”

“Gross! They are middle aged and I bet the tickets must cost a fortune.”

“Yeah. I asked her how they had met; you know what she said?”

“Go on.”

“On a park bench!”

“Bit weird, I’d say. Princess meets Down and Out.”

They laughed loudly.

Iris and Justin were dismissed and Paula and Kat got peacefully and gradually drunk.

Zoe Ainsworth-Grigg

Iris and Justin

Eighteen

A second tale of transportation.

This one's family roots lie in the Midlands of the UK, and the reader may be appreciative that our justice system has improved, in some ways, over the years - especially where children are involved.

ELIZA CRAYTHORNE' STORY -
A Child Convict

The story of Eliza Craythorne, who is my 1st cousin 5 times removed, shows the hard lives of those born in earlier times and the harsh sentences given to individuals, whatever their age, for relatively minor offences, which were often driven by poverty. Eliza was the daughter of Charles Craythorne (the son of Joseph and Ann Crathorne of Kings Norton, Worcestershire) and his second wife Ann Hawker (or Hawkes). Eliza was born on the 26th of March 1833, and she was baptised on the 13th of May 1833 at St Philips church, when her large family were living in Garrison Lane in Birmingham.

In 1847 Eliza was 13 and she was employed as a 'nurse girl' working for 37 year old Mary Westbury who was a midwife and her husband Samuel who was 33, and he was a shoemaker by trade. They accused Eliza of 'stealing one frock and other articles from the person of Sarah Ann Westbury: the property of Samuel Westbury.' Sarah Ann was the two-year old daughter of Mary and Samuel.

Eliza was brought before the Sessions of Peace for the borough of Birmingham within the Public Office on Saturday the 5th June 1847. The 'Learned Recorder' M D Hill, Esq. Q.C., entered court at 9 o'clock, and the following gentlemen were sworn to the Grand Jury. Mr. Arthur Dakin was sworn in as the Foreman, followed by Messrs. William Bolton, John Boucher, John Clive, Benjamin Davidson, William Grundy, Thomas Harwood, Charles Hopkins, Thomas Jones, Charles Thomas Lutwyche, John P. Philpotts, Joseph Rock, Joseph Smout and George Unite.

It had been seven weeks since the last Sessions and there was a total of 82 prisoners to be tried, which was an unusually high number. Eliza's father Charles, who had himself been on the wrong side of the law in 1830 for theft, and served two months in prison, was entered into court records as being present at her trial. Also listed was her mother and some of her brothers and sisters as 'being her relations where she was last residing.'

Due to the heavy calendar the 'Learned Recorder' briefly addressed the Grand Jury stating that he did not think it prudent to detain the Grand Jury with any lengthy observations, and so he asked them to retire to their rooms, and the bills would be sent up to them. Before they retired, and as he had often stated before, it was not the duty of the grand jury to try the guilt or innocence of the prisoners, but merely to ascertain whether there was sufficient evidence against them to call for an answer to the charge.

He further explained that the prisoners were to be tried in that Court, and that every prisoner would have a full and complete opportunity of disproving the charges against them. The Grand Jury then retired, and a short time later the trials of the prisoners were dealt with.

The court was adjourned at 7 o'clock on Saturday evening and all those present were informed that the court would resume again on Monday morning at 9 o'clock, at which hour C. J. Gale, Esq., Q.C. would take his seat at the bench.

Due to the heavy caseload the business of the Sessions were finally concluded on the evening of Tuesday the 8th of June, and the sentences were then passed down to the prisoners. The charges ranged from the stealing of two tons of iron, to a man accused of stealing a handkerchief; the property of a person unknown.

There seems to have been little distinction between types of crimes, or criminal; no one was acquitted, and all received either a prison sentence, or transportation. The court sentenced 14 year old Eliza Craythorne to be transported to Van Diemen's Land (Tasmania) for a term of 7 years.

The sentence of transportation were usually carried out in three parts. It was normal for prisoners under sentence of transportation to spend the first part of their sentence where they had awaited trial, usually in solitary confinement. They remained there until the Secretary of State ordered their removal to a port facility. The second part of their sentence came into force when the prisoner arrived at the port facility where they were held until they were allocated to a prison ship.

After arrival at the port facility the prisoners were generally assessed by the authorities and their chances of actually being deported were dependent on their previous record, and their behaviour whilst in detention. The final stage of the transportation process was when a prisoner finally leaves these shores.

In certain cases, the sentence was overturned and the convict served out their sentence in England. Typically, prisoners were young and from the major cities, with many originating from Dublin in Ireland. Notably, a large proportion of the Irish convicts at that time were orphans; a situation caused since 1845 by the successive failure of the potato crops that bought famine and economic ruin to Ireland. Regardless of this situation young girls and unmarried women were invariably transported as this was seen as a way to rid the country of its criminals, and a way for new colonies to become populated. So, by virtue of her age and gender, the authorities did not intervene, and Eliza's sentence was upheld. However, in reality the fate of Eliza Craythorne had been sealed on the day of her crime.

The second stage of Eliza's sentence was when she arrived at Millbank prison, in Woolwich, London, carrying with her the 'caption papers' stating her offence, the date of conviction and length of sentence. Millbank prison was run using the 'separate system' where prisoners were kept in isolation. The building layout was in the form of a six pointed star around a central core, which made it appear that the prisoners were under constant surveillance. Every prisoner had religious instruction and was quickly put to work turning the 'crank,' picking oakum (picking apart old, tarred rope for water proofing ships), making shoes or stitching mail bags. Millbank, although clean and ventilated, was still very damp and unhealthy due to its locality and fatal outbreaks of cholera occurred. Eliza was probably held here for at least 6 months.

Eventually Eliza was allocated to a ship – which was the 'Elizabeth and Henry,' a converted Navy war ship. Over the coming days the women are given medical examinations. The majority were found to be in 'intolerably good health,' except for one woman who had 'very urgent symptoms of her disease.'

The embarkation began on the 2nd of February 1848. The ship's master was William J. S. Clark and the ship's surgeon was John Smith. Eleven days later on Sunday the 13th of February 1848, the 'Elizabeth and Henry' set sail from the Port of London at dawn. Eliza Craythorne was listed in the leather bound ships log as convict 15903, one of the 170 female convicts who had been tried and convicted in various counties in England, with many being convicted from as far away as Scotland. It was a bitterly cold morning, and Eliza was manacled below deck with her fellow prisoners and their children and were now having to face the stark reality that they were leaving England for the last time. Eliza was just 14 years old; a very tiny girl who stood only 4ft 9" tall in her stocking feet, she was unable to read or write, but she was now sailing down the Thames estuary, alone, and into the unknown.

Conditions on board prison ships were horrific. The ships were generally in a bad state of repair and the cells were inadequate to accommodate so many people, especially those with children and babies. In the absence of proper cells, partitions and chains were used to confine prisoners. The ships were poorly ventilated and often had little or no access to light or air. Prisoners were generally housed below deck, and they were constantly swamped with water in high seas, and seasickness was commonplace. The voyage from London to Van Diemen's Land would take on average about four and a half months, only stopping en route to pick up water and supplies. (It is known that the 'Elizabeth and Henry' called in at the Cape of Good Hope).

The 'Elizabeth & Henry' was at sea for 138 days and the vessel arrived in Hobart Town, Van Diemen's Land on Friday the 30th of June 1848. All but one of the 170 convicts and one of the 25 children who had embarked on this arduous journey had survived. The adult died during the early stages of the journey and the infant died on an unknown date during the voyage.

On arrival all of the prisoners were minutely examined, and all were considered to be in good health. After the medical examinations the personal details for each convict were entered in a separate volume and the date and place of trial, sentence, dates of embarkation and arrival, religion, degree of literacy, crime for which sentenced, gaol and hulk report, whether married and the convict's own statement of her offence. Eliza gives her religion as Protestant and in her own words her crime was listed as 'stole some frocks from two little girls.' The Description Lists are then undertaken on each woman giving the trade, height, age, complexion, head, hair, visage, forehead, eyebrows, eyes, nose, mouth, chin, native place, marks and information on services. Eliza was described in the register as having a round head and a slightly freckled oval face, a low forehead with a long nose and a small mouth and chin. Her hair and eyebrows are brown, and she had hazel eyes. (It was a common belief that all women convicts' were prostitutes but 32% of the women on board the 'Elizabeth and Henry' declared that they were 'ladies of the town'). The women and children were eventually transferred to their respective asylums. John Smith, ships surgeon, was later commended for this by the superintendent surgeon at Hobart.

However, at this point surgeons were no longer in the pay of the ship's master, but their sole responsibility was always for the well-being of the convicts. Importantly, a bonus was paid to the ship charterers for the safe landing of the prisoners, so it served everyone's interests to keep the prisoners as safe and healthy as possible. This being said, it was John Smith's strict discipline during the voyage that ensured there had been as much ventilation as possible within the prison confines, especially in the sweltering heat as the ship neared the equator. Cleanliness within the cells below deck was also of paramount importance to him, with particular attention being given to the cleanliness of the prisoners themselves. He also supervised the prisoner's diet ensuring the prisoners and their children were provided with foods to meet their specific needs.

Tasmania has two stages to the prison sentence. A ticket-of-leave was granted at the satisfactory completion of the probation pass holder stage, and this was eventually followed by the final stage, the granting of a pardon. Women who were eligible to become probation pass holders could be employed privately, usually as domestic servants, and could find work with free settlers, or even convict settlers. The probation pass was linked to conduct and could be revoked for serious breaches and offenders sent to a House of Correction (or Female Factory) for a period of 'punishment, employment and reformation.' Many female convicts were keen to marry very quickly, as it was generally believed that marriage would effectively free a woman convict from her servitude.

The Government actively encouraged marriage between convicts as it was seen as a means of rehabilitation and became the practice that any man wanting to marry one of the female convicts could apply. The women were lined up at the 'factory' and men would drop a scarf or handkerchief at the feet of the woman of his choice. If she picked it up, the marriage was virtually immediate.

The female convicts that had arrived in Van Diemen's Land between the years of 1843 to 1849 were sent to the 'Anson,' a penitentiary housed in a converted naval ship, for a six-month training period in domestic skills. It is known that Eliza spent a period of her sentence on the 'Anson,' which was formerly the HMS Anson. The 'Anson' was built in 1812 in England and was a 74 Gun Ship. After its arrival in 1844 it was refitted as a hulk Probation Station which was then anchored in Prince of Wales Bay on the Derwent river at Risdon near Hobart.

Richard Cooke, also a convict who had been convicted for receiving stolen goods, received a ticket of leave in July 1849, and on the 2nd of October 1849 he sought permission to marry Eliza, who had just turned 16 years old. If a convict, or a freed person, wished to marry an application had to be put forward to the Australian government, which had to be granted. The couple's application was approved, and they married on the 22nd of October 1849 at St Georges Church in Hobart. Richard was about 33 years old, and he was by trade a manufacturing chemist. He was also recorded as a Protestant, and he could read and write.

Richard Cooke had been tried on the 7th of July 1845 in Middlesex, England, although his place of birth was Stroud in Gloucestershire. He was found guilty of receiving stolen goods and sentenced to serve seven years hard labour in Van Diemen's Land. On the 4th of September 1845, two months after his trial, Richard, convict number 33/1/74/17231, left Woolwich, London on board the convict ship "Pestongee Bomangee." He was 26 years old when he arrived in Van Diemen's Land on the 30th of December 1845, after a journey that had taken almost four months. On his arrival he was assessed, and he was described as being 5ft 3ins tall, with an oval face, dark brown hair and whiskers, brown eyes and black eyebrows. Richard had a cast in his left eye, he had a scar between his eyebrows, and he also suffered from a speech impediment.

In 1850 Eliza was given a ticket of leave which was a part of the process which could lead to her eventual freedom. It was during the early part of August of this year that Eliza became pregnant with Richard's child.

Richard received his certificate of freedom in 1851 but around the same time Eliza became involved in various kinds of trouble, which would continue for the next few years. She was reported to have been in breach of her pass on several occasions, absconding whenever she could, and managing at times to travel some distances; for which she served several periods of hard labour. On numerous occasions Eliza was entered into the registers under the heading 'Probation Gang System' and received a number of harsh punishments, but nothing seems to have deterred her.

When Eliza was 18 years old her situation had worsened and it seems she had turned to prostitution. On the 26th of March 1851, and when heavily pregnant, she was prosecuted "for living in a common brothel." Eliza was sentenced to 2 months hard labour at the Cascades Female Factory. On the 5th of April 1851, ten days later, Richard, who has served six years of his seven year sentence, leaves Van Diemen's Land bound for Australia. He left from the port at Launceston under a 'conditional pardon' aboard the 'Swift,' bound for Melbourne in Australia, leaving Eliza who was eight months pregnant to her fate. Richard had received his certificate of freedom and was keen to start a new life. Eliza was still out of control and absconding. Eliza absconded from Cascades and made her way to Hobart town. If so, was she running away in an attempt to find him? She was later recaptured and brought back to Cascades in the south of Hobart to await the birth of her child.

There was a lying-in hospital within the prison. The site was originally a distillery and entirely unsuitable for its purpose. Being located in the shadow of Mount Wellington, on low-lying land adjacent to the Hobart Rivulet, the buildings and grounds were often flooded. Women waded in ankle deep water for three months of the year and little sunlight fell over the area to dry it out. Like all female convicts, Eliza was required to wear a uniform, this comprised of a grey wool dress, white cap and apron, and although pregnant she was set to work immediately. Cascades was a place of punishment but also a centre for different industries, hence the name 'Female Factory.' Prisoners are assigned to blanket making, sewing clothes or doing washing brought in from the outside. Women were also hired out.

On the 4th of May 1851, four weeks after Richard left for Melbourne, Eliza gave birth to a son at Cascades, and she named the child Richard Charles Cooke, after his father and his maternal grandfather. Sadly, on the 13th of May 1851 Richard died of acute dysentery aged just nine days. It was the practice to wean babies from their mothers as early as two weeks so their mothers could continue to work. The nursery was overcrowded and filthy and the children were given only the basic rations. If a child survived the nursery, they were moved to the orphanage where conditions were no better.

Two months after her son's death, on the 14th of July 1851, Eliza received another 3 month sentence for hard labour for 'not proceeding according to her pass.' Following this episode Eliza's life appears to settle down for a period but the following year she absconds again. She was probably at liberty for some time, but she was finally apprehended in Victoria and brought back to face the magistrate, and this takes place on the 20th of September 1852, but due to her previous record for absconding and prostitution, the court imposes a harsher sentence, and she was sentenced to 6 months hard labour and her ticket of leave was revoked, which had been granted to her two years earlier.

Following this Eliza appears to have settled down, and on the 6th of June 1854 Eliza Craythorne was given her certificate of freedom and two and a half years later she married Benjamin Flukes, a sawyer and ex-convict who had been born in Brierley Hill, Staffordshire about 1826. Benjamin had been convicted 'for stealing a pot containing the life savings of employer' and he came out aboard the 'Theresa,' Convict No. 2287, arriving in Van Diemen's Land on the 4th of July 1845 with 219 other male prisoners.

Eliza married Benjamin Flukes as Eliza Craythorne and that she was a spinster. Did she disclose her marriage to Richard Cooke, or to the Authorities? Previously married convicts were permitted to remarry after seven years' separation as long as their spouse was abroad, even if they were still living. Eliza was fully aware that Richard Cooke had left Tasmania for Australia in 1851 as her marriage to Benjamin Flukes was carefully arranged to be registered on the 30th of October 1856 at the British Church, Swansea, Tasmania; after 7 years, 1 week and 1 day had elapsed since she had married Richard Cooke in Hobart on the 22nd of October 1849. It appears that Eliza and Benjamin, or just Eliza did not want to break any more laws!!

Five years later, on Tuesday the 31st of December 1861, Eliza, together with three other women and a man were at the Police Office facing charges of assault and theft. Eliza was charged under her maiden name of Craythorne. Although there was evidence of violence, theft and drunkenness it was decided that there being no other evidence, and the property not having been found His Worship discharged the prisoners. An article concerning the case was published in the Mercury Newspaper, Launceston, on New Years Day 1862.

Eliza and Benjamin's marriage was probably short and there is no evidence of any children from this union. There is little doubt that Eliza suffered emotionally. She was little more than a child when she was convicted of theft, taken from her family home and transported halfway around the world to a penal colony, which had the reputation as the harshest of all the penal colonies at that time.

Eliza had married Benjamin Flukes in 1856 but he 'married' a woman named Mary Doyle in 1869, thirteen years later, although Eliza was still alive and was not living too far away from her 'husband.' Benjamin and Mary may have had a family together, although Mary had died in 1871. The following year, on the 26th of December 1872 Benjamin married again, this time to Catherine

Wilson, and the marriage took place at Emu Bay, a port city on the north-west coast of Tasmania.

Benjamin Flukes died in 1905 in Tasmania. Eliza died in Launceston. Her death was registered there on the 19th of August 1883 aged 54 years, and interestingly her death was registered under the name of Eliza Cooke.

Patricia Simpson

Nineteen

"I can tell thee all a tale" offered a middle-aged man in an accent with a discernible, rustic tinge.

"It were told to I by me pa, just afore he passed away.

It concerned a couple he had living close by to him and he insisted it were true but, knowing him as I did, I has me doubts."

His fellow passenger settled back in her seat and closed her eyes as the story began ...

WITH A NOD TO WILLIAM SHAKESPEARE

Married couple Antonio and Julia Winklethorp lived in a small, rural location just north of Bury St Edmunds in Suffolk. Pleased to escape many years previously from North London suburbia, they quickly adapted to village life. Both became ardent members of the local nudist leapfrog ensemble, though only in summer months.

Antonio also found pleasure in hiking through the woods in nearby Dixons Covert whilst his wife was happy at home making jams and baking cakes for the local branch of the W.I. This particular group really came into their own when baking, especially bespoke cakes. Several of the women were very skilled at icing, and on a Saturday morning many people could be found lining the streets outside of their antiquated shop, wanting to purchase anything which was home-made. Anywhere between sixty and one hundred cakes could be selected, wrapped in Clingfilm and sold during a two-hour time slot, that's without including the chutneys, jams and the questionable pickled objects which were also on display.

It was when hiking one day that Antonio met Rosalind, who came from Thetford in Norfolk.

Quite out of character for Antonio, he eventually asked her if she would like to come out for a meal to a discreet Mexican place that he knew where the only lighting was by candles and subtle Mariachi music was piped through hidden speakers. This is also where, according to their advertisement, one "could always get a square meal on a round plate."

Rosalind was pleased; she had been hoping that Antonio would ask her out, even though she knew he had a wife at home.

"I like a nice Mexican," was the perhaps overly enthusiastic exclamation she made to Antonio in reply.

Things were therefore settled.

Tuesday evening at seven, wearing an angora sombrero to set the mood, he would pick her up and drive them both the four miles out into the countryside of Norfolk for their dinner date.

Edmund, a pal of Antonio's, was one of the waiters. He showed them to their table in a secluded corner. Antonio took a seat but was immediately asked to bring it back. He and Rosalind then sat. After studying the comprehensive menu, they both settled for a platter consisting of Santa Fe Nachos, Wings, Quesadilla and Mexican Taquitos served with guacamole, Pico de Gallo, sour cream and ketchup.

Whilst waiting for their order to arrive Antonio gazed around the room. He made Rosalind aware of a chap sat at a table, with two others, by the window. This was Sebastian Peasmould, he told her, well known raconteur and all-round boring bloke.

Next to him was Roland Butta, his aboriginal manservant. Friends called him Maki, meaning 'moon,' because it was something he did quite often. He, Roland, also owned a condiment set which he took everywhere with him. The sea-salt cellar was shaped like a crude-posturing giraffe and the peppermill resembled another indefinable tall beast.

The third member of this troupe of humdrum diners was Helena, an overweight ex-waitress, who had developed a liking for large dogs after her Pekinese had been flattened by a road-roller. Helena was also the ex-spokesperson of The Pevensey Bay ladies blow-football team, The Puffing Nannies.

Rosalind asked Antonio how he had met his wife and he told Rosalind that he had encountered her when he was on a cycling trip to Amsterdam whilst in his early twenties. She was in TibetWinkel on Spuistraat when he entered; he was looking for a CD of Tibetan sea-shanties. They got chatting and then went for a coffee and a reefer just up the road in 'The Grey Area' coffee-shop. Inside two men were playing a game of dart. (Two of the coffee-shop's set of darts had been stolen). We later shared a hotel room he told her and were married six months after returning to England.

Seated in the opposite corner was another local luminary, Harvey. He was Nicole's partner, and he was keen to watch the performance of a rain-dance group she was in, along with Moon Wellington, an American Indian, and another Englander from Greenland who also imports Spanish spinach and sells it to an Italian priest so that he, the priest, can continue making his range of delicacies and therefore go on catering for the congregation of the church in the Italian quarter when they all gather in the village to take a part in a short- story writing competition.

During the meal Antonio gave Rosalind the following information:

"In Mexico the government once tried to impose VAT, previously a taboo subject, on nachos and sombreros, and were also expecting the people to pay an extra centavo or two on every transaction at the filling station. This, quite rightly, upset a lot of folk and almost led to riots before the government did a U-turn."

Rosalind nodded in complete incomprehension. Their conversation later turned to a shared interest in classical music.

"If you like Wagner," he said, "Then my set of bootleg recordings by the Bournemouth Sinfonia, made whilst they were touring West Germany, is of a standard you are unlikely ever to hear again, especially the Gotterdammerung funeral music; a piece to die for."

After the meal Rosalind asked Antonio, in her broad, Norfolk burr,

"Can't thee climb the mound and share the cockshut with I?"

Thinking she was offering some sort of intimate gratification; he responded as any red-blooded male would do; he showed her his collection of pre-war Norfolk bus-timetables. But she quickly explained that she was only inviting him to watch the sunset with her. Antonio said he would like that.

Because Edmund didn't have a great deal to do, he decided to slink outside for a smoke. As he looked up the road, he saw Julia striding purposefully towards the restaurant. Edmund dashed back inside to warn Antonio.

“Your wife’s on her way here” he told him.

“Damn.”

He paused, “What am I going to do with Rosalind?.”

“Take her through the back door,” Edmund hastened, “But make it quick, before Julia sees her.”

Fergal McDolomy

Twenty

Those of a certain age are sometimes reluctant to embrace modern technology.

However, circumstances which are often beyond their control can lead this demographic to cast their boat into, for them, unchartered waters.

Often the experience isn't as foreboding as expected, as the following tale will show.

Pat, the storyteller, recounted this amusing tale to her fellow passenger on a long coach trip to Teignmouth made even longer by the inevitable traffic problems. She insists it is true!

ONCE UPON ANOTHER TIME

The Book Circle started off as four or five people coming together who simply liked books, or the idea of books, or who even liked the idea of saying that they were readers of books to their friends. It was quite a prestigious thing to belong to a book group, so they decided to form one and it began to grow.

They were an odd bunch really. Millie (Millicent, not just Millie) was a farmer's lass and each month on Book Circle Day she brought eggs for her friends. They began to look forward to them, they were duck eggs too. Josephine knitted, she took her knitting everywhere, she would sit through the two hours knitting complicated patterns discussing books and whatever subject came up, the latter often being at a tangent to the original subject. Her only distraction was that when it was her turn to make the tea, then, and only then, did she lay the knitting down. At Christmas time everyone got a hat and mittens in brightly coloured yarn.

Fred and Myrtle on the other hand did not actually read the books; they came along, nodded appropriately, listened then marked the books as if they had. An attempt to make one of them go first by the wily Group Leader was always well fielded by either Fred or Myrtle. They did not want to say that they loved the books if the majority didn't or vice versa. Fred uttered ''Twas a fair book, aye, I need to collect me thoughts" and Myrtle "it's me bladder you know, I must just go to the little girls' room." So they carried on without her. When she arrived back, some five minutes or so later, the discussion was in full flow.

Then there was Brexit. Would you believe such an event could divide people down the middle, send them all off in different, and sometimes very peculiar, directions, everyone with views of their own. Mike had voted in, Jerry out and at one Book Circle meeting, there were fisticuffs. Seeing it on this scale, there is no wonder that parliament has issues, for this was like a government in crisis. Josephine wrote to the PM offering her services to make her tea and sending her a hat carefully constructed in stripes of red, white and blue. Strangely she was never seen on television wearing it, Josephine often pondered on this and wondered if she had dropped a stitch or something. Millie didn't think that anyone deserved an egg anymore, arguing about such things and grown men with pistols at dawn, it was something out of the Middle Ages, something in fact out of one of the books that they had been reading. 'Defend your honour' comes to mind.

Fred and Myrtle didn't care, they missed the discussions but no one wanted to talk about books anymore, quickly dismissing the discussion in favour of something more exciting: Brexit. However, a miracle of miracles in its way, Fred and Myrtle began in earnest to read the books. They read them together a couple of chapters at a time.

At the next meeting after yet another failed trip to Brussels by the PM the arguments began again, lots of leering; Fred, in a very uncharacteristic manner, stood up and declared in a loud voice:

"This was an excellent book, me and Myrtle loved it, it wasn't about fighting, it was about love, like what we 'ad ere' before you lot started your loggerheads."

There was complete silence, everyone looked at each other; they hadn't bothered to read the book, completely passing it over as being of complete insignificance to what was going on in the real world. However, they listened to Fred.

You see, in his own way, Fred knew what mattered and what a Book Circle was all about. Fred knew that sometimes you had to shut out the horrors and inadequacies of the real world and indulge in fantasy, in books and it seems that at that time the two were mutually exclusive.

New beginnings Fred, well done.

Brexit passed and Mike and Jerry actually shook hands. Slowly the Book Circle came back together.

Then came Covid.

They met at the last possible meeting that they could go to, sad desolate faces. No one had any idea about technology. They spoke of something that they had heard of called SKYPE or

ZOOM. Face timing went way beyond every single one of them. They had chosen a book and got it from the library, not knowingly aware that soon the libraries would be closed and they would not be able to return them. They promised that they would ring each other but in their heart of hearts they knew the pandemic was not on their sides.

Soon came self-isolation, shielding for Millie and Josephine. Fred and Myrtle did not have to shield but they had to be very careful.

They decided that they would go to the early morning Pensioners' shop at Waitrose, it looked calmer and a more disciplined approach. They set their alarm for 6 a.m......who on the earth sets an alarm for that time at their age, were they stark raving mad? Myrtle was the most reluctant to get up, rightly complaining that 'she might be in lockdown but that did not mean that she had to do uncivil.'

They were in the car by 7:25 a.m. expecting to be stopped by the thought police on the way - 'why have you left home, what right have you to be out?' Fred had a good answer ready but he would always be polite, not voicing what he was really thinking. Myrtle not quite so much so and Fred was hoping against hope that they would not be stopped. They had tried very hard to get an online shop but had not been successful so Myrtle had her replies good and ready and after all, when you have been forced from sleep at the crack of dawn, you deserve to be grumpy.

They arrived at the car park at 7:50 a.m. There were many people already there. They donned their masks and sanitised their trolley, joining the queue. Fred exclaimed in a somewhat too loud voice, "I would willingly swap my 70 years for those of that young girl in front there." She was 30 if a day. Myrtle immediately alert exclaimed "Eyes front, Fred, stop ogling." Fred decided that the girl could not be NHS, not in those skimpy clothes! It didn't occur to him that there was actually a life outside the NHS at the moment, albeit perhaps a very slim one.

Myrtle was agonising about what he would do about the sex change though if he swapped his 70 years. She decided 'no, not

Fred, he was her man always,' of that she was very certain. A small giggle escaped her lips, he might be 70 but….

In they went, booming voices: "Keep two metres apart, there are too many people in aisle one, please move." Now they had just read 1984 in Book Circle so Fred and Myrtle were used to this sort of thing with the thought police. They giggled to themselves that this was really coming true. Never in their lives had Fred and Myrtle spent so much money in one food shop. They weren't over stocking, just necessities or so they felt, as they had always felt, that what would be would be and that it was and they had their little garden and their son had something called 'Prime' so anything they wanted he got for them.

However, Fred wasn't happy about his Book Circle friends.

One morning Fred was talking to his son, who suggested that they held the meetings on Zoom.

"What," said Fred, "What's this Zoom thing? Never 'eard of it, I 'ain't doing any of this stuff that others can get into and see my things."

Fred's son began to explain. He was a very good and patient son. At first Fred wanted nothing to do with this 'techie rubbish' but, after a lot of protesting, he began to listen.

Fred and Myrtle did have a computer but their son said that he would get them a tablet and it wasn't long before the Great God of Online Purchasing a.k.a. Amazon, delivered one such thing by Courier Van, depositing said package on the doorstep and running away. Fred likened it to 'knock down ginger,' a game that had got him into no end of trouble as a youth. Myrtle wanted the poor man to come and have a cup of tea as all of that knocking and running must have exhausted him. "Social distancing" boomed Fred as if he had invented the term.

Said son collected the tablet from their doorstep. Myrtle left him a bag of goodies for the grandchildren, cakes and sweets from her secret stash. She seemed to have got the idea of social distancing by now and even opened the door in her mask. On one letter that she wrote to her sister she wrote a message across the back, "now wash your hands please and use the sanitiser before opening."

The tablet arrived back duly configured with Zoom, downloaded with full instructions. There was a Zoom message asking Fred and Myrtle to join their son in a meeting scheduled for 11 a.m. the next day.

"I 'ain't having no meeting with my own son on a screen," said a very reluctant Myrtle but Fred pushed her on. He followed all the instructions to join, pressed the right buttons, made a note of the passwords and found himself in a waiting room, not quite the sort he was used to at the Doctor's surgery or the Dentist, but, nevertheless, that is what it said. Then 'ping' ....'joining meeting' and there he was and a grinning grandson in another box, calling out "press video Granddad." Myrtle, on hearing her beloved grandson's voice, forgot her resistance and joined in. It was great, Fred felt as if he had conquered Everest all on his own.

Now to convince Zany Zara, she was the Book Circle Co-ordinator or Group Leader. She very much liked to be in control. Myrtle felt that she was 'up herself,' if she dared to use that expression, often choosing books that she felt might be on a different wavelength to some of the others. Really, she was probably on another planet, however, everyone loved her, probably because she was as she was and hey, it didn't matter because they got to choose books too so it was quite democratic. Fred and Myrtle called her ZZ partly because she sent them to sleep half the time and partly because it was their secret and they had invented the Zany bit, once they had looked up its meaning to ensure that they were using it correctly.

ZZ had a tablet of course but because she was ZZ she had to be responsible and, needless to say as such was not a bit responsive to Fred. Everyone in the circle had an email address as that was their way of communicating but beyond that not much knowledge by way of social media. Some of them had these smart phone things but they only used them for phones and the odd communication really.

The next day an email popped into everyone's box saying "Good news everyone, I have now discovered something very exciting. Being a bit of a techie myself I have personally set up Zoom on my computer and we will have a Book Circle meeting. It is the simplest thing in the world to set up, just follow my instructions."

Fred and Myrtle read this but they just shrugged their shoulders, if it worked it would be a good thing. ZZ needed to be in control, they understood this and so be it.

There was panic of course; some people did not even know how to download. Fred made phone calls. In his heart of heart he did not want folk to be embarrassed by ZZ, who once in control, could be, with the best will in the world, well just a little, well, controlling. Fred and Myrtle had, of course, read the library book and were prepared. ZZ was there waiting for them.

Getting everyone online was a different matter. There were seven of them now, membership having hovered a bit after Brexit. Millie could be heard, "I can't get a picture, are you there?"

"Press the video Millie."

Sound gone, they couldn't hear but she could hear them. Fred excitedly

"Press sound Millie, you are muted," proud of himself with his new technological knowledge. Millie appeared on screen but her not seeing them.

"No, Millie, we can't hear you, press the button, the button, we can't hear you, we can see you though."

"I'm not deaf, why did you say I was a mute."

"Not a mute, Millie, it means simply you are silent to us."

ZZ looking exasperated. Josephine in the waiting room frustratingly not able to get any further, Mike and Jerry came on. Fred and Myrtle seeing one flash to another, not seeing everyone together. They had seen it on TV, and then they discovered the group view button - not bad, five now.

"Can you hear me" and then she could and she them. Six. Poor Josephine still on 'waiting to join meeting' mode. Everyone now shouting seemingly oblivious to the fact that she couldn't hear them.

'Ping' - suddenly she was there. Eureka! Knitting NHS dolls. Book Circle reunited or not. ZZ was not there; her space on screen was missing. Everyone posed. No signs, no return. Half of the meeting time gone already. They started talking amongst themselves. Not about the book, somehow it seemed ZZ's territory.

"Do you know" said Josephine, "I have made a bucket list, what I would like to do before I go, this has brought it home to me."

"We have all got things like that I guess," said Jerry. "My wife and I want to travel more while we can."

Fred and Myrtle wanted to go to Australia, their daughter and family were there. They had been planning it but now it was on hold. They had not told anyone; it was their secret but they mentioned it now. Millie wanted to go to London and up the Shard, Mike wanted a shed and a garden makeover, secretly hoping to get on 'Garden Rescue.' Josephine, who had started this conversation, blushed as everyone waited. "I want to go skinny dipping," she said as she knitted on. How could you compare a shed with that? Fred and Myrtle smiled to each other, this would not be on their bucket list because 'yes,' way back when, in a deserted cove of an idyllic Greek Island, they had done just that. They really hoped that Josephine would get there, she deserved to, a fanciful fantasy dream in the middle of a shielding lockdown, pure escapism. She was shutting the pandemic out. Everyone secretly wondered what ZZ's bucket list would be if she was there.

Eventually, with the time nearly up, ZZ did manage to return, flamboyantly taking her place. She seemed to think that her absence had not been noticed. She was amazed at how many people were present. “Sorry,” she said, “ I was called away to another meeting, how was the book?” Everyone looked aghast, Fred piped up “We were waiting for you.”

“Well I am afraid that the time has passed we will meet again next week.”

So the meeting was adjourned. ZZ did manage to apologise and set up a meeting for next week. Emails passed amongst them, some wanted ZZ to go but Fred and Myrtle persuaded them that they had got this far so let it be. Hadn’t they been reunited? Wasn’t the book club back together? Were they not technophobes, he had learnt that word from his grandson.

Everyone looked forward to the next meeting; it is strange how they all felt that they had achieved something. They were living in the modern world.

The next week came around very quickly. Fred and Myrtle got themselves ready, dressed in their good clothes. Book and notes in hand. At the appointed hour everyone pinged in until all seven were there. Millie had brought eggs; no one quite knew why or what she was going to do with them. Fred said he would collect and deliver them. She was wearing a mask. When he said that he wanted to play knock down ginger no one seemed to understand. Josephine was knitting masks and although people thought they might be somewhat uncomfortable, no one commented. ZZ seemed a little humble. She asked Myrtle to lead on the book but Myrtle was more than prepared and even gave the book a score.

Jerry had always appeared to be a very assertive sort of character totally in charge of his feelings as had been apparent in the Brexit war. He was just giving his opinion on the book when a very fierce female voice screamed out in the background,

“Jerry you haven’t cleaned the shower, you dirty imbecile.” Jerry crept back, showing a humility never before seen.

Suddenly a vision appeared on ZZ’s screen, in high heels and mini skirt, lips a-glow with a bright red hue. Waving and saying ‘hello everyone.' Yes it was ZZ's husband, cross dressing and choosing this moment to show his pride in the fact. ZZ seemed to take it in her stride but then was tempted to turn the camera off, wondering whether, after all, Zoom was such a brilliant deal. You couldn't hide anything for the camera never lies? Josephine knitted on. Millie excused herself to go to the loo and her place was taken by a big fluffy cat that kept meowing into the screen, obviously wanting the attention and the company of others. When she returned she pushed him out of the way, 'Down Willy" she said. She had made the tea and would be serving it. Did she really believe that this was possible but as Fred said later to Myrtle,

"It's as real as you want it to be lass."

Well done, Fred, new beginnings again, albeit somewhat strange in parts.

Let's escape again to the world of fantasy and maybe when it's all over we can even stay there for a while.

Oh and no one ever found out what was on ZZ's bucket list.

Pat Mabberley

Twenty One

The term 'dementia' is commonplace nowadays.

It is a condition that most people hope they will not have to deal with; watching a loved one deteriorate into someone they no longer recognise.

The next, poignant, tale addresses this distressing condition from the sufferer's perspective; one not often considered.

LET ME GO GENTLY

I have dementia. I knew I had dementia long before the GP told me that I did. The poor sleep, the trips and falls, the weight loss, the word finding difficulty, getting lost... I am an expert. I know about these things. I went around the country lecturing about dementia. Talking to nurses and carers; doctors and dentists; anyone else who had had an interest. Mixed dementia he said. Yes, I know!

I don't talk much now. Talking was what I did for a living but where are the words now when I need them? I can't talk much but I can think and feel and hear. I hear the slight note of exasperation in the nurse's voice when I don't understand what she wants me to do. I hear the sadness in my grandson Jack's voice, when he tells me about his day teaching PE at the local grammar school and he thinks I don't understand. I don't always call him Jack. Sometimes I call him Ben or Tom. These are his brothers. People think I'm confused but I'm not. I've just made a mistake. I've just said the wrong word. I don't call him Michael or David or Martin, do I? Just because I get his name wrong, doesn't mean I don't know who he is. I wish I could tell him how much I like him coming to see me, but I can't say the words. I can only think them, and the words get stuck somewhere in my rapidly shrinking brain. He brings in his black Labrador, Ruby. She comes and puts her head in my lap. No exasperation. No sadness. Just contentment that I am rubbing her head. I can do that. It's automatic, isn't it? Stroking an animal's head. Sometimes he brings in his baby. I might forget many things, but does a woman ever forget how to hold a baby?

Ben sometimes comes to see me. Or it might be Tom. Someone that I love anyway. Someone who loves me. He brings his guitar and sings John Denver. How is it I can sing 'Take Me Home, Country Roads,' but can't say 'Take me to the toilet?' I clap along and laugh.

"I bet you were a right little raver when you were young, Grandma," he says.

Was I? Maybe. I smile and he smiles back and does a little dance around the room. I have agnosia. I don't really know what that means anymore, I just know I don't recognise faces, but I know it's my daughter by the way she speaks to me and holds my hand and says

"Hello Mum. It's me. Joanna."

She thinks I don't recognise her, but I do. I recognise the feelings she shows me. She never expects anything from me but will bring things in for me to look at. Yesterday, or perhaps it was last week, she brought in a little toy wombat. She says,

"You brought this home when you and Dad visited Australia."

"Your dad gave me this," I say.

She smiles, glad that I remember.

She never says, 'Who am I?' or 'Do you remember…?'' She says,

"I remember when you brought that wombat home. You said its fur was as soft as Dad's beard and we all laughed."

I do remember a bit. I rub the little wombat against my cheek, and it does sort of remind me of Barry's beard. Where is Barry? I wish he was here. I wish I was with him. Where is he? I want to be with him. I wish I could get a chest infection and die. If I didn't have this bloody awful dementia I could say, 'Don't treat me. Let me go gently in my sleep.' But I don't. I can't tell them how I feel.

No, even though I have dementia, they have to treat me. They wouldn't want to be in my position, but they treat me whenever I have something wrong with me.

It's what they do, isn't it? Doctors and nurses? It's what I did all those years ago when nurses wore cardboard hats and silver buckles and blue dresses instead of those pyjamas they wear now. If I could, I would go to Switzerland, or is it Austria? Or Australia? Somewhere overseas anyway. I'd go on holiday. No,

I wouldn't. What am I thinking of? I'd go for an injection. I'd have an injection and join Barry.
Joanna is talking to me.

"All three boys are coming home for Christmas Mum."

Christmas? Christmas? Why is she talking about Christmas? That explains the paper hanging from the ceiling. I can't see colours any more except red. I thought it was just dust hanging down. "Ben will come and see you Christmas Day."

"That will be nice," I say. But I don't think I can tell one day from another. If she told me it was Christmas Day today, I'd believe her. But she doesn't lie, my Joanna. She bends down and kisses my cheek.

"Love you, Mum."

I feel the wetness on my cheek and think she must be crying. I feel like crying too. Crying that I will still be here tomorrow. Crying that I will be here for another Christmas. I smile.

"Love you too."

At least I can say that to her. Words I have said a hundred times to her. I can't tell her how much I love her. I can't always say her name. I don't have the words anymore. I can't tell her how sorry I am that I am still here, but perhaps that is just as well. She comes once a week. Or it might be once a day. I don't know any more. Time stretches and contracts. I have a clock, but I don't know what it says. It looks like a face, and it frightens me until I realise that it's nothing to be frightened of. I'm often frightened. The banana on the table that looks like a snake until I move my head and it disappears. The dark purple rug that looks like a hole and I wonder why there is a hole in my bedroom floor. When it is dark, I go to bed and pray that I won't wake up in the morning. But here I am.

I lie here and look at the curtains. Whoever chose them? What happened to the lovely blue velvet ones, Barry and I bought when we moved into our new home. Barry has gone. I forgot. But the pain of loss never goes away, does it?

Christmas has come and gone. I am lying in bed on my side. I don't get out of bed anymore. My legs won't hold me up. Joanna is sitting beside me. I don't recognise her face, but I know it is her by the way she holds my hand and talks to me. Her voice gentle and soft. Talking about the boys.

"Joanna," I say.

"Yes Mum. It's me."

"Joanna."

This is the most important word in the whole world. I need her to know that I know her, and that I know she is here with me. That I love her. She is crying. I know she is, even though my eyes are closed.

"It's OK Mum, you can go now."

She tucks the little wombat next to my cheek and I smile.

"Joanna." It is the last word I will ever say.

She drifts off into the last sleep she will ever have. The wombat fur, that is just like Barry's beard, is next to her cheek.

Judith Paice

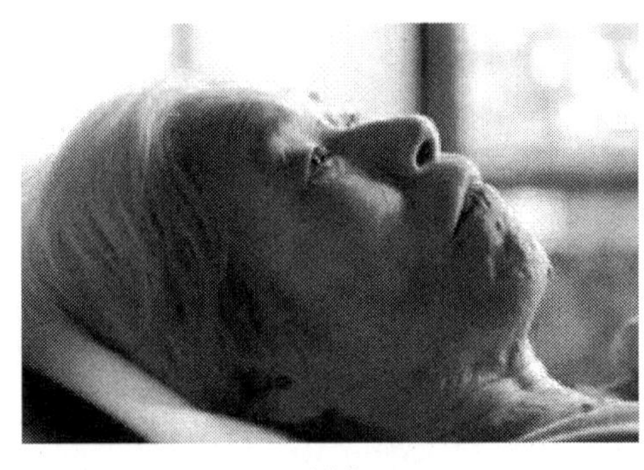

Twenty two

The majority of natural births are without incident. There are, however, those which leave the newborn with life-long problems when competing within a "normal" lifestyle.

There follows an account of one such incident; rare but not unknown – except maybe in the period where the story is set.

The storyteller insists it is true and it is all there in the history books!

PORTENT

I loved my girls from the first moment I saw them. The midwife was slow to show me. "I don't know what we 'ave 'ere Mistress Herring" she said as she wrapped the newborn bundle tightly in a sheet and handed it to me.

I was puzzled. Never before had my labour produced anything strange. Me and my husband had five living children, five mouths to feed, and we hoped we would have a sixth. But as I looked down at the bundle I saw to my surprise two little heads, two mouths, and two sets of eyes. Yet only one child had emerged from my womb, surely?

"You need to see what it is, Missus." the midwife said in a soft voice which trembled, "Don't be affeared now" she went on, although her voice betrayed that she was a little afraid of what she had witnessed, "It'll be God's will…but I doubt the creature will live for long so you should be prepared for that."

I looked up at her then, trying to gather some meaning from her words. But she bent over and carefully unwrapped the sheeted package until I could see what she meant. There before me were two bodies, four arms and four legs.

Everything seemed normal save that the bodies were linked together, fastened tighter than two men wrestling together. I smiled at the little faces which were searching mine for recognition. Whatever it was, it wanted my love, nay needed my love, and I felt that affection surge through me like a warm wind on a summer's day.

"It's two girls, Mistress," the midwife explained. "I have heard such cases exist but never seen one. You see how their tiny bodies are joined together? It seems they share one skin." she continued, wrapping my girls up again to keep them warm.

"How.?'" I began as I cradled the bundle in my arms and felt my breasts start to swell with the milk they would need. Would they, though? So many questions were passing through my head.

“I can’t say how it happened.” the midwife said, starting to tidy up the room for my husband’s visit. Having delivered the girls she seemed anxious to leave, no doubt fearing the reactions which were to come and anxious to avoid taking the blame for this calamity.

“What shall I tell ‘im?” I pleaded with her. The girls were crying now. It was not exactly the full throated yells of my other newborns, who had come into the world with clenched fists, their strong legs kicking the air as the midwife held them up by the neck like skinned rabbits. The sound coming from these tiny mouths was more like that of a pair of mewing cats, and I got the impression that the noise each made was as much for the other’s benefit as it was intended to get my attention.

Above the soft sound of my new daughters’ voices we could hear my husband approaching the door. He had been called from the fields when my pains reached the stage that meant my womb was ready to expel the child. He had been left pacing outside, anxious to return to his work before he got his wages docked, while the delivery of the girls took longer than any of my previous children.

“I’ll explain to ‘e, so ‘e’s prepared afore ‘e sees it.” she said, nodding towards the girls. “ Nothing like this ever in Isle Brewers.” She shook her head then, taking off her apron and folding it, she passed through the door to deliver her news.

I gazed down at my little girls who had quietened down, their four eyelids drooping. As they dropped into sleep I rocked them gently and sang a lullaby like I had to all my babies. The midwife had said they might not live for long. I wanted to make them as comfortable as I could. That is how my husband found us as he crept into the room, his cap clutched nervously in his hands.

“What ‘ave we ‘ere, wife?” he asked softly, almost creeping over to the bed as if afraid of what he might see.

I raised the bundle to his eye level. “Two beautiful girls,” I told him, “Save that they are ..” my voice broke a little, ”Oh dearest husband, their bodies are joined together, their little bodies are one.” A tear ran down my face then, followed by a torrent of others and many sobs. While my body shook with emotion my husband took the bundle from me. I was afraid at first at what he might do, but he cradled them as I had and carefully peeled away the sheet to see if what he had been told was true, all the while whispering " Lord save us! Lord save us! How can this be?"

After a while he seemed to find some resolve. The midwife was long gone so we were left to think what to do. With one of his large, rough hands, my husband picked up the cap he had left on the bed while with the other he carefully gave the girls back to me.

"Midwife thinks they may not last long, so vicar needs to come." he said with determination. "I'll call at the church on my way back to the fields." He looked at me as if he felt guilty at going." I 'ave to keep the job." he said earnestly. "Two more mouths to feed!" he joked, then almost broke down himself.

"What'll folk say?" he muttered as he left the room.

Exhausted, the bundle and I slept, only to be disturbed a while later by a rattle on the door and the entry of a procession. Headed by the vicar, closely followed by the sexton and the local apothecary, a queue of curious men entered the room with urgency, then stopped abruptly when they realised the thing they were intrigued by, or afraid of, or affronted by, was no more than a woman in childbed with two small faces lying alongside her.

Those early days were hard. We had the babies christened 10 days after they were born, on 29 May. This was in the year 1680. The baptism was done by the Reverend Paschall, the vicar of Chedzoy who, I recall, was hesitant about holding the little ones. We called the girls after Aquila and Priscilla who were friends of St Paul, the Good Book says, and helped him to spread the Gospel. Many neighbours had gathered to see our daughters for themselves as word had spread. After some persuading, my sister and brother-in-law stood as godparents, but they wouldn't hold the girls after the vicar had poured the oil and the water on them. They seemed to think it might bring them bad luck.

So, our lives moved on. These new daughters needed a lot of feeding. I took to carrying them about with me, tied to my chest as I worked, so that I could satisfy them when needed. For clothes, I sewed two smocks together to create a strange looking garment that would fit them both. As they grew and started to wriggle around it was a task to get them dressed, I can tell you! Once they got used to the sight of them, the other children quickly got to love them and petted their new sisters. Our eldest fashioned a cart for them using bits of wood my husband found on the farm and the pair enjoyed being wheeled around the place by their brothers and sisters. On fine days, when the chores and schoolwork were done, we would take the girls to the river; Isle it is called, hence the name of our village.

The children would throw sticks into the flowing waters to amuse the girls, which made them giggle. Those were the good things. Our family learning to look after our latest arrivals. It wasn't easy to keep everyone fed on my husband's wages as a farm labourer, but we managed. The bad things came from outside the home. Word soon spread around the south of the county of Somerset, where we lived, and we had to cope with a lot of intrusion from strangers. Then someone in Taunton issued a pamphlet about the twins which even got circulated among the folk in the streets of London!

That led to crowds coming to see the girls, which was not good for them or for us. They even made a commemorative china plate in Ilminster to sell to the visitors. It was yellow with a picture of the girls on it. The attention made my husband irritable. We were just poor, God-fearing folk, trying to make a living off the land and eating our meagre meals off wooden platters.

Just as things were getting bad, they got worse. Aquila and Priscilla were lost to us. The way it happened was this. Lots of visitors were coming every day. It was hard work to keep the place clean and tidy, prepare the food and do the washing for all of us, let alone entertain strangers wanting to gawp at my children. I have no idea who these visitors were. Some came in pairs, some in large groups. Men and women, young and old. Of course, they were folk with leisure enough to take the time to seek us out, not people toiling in the fields like the children's father.

As I later heard, among those who came to stare must have been a certain Mister Henry Walrond. He was a local JP and lived in a big house, Walrond Hall, near our village. All I know is, I was tired and busy and somehow in the course of his visit he, helped by his friend, Sir Edward Phelips of Montacute House, took the girls away! They probably wanted to make money out of them, the vicar told me later. Of course, we were distraught ,and wanted the girls to be returned, but what could we do against a JP and a Sir?

I tried to make inquiries about my daughters' welfare of the staff at Walrond Hall, when I could manage to run into them on market days. They were sympathetic but evasive and not very helpful. Eventually I learnt my little girls had passed away. They would have been but three years old. No one knows how exactly they died, but I know they would have been missing the love of their father and mother and the company of their brothers and sisters and that makes me sad. I believe the perpetrators will be brought before the law for their shame and dishonour. I also heard that they are making a china plate about the abduction too. China plates won't bring my daughters back.

The Duke of Monmouth swept through our land stirring rebellion some two years after the girls died. Reverend Paschall took the side of the King and wrote to warn him, citing the birth of my children as an evil portent and describing what happened as a monstrous birth! Well, they were not monstrous. As I see it, it was God's will that they be born and they brought much happiness to my family until they were cruelly snatched away.

My husband and I are adjusting to life without our twin daughters. We certainly do not miss the crowds of visitors! Our other children are growing older now, but we often walk to the river together and talk about them. Then we throw some sticks into the flowing water and, if you listen carefully, you can hear the girls giggling still.

Catherine Cooper

Portent

Twenty three

Discussion groups meet, nationwide, on a regular basis. The subject matter can be wide-ranging. Sometimes it can be political, or tackling subjects of local interest, whilst others meet purely as a social get-together.

Now and then controversial issues are raised.

This is a story of one such gathering which may, or may not, have occurred in Norfolk, retold with considerable relish (and chuckling) on a long coach journey.

THE MEETING

Gregory once attended a meeting, advertised as a discussion group, at number twelve, after making an application on-line. He had had to provide his personal details, (name, address, d.o.b. etc.), and then give his vital statistics, including shoe size, and finally choose an eleven-letter username and a security question. The username he chose was 'Goatsniffer,' which was, evidently, a rhyming-slang term, though he had never been able to fathom out what it meant. The security question he chose was "What is the name of the industrial metal album, released in 2000, by German band Megahertz?" the answer of course being 'Himmelfahrt.'

Whilst it was easy to enter the front door at Dr. Gibson's as it was ajar, a computer was in control of the opening of the inner two doors. Menus are brought up on a screen, but one has to enter one's username before access is allowed. Once through the first door, one's shoes must be removed and the security question answered. Gregory looked over the shoulder of an obviously non-security-conscious young lady on the evening he attended and, although he didn't see the question, he noticed that her answer was "I like the solitude, but I don't like doing it on my own." One then steps on to a plate which digitally measures the size of both of your feet when placed toe to heel, before allowing you access, through the second door and into the open-plan, downstairs area.

As Gregory headed towards the rest of the people in the room, he saw they were sat, in an ellipse of ex-cinema seats, and as he approached the group, he noticed that in the centre of the seats was a damaged coffee-table, one leg was propped up on a copy of Tolstoy's War and Peace, with plates of cheese and biscuits arranged in an inverted ellipse upon it. The cheddar was cut into rectangles and the brie was cut in slices and each slice was served on a water biscuit. There was also a coffee-pot from Woolworth, a 1950's Limoges Bernardaud Nankin pattern sugar bowl and a tureen of the same design containing decaf teabags.

Dr Gibson rose from his chair as Gregory approached and brushed away the songbird which had been perched on his, the Doctor's, shoulder. He told Gregory that, as he was the last one to arrive, then perhaps he could introduce himself to the others before sitting and say a sentence or three about himself. The others would, in turn, then introduce themselves.

Gregory looked around him, and apart from Dr Gibson and Gregory the group consisted of three women, one of them a pygmy, and three other men. So, Gregory gave his name and added,

"I once worked for 'Blendex,' the company that made food-blenders but which has now, sadly, gone into liquidation. My sister studied the Racecourse Betting Act at Clyde university, which only goes to show that anybody, in fact, can turn out to be a distinguished turf accountant. I have mild Asperger's syndrome, hail from Grene Forda, a small village west of London, though I nowadays live at number 1. I'm divorced and have a daughter who is a lesbian. Finally, I have little time for people who aren't smart enough to realise that they are stupid."

After Gregory's mini speech everyone stood up and moved one seat to the left before sitting down again. The pygmy needed help climbing on to her seat but a man in a deerstalker hat came to her aid.

Gregory then sat down. During the ensuing introductions, Gregory noticed that the far wall had been decorated in such a way as to appear as if one was looking at a view of Mount Korab in Albania. But it was an optical illusion; a fine example of trompe l'œil, a rival to anything by Daniela Benedini.

Dr. Gibson introduced himself first; raising himself up on tiptoe he proclaimed,

"My full title is Dr. Ricardo St. John le Baptiste Gibson B.A., B.Sc., C.C., and I come from Diss in Norfolk.

"How about Dick for short?" quipped a male-sounding voice, though nobody's lips moved.

The Doctor ignored the remark and went on to say that he is Doctor of psychology, a bachelor and one day, whilst stood at the ATM he decided that he would like to buy a semi-detached bungalow, with a thatched roof, somewhere near to Castle Rising in Norfolk. But he's not quite there yet.

A lady with a shrill voice was the next to stand up and speak,

"Er, hello all. My, er, name is Maureen Mentumme, Mo for short, I am, er, English but of French parentage and I like camping at Blakeney. I, er, refer to myself as an 'attic poet' and also must admit that I er always wear a knee-length petticoat, er, even with a mini-skirt."

Gregory idly wondered if she had a petticoat underneath the checked, tweed slacks she was sporting today.

A moustachioed man calling himself Harry Walls-Wylde was next to speak. He firstly asked Mo if "an attic poet was akin to a closet-lesbian." He giggled, but nobody else did.

"I shall ignore that remark," said Mo, so Harry continued,

"I am here on an involuntary basis only, I run a TV research company and the board consider that it would be interesting to see what occurred at these meetings. I'm married, with two school-age children, and own a Golden Guernsey goat. I just want to add that there are some men, when in a gent's public loo, who prefer to lock themselves into a cubicle to pee rather than use the urinal. I'm not one of those though."

'More information than some folk needed,' thought Gregory, and there were a couple of coughs of embarrassment from the group.

A man in the deerstalker hat and baggy, corduroy trousers spoke next; raising himself noisily he told the rest that he was named Percy Vere and was originally from Bury St. Edmunds. He had served a short custodial sentence for poaching but was now a gamekeeper on a large local estate owned by a member of the gentry.

"Poaching and game-keeping goes cap in hand," he added, "that's how I learned my trade."

The next female to introduce herself was a tall, buxom, chubby lady named Helen Brownstone. Gregory had to raise his sightline when she stood up.

"Before I start," she said, "I must first ask Percy, why do you have two pairs of gamebirds over each shoulder, with their beaks attached to your trousers?"

"Them's my braces," replied Percy.

Helen sniffed and went on,

"I helped to win a bronze medal in a relay race at the Highland Games ten years ago, and, whilst there, I also assisted with the haggis address. I am married with one son and play the alto clarinet." She added, "My son boasts I am a phenomenal bassoonist, even though it was a clarinet recital that he came to, to watch me play."

The final lady, the pygmy, said her name was Colleen Hakizimana-Murphy, and she added "I was born in Burundi but brought up in Eire from the age of five by my adoptive parents. I have often wondered - can Irishmen, and women, be taught to speak Mandarin Chinese? I am lonely, unmarried, looking for love from either gender, life is passing me by. However, I believe that the recent shortage in Eire's grain crop was mainly caused by the wheat tops being eaten by carrier pigeons. I am employed, part-time, as a trainer, showing how to survive in harsh weather and on unfriendly terrain."

"Finally," she said, "How can one have the four corners of the earth when the earth is a globe?"

The final male, bearded but effeminate, introduced himself as Al Packer. He was single but had a friend, (gender, or species, undisclosed) kept a mini herd of three, small llamas and added that he had various I-pod apps, including one which converts metric weight to avoirdupois. He believed for ages that Kvasir was the Norse god of odd socks, but he later discovered this was false, and he was, in fact, the Norse God of inspiration, who was killed by a pack of marauding dwarves.

"So who is the God of odd socks?" Helen asked, but Al didn't know

Once the introductions were finalised, the Doctor said he would move around the circle to ascertain which particular subject each individual wanted to comment upon during this meeting.

"Why don't you begin?" he said, indicating Mo, the lady with the shrill voice.

She cleared her throat and shrieked,
"I would just like to recite something I wrote whilst having a slice of toast and lime marmalade this morning," and before anyone could object, she continued, in the key of F♯ minor,

"Somewhere in the atmosphere something strange exists.
Its annual appearance is surrounded by thick mists.
At midnight-time on Halloween an eerie sound is heard.
A noise that's been mistaken for an Australian lyrebird.
People who investigate those noises from the glen
Soon get shrouded by miasma and are never seen again"

"That's quite good," said Doctor Gibson, "but is it poems that you wanted to discuss?"

"Not today," she said.

"That's a shame," said Al, "I thought you might want to explain the vagaries of a villanelle."

Gregory had the distinct impression that he, Al, was aiming to make Mo look stupid. But without batting an eyelid she replied ,

"A villanelle is a 19-line poem of fixed form consisting of five tercets and a final quatrain on two rhymes, with the first and third lines of the first tercet repeated alternately as a refrain closing the succeeding stanzas and joined as the final couplet of the quatrain. Good enough for you, Mr Nit-picker?" Al said nothing, so Mo continued,

"My point is that I am concerned about the facilities for Art at Clyde university. The department is too small and is therefore cramped. The university management appear to have an elitist leaning towards the literati. The kid I chased from the art-room just would not stop harping on about the Ides of March and the assassination of Julius Caesar."

"But anyone can read a book," she added with a tone of annoyance in her voice, then added, "so why not have a team of students build a new art-room, or an atelier perhaps, so that the more gifted of the arty-farty crowd can concentrate on copying, or embellishing, works from the pre-Raphaelite period."

"That's a very valid point" said the Doctor, who secretly didn't have a clue what she was talking about. He leant forward to nudge the table. This was probably done, surmised Gregory, to establish whether or not his table's centre of gravity had moved. Obviously satisfied, the Doctor leant back again and asked if anyone would like to comment on Mo's interesting comment. After a few moments of silence Gregory said,

"Maybe they could decrease the size of the stage. It is huge and greatly underused on the majority of occasions. This would free up a lot of space which could be put to alternative use."

He was beginning to get warmed up and, leaning slightly forward, was expecting a lively debate. However, everyone else just sat in stony silence. It was Harry who finally said

"I have never been inside Clyde uni, so I couldn't rightly comment," and one or two others concurred by saying "Hmmmm."

"Well perhaps we'll return to this," the Doctor proclaimed after a while realising that nobody was either willing, or able, to comment further. Gregory nodded his agreement. The Doctor then asked Harry what *he* would like to discuss. Harry stood up, wobbled a little and then sat back down again before saying,

"I would like to speak to a member of the coalition, remind them about their promise to make the phone-masts in this town an omnidirectional functioning system, and to ascertain why, for their spin doctors, scripts do no good in altering people's perceptions of the party's rhetoric and, finally, ask if their angle can be interchangeable with that of their electorate."

Gregory looked around the group, and their open-mouthed expressions exquisitely belied any belief that they had understood anything Harry had said. Gregory noticed that the Doctor's body-language indicated that he shared Gregory's' unspoken opinion. But he said anyway,

"Does anyone have a comment to make on Harry's point?"

Al gave a cough and then said, "We are all blind to the future but hindsight gives us 20/20 vision."

"Which means what?" asked Helen.

"Well," answered Al, "My dad navigates using these phone-masts when he's travelling and having no omnidirectional functioning system is a distinct disadvantage."

Helen replied "If he knows this then why could he not have bought himself a book of maps instead?"

Gregory noticed the look that Al gave to Helen, one which implied 'Stupid woman' before he answered her. With a deep sigh, he said

"Well, lady, he knows that there *are* other avenues to explore, but some of them have no trees."

"There's no need to talk down to me, I'm a celebrity," Helen replied.

"Keep your shirt on, Missy," said Al, "You may consider yourself as some sort of sporty, UK heroine, but being the third runner in a relay team doesn't impress me at all. If life was one of the imaginary 'lines' which circles Earth, then it would be sometimes rocky enough to register on the Richter scale."

“Well, I'm actually a model now,” Helen replied haughtily and added,

“Mind you, even though I wear the latest in mascara, and have herbal conditioner on my hair, my life as a model still has no direction. I often think that maybe my tendency towards embonpoint (ombonpwarn) had a bearing on this.”

Al snorted and said,

“During the bus-journey of our lives we encounter many stops; the request stops we can ignore if we require but not those which are mandatory.”

Gregory thought ' Well this bloke is definitely a misogynist, and no doubt a complete misanthrope, but I'm baffled by his need to always speak in metaphors.’

The Doctor then interjected “I think we'll leave this point for now and move on to another.”

“That's ok by me,” said Harry.

“Al, do you have a point of your own that you would like to present to the group?,” asked the Doc.

“Yes,” said Al, “I wondered why the phenomenon exists of folk wanting to abbreviate or shorten a lot of things in daily life?”

“Could you elaborate?” asked Percy.

“Yes, I can” said Al, and after sneezing and someone else saying ‘Gesundheit’ he continued,

“The main point is how names of TV programmes are shortened. Like that Essex programme being shortened to ‘towie,’ and Coronation Street to ‘corrie,’ or Enders, or bloody Strictly. I mean that vacuous, Sickly Come Dancing programme used to be named just 'Come Dancing,’ and I can't help but think that it's a good job nobody thought of abbreviating it back then. Is it a form of laziness, or are people all jumping on the bandwagon of modern-day easy-speak?"

"Hmm, another good point," said the doc, "Does anyone want to comment on this?"

There were one or two giggles before Percy asked,

"Have any of you ever come across what I term as the 'repeat story syndrome?' By this I mean that there are people who would tell an anecdote of some kind. If the tale was, or was meant to be, amusing then they would chuckle about it. Quickly afterwards, just in case they weren't heard the first time, the person will say "Yeah!" and then repeat their tale again straight afterwards, verbatim, even chuckling in the same places as they did on the first time of telling."

Seven of the eight attendees confirmed they had also had this experience, all except Colleen who stated that she had never had any type of experience, including sexual. After giving this information, she asked if she might ask a question.

"Of course," answered Doctor Gibson, swiftly rushing past any embarrassed coughs.

"How is it," began Colleen, "that the people who die in accidents, crashes etc. are always reported in the press as being such popular people and loved by everyone they knew. Don't *miserable* people ever die? One never hears the term 'He was a miserable git, and nobody liked him, so he won't be missed at all.' Also, many of the people who turn up for a person's funeral never gave a thought to visiting the deceased when they were living. Why is this? Is it peculiar to western culture?"

'That sort of comment could well ruffle a few feathers,' thought Gregory.

"I think this is a concept that most folk would agree with, but it's doubtful that those same folks would admit to the fact that they concur," Colleen concluded.

Mo spoke first saying,

"Only a select few came to *my* husband's funeral. He had no family except an estranged sister and wasn't a popular person as such because of his miserable demeanour, but I loved him. I can remember when I first met him, he was my boss before we married, and one of the first things he said to me was,

"If you can force sales with a winning smile then you and I will go off to Bognor; forty miles from here, as the crow flies. So, we did; we had a dirty weekend and fell in love. I agree with Coleen's point."

Al Packer said that he understood, too. He added,

"My first partner had few friends or visitors to his place, something I noticed once I started staying there two or three times a week. He used to look at himself in a mirror and say things like 'There's nothing manlier than wearing taupe, stretch-elastic jodhpurs, a pink roll-neck jumper and clutching a paisley duffel-bag containing spare briefs and a bottle of mineral water.' He would pose, often with my goats, whilst I painted a caricature of him."

"The finished article may be worthy of praise," he once said, "but there are only a limited number of ways one can hold a paintbrush. Although we didn't stay together for very long - he died of a heart attack - so many people that I had never met turned up to see him laid to rest. I have never seen any of these people since, though."

Helen said that she thought the point raised by Colleen was crying out for further discussion. So, she asked Colleen if she fancied coming along to one of their Sunday concerts; have a chat over a couple of drinks and then partner her in some of the country dances. Colleen told her she would love to, but only after she had returned from Paris.

"You're going to Paris?" Helen asked.

"Mais oui," came the reply.

"Take one of the slip-roads off the Périphérique and try to wind your way down to 'old' Paris; you will not be disappointed, especially with Le Marais."

"I'll give you my number before we leave," mouthed Colleen to Helen, who nodded agreement.

The Doctor looked as if he was going to interject but Harry spoke first,

"I lived with my uncle for the last three years of his life. He was a part-time, stand-up comic who suffered terribly from stage fright but usually, after the first gag had been told, he relaxed and was full of confidence. He was seen by thousands of people during his comedy career who laughed at, and with, him. His funeral cortège was huge. But as far as I'm aware his visitors were, and appeared to always have been, few and far between. He never socialised either. So, I would say he was popular, but without ever realising it."

Helen then said to Mo,

"I'm sometimes reminded of a woman I met near Paris one day, and she inspired me to write a little poem about her. I know it by heart so I'll recite it if I may."

She glanced at the Doctor as if seeking approval and he nodded. Then was a general murmur of consent from the others too. Helen took a deep breath and recited the following:

"I met Hilda in the Ile de France as she was about to jump into the Seine.
She told me she had missed the first time so was ready to try it again.
I grabbed hold of her sleeve that flapped in the breeze and pulled her away from all harm.
Obviously hateful, and not at all grateful, she asked "Are you a gendarme?"
I replied that I was just a passer-by and not a good friend of the law.

She said "You don't know me, there's nothing you owe me, what are you bothering for?"
I said "I have empathy, and also sympathy, for someone with the blues."
And added "But if you are determined to jump then please can I have your shoes?"
That remark, in that place, made the look on her face change to joy from deep sorrow.
Then as we walked away she said "I'll forget today. Stay with me till tomorrow."
Then said "Come with me back to Saint Denis for a KFC and a white wine.
When we're replete we'll just cross the street to my flat, where we'll have a good time."

There was a small ripple of applause and Mo said that she found the verse quite entertaining.

"I didn't leave for 72 hours," said Helen, and then continued,

"Yes, miserable sods do die, though mostly not as quickly as others would prefer, but it's the coverage of these deaths that you don't see anywhere. The death of a miserable git doesn't sell as many newspapers as, perhaps, that of a local hero. Also, whilst on this subject, it seems to me that every 'disaster,' whether it be flood, famine, typhoon or earthquake, only ever refers to the devastation in terms of the loss of either human lives or their property. Animal deaths are never mentioned. It's as if they're to be totally disregarded."

The Doctor asked Gregory if he would like to comment and Gregory replied,

"Death is still very much a taboo subject and I think Colleen has a very valid point. The powers that be, in 'developed' countries like ours, are willing to spend vast sums of money trying to keep people alive for as long as possible, irrespective of their state of health or quality of life. An animal in a similar circumstance would be put to sleep because it would be cruel to do otherwise. Countless millions of pounds are spent annually, across the globe, on trying to find a cure for cancer, a disease that is responsible for killing at least 10 million people annually worldwide but is one of nature's ways of controlling population. Again, the question must be asked; what if all of the people lived. There's at least another 150 million people in 15 years or so years, swiftly made into a quarter of a billion by reproduction. They talk about avoidable deaths, caused by medical negligence, or 'premature deaths,' caused by air pollution, but what exactly is a premature or avoidable death? We're all going to die, that's a certainty. We're all of us 'only immortal for a limited time.'"

"If I might just..." began the Doctor, but Gregory was in full flow now.

"No, let me finish. I'm here to make a point so please allow me to do so."

The Doc gestured for Gregory to continue.

"I saw on TV yesterday, and not for the first time, an appeal for money. This particular appeal informs us, using graphic images, that 4,000 children all across Africa are dying every day, either due to lack of water, or maybe hunger or a disease of some kind. Knowing the outrage that is caused when one child in the UK dies, either through neglect, or abuse of some description or, heaven forbid, an accident, then multiplying this by a factor of 4,000 is a scenario we, in our supposedly civilised society, just cannot comprehend. However awful or heart-wrenching these images may be though, does anyone ever stop to consider 'What if these children didn't die?' If all the poverty and abuse halted tomorrow, and those 4,000 lives lost daily were saved by this occurring, then one only has to do a simple calculation to find out how much of a problem this will present us with, beginning in approximately 15 years' time: 4,000 X 365 X 15 equals nearly another 22 million people this planet will have to feed, find clean water for, construct a house for and find them a way of earning a living. Then, of course, in 15 years from tomorrow, and for the next however many years, a high percentage of these people are going to procreate, which can only compound the problem. So instead of sending billions of pounds to African despots so that they can have a lavish lifestyle, or build a rocket to send into space where the Yanks, Russians and Chinese have already been, why not channel that cash into finding a method of stopping those 4,000 children being born in the first place? That's my point of discussion."

Gregory took a deep breath and gazed at the others, who seemed shocked into silence. Finally, the Doctor said,

"Well, Gregory, it seems you have touched on a controversial subject, and I wonder if any other members of the group see the super-ego exhibited here?."

"I'll take everyone's silence as meaning No," Gregory quickly said, and then without waiting for a reply continued,

"Let's look at a typical example of super something – the constabulary will diligently search somewhere, perhaps a local clay pit, to try to locate the remains of a murder victim which, after twenty or so years, will just be a pile of bones. Then, if they do locate said remains, what do they do but dig them up just so that the bones can be re-buried in another spot, usually at vast expense. What is the point, I ask? Why not just remember the victim as you last saw them? Yes, I can empathise with the victim's next of kin, but once a person has died then their body becomes no more than a useless, empty vessel."

Helen said, "You wouldn't be saying that if it was your child buried out there on some lonely moor."

"Yes, I would," came Gregory's quick response, "Their body would be of no use to me at all. It just becomes an article that I will have to pay some licensed bandit disguised as a funeral director an awful lot of cash to dispose of, in a manner that is deemed as good and proper. Graves are pointless in the vast majority of cases because people who have died will still live on in the hearts and minds of those they leave behind, though once those from living memory, say grandchildren, die off, then the grave will doubtless remain unattended for eternity."

The Doctor said,

"I admit that I do not hold with this business of people leaving flowers at the site of a person's death; surely better to give some cash to a trust for the bereaved, to help them with those abominable funeral expenses at least."

He paused before turning straight to Gregory and saying,

"However, you may wish to portray yourself as being a kind of eccentric, but I for one believe this to be a cheap confidence trick. You obviously have no compassion for others less fortunate than you, and you also have a warped sense of dogma. Maybe you would like to leave us while we have our cheese and biscuits and come back in twenty minutes or so with something sensible to discuss."

Gregory was flabbergasted at the Doctor's vehemence, and the opprobrium it incurred in him just made him stand up and say,

"Not only are you wrong, Doctor, but you're also very narrow-minded. Yes, I will leave, and I'll not return."

The last thing Gregory heard as he was leaving was Mo's shrill voice proclaiming,

"The man does have a point, you know."

.

But the Doctor said something that Gregory didn't hear. Gregory just put his shoes back on, had a pee in the tuba resting in one corner and slammed the door on his way out. He returned to his vantage point at home, just as the sun was turning the sky a deep crimson, and it was only a few moments later that he saw Helen and Colleen leaving No. 12, holding hands, and almost immediately they were followed by Roger and Percy, not holding hands. 'Hmm!,' thought Gregory, 'I guess I maybe upset a few folk.' He soon regained his sense of humour and smiled to himself at the whole episode.

The discussion group must have continued for at least one more meeting after Gregory's only visit, but then it dried up. The Doctor evidently took up crochet and he made a range of bespoke antimacassars for his family. From the comfort of his chair Gregory reached over, put on his touch-lamp and retrieved from his duffle-bag the copy of "Morse's Dash" that a friend had passed to him. ‘This might be more interesting than “A Compendium of English Cheeses“ by Wesley Dale,’ thought Gregory, as he stretched out.

‘At the very least it will put me to sleep.’

M.C. Evans

The Meeting

Twenty four

"Let me tell you a story," said an older female,

"about the time I spent in France as a student.

It is an experience I will, mostly, never forget, for

many reasons.

Some of which I needn't divulge."

SOJOURN IN FRANCE

Have you ever been a guinea pig? I have.

In 1963, with about 70 other students, I spent six months in France at Tours, part of the university of Poitiers. We were some of the first cohort of students to follow a three-year course of teacher training. The syllabus had previously been covered in two years, so the authorities had to find a way of filling the extra time. As the main course we all followed was French, they sent us to France to study and practice the language as part of our course.

We travelled by train from London to Tours. There was no tunnel at that time, but I have no recollection of the channel crossing. We travelled as a group from various colleges and arrived at Tours station to be allocated our 'digs.' I was sharing with a fellow student from my college, called Pat. We were billeted in a town house in Rue d'Amboise and were surprised when we arrived to be asked to take off our shoes and scoot along the wooden, polished floor on little pads. We thought this a novel way to keep the floor shining and dust free!

Our room had two beds and behind a screen was a toilet, washbasin and another toilet-looking appliance whose use we were not sure of. Was it to wash your feet, your hair or something else? Only later did we learn the purpose and its name – it was a bidet! Breakfast was provided by madame and consisted of delicious bread, unsalted butter and home-made jam which we ate in the kitchen before leaving for lectures at the college.

The mornings were spent practicing the French language and at mid-day we were dismissed to walk to the university restaurant where we were introduced to the delights and wonders of French cuisine. Meals at that time were very different to those we were used to in England. A couple of sardines would appear with a basket of bread. This turned out to be the first course of several. It was followed by meat of some kind and then some vegetables, often beans. Dessert sometimes consisted of a little glass pot or small bottle containing a creamy substance which tasted rather sharp and was, of course, yoghurt which had not made its way across the English Channel at that time. Another strange dessert was a little paper roll containing cream cheese which was served with sugar.

The afternoons were spent exploring the city of Tours with our compatriots. We spent many happy hours in the warm summer months wandering between the two rivers, the Loire and the Cher, which flow through the city. We were fascinated to learn that the Loire supplied the city with its water which was filtered through the sand and otherwise, at that time, was untreated.

The house that Pat and I stayed in had no bathroom (that we were able to use), so each week we would visit the municipal baths where, for a small fee, one could have a nice, hot soak. At that time the sanitary facilities in France were more primitive than in England. One flat near the cathedral that housed some of the students had a toilet which consisted of a perpendicular drop from four floors up straight down to the sewer below, with no S bend! Needless to say, it was rather smelly. The mother of one of the girls in this house was so worried to hear of this that she sent her daughter a bottle of bleach through the post.

The river Loire is famous for its chateaux. In years gone by the area was part of the estate of the kings of France and, being mostly forested at that time, was used for hunting. The chateaux were the hunting lodges used by the king and his court, together with many servants. As penniless students we used the weekends, when we had no lectures, to visit the chateaux. Many are in open countryside, so in order to visit them we would hitchhike in pairs. At the time this was a common pursuit of students! We soaked up the culture of the region and learnt a lot of history, most of which is long forgotten. During the war, the Loire was the border between occupied France to the north and Vichy France. As a result, the allies bombed many of the bridges and the local inhabitants were not always well disposed towards the British. They had suffered very badly and were still way behind us in many respects. However, we had many interesting experiences with our hosts.

Pat and I were taken to the 'allotment' of our landlord which was a few kilometres outside the city and had a small stone building on it with few facilities where they would spend the weekends. Other students were taken on wild boar hunts during the season.

As we grew used to hitchhiking as a means to travel, we became more ambitious in our choice of destination, until it turned into a competition to see who could travel the furthest in a weekend. Once, Pat and I decided to aim for Germany. I spent a couple of months in Stuttgart as an au pair when I was still at school, so we decided to visit my family there. We had some interesting lifts in various vehicles and did manage to reach Stuttgart. Unfortunately, we had to be back in Tours by Monday, so we did not have time to visit the family I stayed with. My memory of that trip is walking down an avenue of horse chestnut trees in Alsace. It was autumn, and the ripe, spiky chestnuts were falling to the ground around us with a small explosion as they burst open. Another weekend a friend (now my husband) and I hitchhiked all the way to Spain via Biarritz. We had to turn around then as the weekend was short. Our lift back to Tours was with an American serviceman who was stationed there. He was glad to have company in his car to prevent him from falling asleep. I think he was also glad to have English speaking passengers, but it did not help our French!

Most of us had not yet learned to drive, but one of the students who was slightly older offered to hire a car so that we could visit the Dordogne, and a place called Lascaux Caves which had only just been discovered by a man walking his dog. These caves contain prehistoric paintings from twenty thousand years ago. Four of us drove down in a Renault Dauphine, found the caves and stayed in a youth hostel nearby, the key of which was kept by the local mayor. We were shown around the caves and were amazed at the clarity of the images. They could have been painted yesterday. There were horses, deer and bison in various shades of red, orange and black, made from natural ochres. We later learned how fortunate we were to have seen them because within a year the caves were closed to the public due to the moisture in the breath of people affecting the walls. If you go to see the paintings today, you will see an exact replica built nearby.

As the months passed and autumn became winter, the weather in Tours became much cooler and we were forced to spend a lot of time in the evenings in cafes. We discovered the delights of the local wine called Vouvray, named after the village of its origin just along the river Cher from Tours. We also discovered the warming properties of a drink called 'grog.' I believe it was made with rum, warm water and lemon and was delicious. A group of us decided to have a proper French meal at a 'posh' restaurant one evening. We saved our money and booked the 'Chantecler.' Arriving at about 7 o'clock in the evening, we were treated to at least six courses of delicious French cuisine - something quite new to us all.

Our stay in Tours was nearly over. We returned home in December, just in time for Christmas, with many happy memories and a love of France and her people which remains to this day and has been passed on to our children.

Debbie Knight

Twenty five

"We have all been here before" to quote a line from a song released in 1970.

It is also a mainstay of several beliefs. Many people are convinced that this is a possibility; others are sceptical.

The following narrative leans heavily towards the former as those who were privileged to hear it, told in hushed tones on a near silent coach.

THE AIRING CUPBOARD

I spent the first three months of my life in the airing cupboard. I was born at 11.59pm on one of the coldest nights of the winter. The air, apparently, was cracking with cold, the snow was deep, drifted, frozen into obscure shapes.

In our street deep channels had been ploughed down the road to give access, paths to front doors were shovelled clear on an almost daily basis. Boots of all shapes and sizes were left on doorsteps to avoid bringing in the grit and salt spread on the roads and pavements, the grey ashes spread on pathways. No-one wanted that muck brought in underfoot to melt and ooze onto their polished floors, floral carpets, dingy lino. Apparently. I was there but have no memory.

I was born at home. My father was absent, working the night shift, my siblings were all asleep, apparently. The snow was falling when the midwife struggled in. She helped my mother upstairs, checked on the sleeping children and banked up the fire. Apparently. My arm was wound around my head, my index finger embedded in my cheek, so the doctor was called. The midwife, whose glass must always have been half empty, with gloomy relish told my mother to hang on and hope the doctor would be able to get there in time. He did, apparently. Having freed the obstruction holding me in, I rushed out into that cold night.

Another girl, with a divet in her cheek, still here to this day. I was held up by my ankles and given a slap on my bottom. As my lungs filled and gave vent to my cries the doctor, an avid fly fisherman, beamed at my mother 'A big one,' he chuckled 'imagine that as a nice pink salmon.' I was washed, clothed and fed, wrapped in a shawl, put in a cardboard box and put in the airing cupboard, the warmest place in the house. Apparently. I was there but have no memory.

By now it was the next day. At almost the same time as I was rushing into the world with my whole life ahead of me, or maybe a few moments earlier, Mrs Gibbs was leaving the world. Her precise time of departure was never accurately determined but during that long cold night she had left the side of her sleeping husband, kissed her two sleeping children and firmly closed their bedroom door. She had placed a pillow from her bed to stop the gap under the door and gone downstairs into the kitchen. Applying the same objective with rolled up towels to doors (locked) and windows, she had turned on the gas, sat down on the floor and placed her head, cushioned on the tea cosy, in the oven. It quite overshadowed my birth, understandably.

So, I lived in a box in the airing cupboard, presumably being taken out to be fed and changed until the cold winter gave up its grip and warmer winds began to blow. Like a migrating bird I moved out of the airing cupboard (still in my box) into my parents' bedroom. Then to a cot, then to the bottom bunk in the back bedroom and eventually to the top bunk. Older siblings had migrated altogether, possibly to return, but never to the nest. Beneath me was my only brother, a sunny Sunday baby as fair and rosy as the June in which he had been born.

Myself, I am winter. I am sure of that. On my birthday, as I opened my mouth to fill my lungs, winter entered my body, my bloodstream, my very being. I am always cold, with ice within that never melts. Even in summer I sleep with a hot water bottle squashed between my rag doll and my underdeveloped chest. I am pale, thin, a sunless creature. I long to be able to crawl back into my airing cupboard existence. Only my flaming red hair gives any colour to my person, the flaming red of a winter sunset seen between the stark bare branches of a December oak tree, its boughs and shoots and twigs held high in naked dignity.

Just as much as winter was a part of my life, so too was Mrs Gibbs. I could never forget her. Somehow, she was intricately caught up in my life. I thought of her each year on my birthday. I could not open an oven door without thinking of her.

When I was younger there was so much I did not understand. I did not know what a cuckold was, or a slut or a bastard, or why the children were poor mites, or why Mr Gibbs was a poor man. And what was so odd about Mrs Gibbs, why was she considered strange, why had no-one liked her? And why the oven?

Once when I was alone in the house (a rare occurrence) I opened our oven door, sat on the floor and cradled my head on the tea cosy I had placed inside. It was very uncomfortable, and that worried me greatly. Poor Mrs Gibbs, to be in such physical discomfort, surely her mental anguish was enough.

When I was older, but before I departed, I found out something that I did not understand, would never understand. This newfound knowledge sealed my fate. Mrs Gibbs would always be a part of my life, and I did not know who to blame.

In time I came to know much of what there was to know about Mrs Gibbs. She had married Mr Gibbs when she was very young, only 17. This was because she was pregnant with her first child, Juliet. Her second daughter, Ophelia, was born twelve months later. When I discovered Shakespeare it all became clear to me. She was considered strange because she was educated. She was unhappy in her marriage. Hardly surprising really, anyone who loved Shakespeare enough to name her daughters after these two tragic heroines had no business being married to a man like Mr Gibbs. Then she had met her alter ego. He must have been, or so I convinced myself. He was a student, educated, attractive (at least, in my imagination, I wanted him to be.) Her affair, her grand passion, was discovered. The lover (bastard) left and the husband (cuckold) stood by his wife (slut). But she could not live any more, she just could not. So that was why she had, on that cold night, put her head in the oven.

I was different from my siblings and my peers, an outsider, a loner. From a very early age I had come to understand that. As I grew, so did the divide. It wasn't just that I looked different (always winter, never summer) it was more than that. I read books. I read everything and anything I could lay my hands on. I would rather read than go out and play in the street. I liked school. I wanted to learn. I wanted something different, something that would take me away from my life as I knew it. There must be more. I was certain there was more. Mrs Gibbs also was different, apparently; I couldn't judge. Although I was there (but only just) I have no memory.

One thing I could never understand was why Mr Gibbs and his daughters stayed. Why did they not leave? And why did the girls stay when they were no longer girls but young women, why did they not escape? Their mother had wanted to, and in the end she did escape, but not in the way perhaps that she had envisaged. I was forever plotting my escape. It was the only time I came near to melting my frozen core. As soon as I could, I would be gone. I had a way out and (hopefully) the ability to achieve it. I counted off the days through the long, grey drabness, the absolute sameness, of my hidebound adolescence. I worked and read and achieved, all for the ultimate goal of escape. And I succeeded.

Yet when I announced my plan, as a fait accompli, I found myself, pathetically, hurt by the reaction: incredulous, negative, so utterly redolent of the defeatist mentality that surrounded me. Was I surprised? Not really. Deep down I knew I could never be accorded the approval and pride that I craved from my family.

I thought I would be elated when I finally left, but in the event it was a non-event. I packed, said goodbye and shut the door behind me. But I took winter with me and Mrs Gibbs, neither of these could I leave behind.

The wide world of academia thrilled me. I embraced it with all my being, and thought I felt the beginnings of a thaw within. Foolish child to think this would last. I may have thought I was thawing within, but I was still winter without. I was different, and that was my lot. Having been alone for so long, the longing to be included became a physical pain. But try as I did I lacked something, something inherent in my peers but denied to me. Relationships, friendships, were peripheral. I existed as an opaque being, suspended on the outside edge. Once again I retreated into my only known world. But this time it was not enough. The thaw was only temporary, like a sudden mild day in the middle of February when the spiteful wind blows a breath of spring only to snatch it away icily from the unsuspecting eagerly bared head.

Then I met someone who became the focus of my life.

Without knowing when or how I, one day, realised that I loved him. The pain was unbearable, yet I did bear it, finding release in the enveloping ache of my longing. I knew he was twice my age, and as unobtainable to me as the heat of the sun. He was the only person who had ever called me by my non-shortened name and I wanted him so badly.

He barely saw me to begin with, but one day, as if he had been refocusing his lens on a more distant object, I suddenly came into his view, clarified, real. He became everything to me. I grew in his presence, fretted in his absence, needed to know everything about him, regretted I had no life until now to tell him. When he took me to his bed and tenderly loved me I felt myself unfolding into his embrace like a pale crocus, pushing through the hard cold earth and opening out to the first rays of sun. I began once again to thaw.

But in the end, because in the permafrost of my very inner core I always knew there would be an end, I slipped out of his focus once more.

It was then that I discovered, by one of those inexplicable twists of fate, that my lover had been the cause of the heartbreak and despair of Mrs Gibbs. I felt no great surprise at this knowledge, indeed I felt released, as if the burden bearing down on me had at last been lifted. I felt purged, cleansed, weightless. And I knew absolutely what I had to do, what I had always known but never clearly acknowledged.

There would be no tea-cosy in the oven for me, that way was no longer possible. Neither could I crawl back into the safety of my airing cupboard. I had long outgrown that space. But warmth was what I craved. So with my newly purchased electric blanket and my exactly counted 89 pills, I filled my hot water bottle and climbed into bed. Then I wrote a letter to Mrs Gibbs. I wanted to tell her how I felt, how sorry I was, how she had been with me all my life, and how much I wanted to be with her. For the first time I addressed her by her name.

Dear Rosalind.

I signed my name and took my pills. As I lay in increasing warmth, with my world slipping away, I thought I heard Mrs Gibbs call out to me. I struggled to listen but it was a faint and far away sound and I could not keep awake. I slid into sleep.

The light dazzled me, so I kept my eyes closed. Except I was still blinded. I heard a voice. I tried to ignore it, but it was so insistent that in the end I opened my eyes. I tried to raise my hand to block out the light, but I couldn't move, my arm was leaden.

The world eventually came back into focus. The blurred face in front of me cleared to a pair of warm blue eyes and I felt the warmth as the breath of the voice touched my face.

Hello Rosalind.

Pia Staniland

Twenty six

"I know a story." a young, twenty-something man, sitting on his own near the back of the coach said. "My grandfather related it to me. It occurred, evidently, on the estate where he and his brother, as teenagers, were once employed."

"I have no reason to doubt its veracity."

THE BUTLER, HIS SON AND THE BRONCO-BUSTING PARSON

This is a snapshot of village life in Miserden in the 1920s, a time before motorways with their frustrating holdups and a time when the national speed limit for cars was 20 mph. No social media either, apart from possibly the parish magazine and the front page of The Times.

It starts when 46 year old William arrives there with his family in 1920 to take up the post of butler to Mr Noel Wills of the Wills Tobacco Company. At that time William had a 7 year old son called Cecil and Miserden was a great place for young boys like him to grow up. The Wills estate was very large, with a small river, a lake and lots of woods, ideal for 'Cowboys and Indians.' It was good for William too. He was able to enjoy the fishing there, as the estate was well stocked with trout and he was a very good fly fisher. He was also an excellent shot and sometimes he and Cecil would go pigeon shooting together. They put out dummy wooden pigeons to attract the birds then sat in a hide and waited. When the pigeons came flying in William would discharge his double-barrelled gun with great success. They would take the birds home for his wife Emily to pluck and prepare for eating. They also fed well with rabbits and the occasional pheasant. Fresh milk was provided by a goat they had brought with them to Miserden.

One of the games the boys of Miserden used to play was 'Jack, Jack, show your light,' which took place in the fields at night. Two boys would set off with a torch. The rest of them would then give chase and try to catch them, calling on them to 'Show the light Jack.' This could go on for quite some time as the two with the torch could double back and forth for ages. If the pursuers didn't catch them tempers began to fray and arguments develop over the lack of torch flashes. It was healthy exercise that kept them out of mischief.

Cecil quickly made new friends at school but at one stage a gang formed under the leadership of a certain bully. For anyone not in the gang life was unpleasant and they were treated as an outcast or subjected to bullying of various kinds. Eventually things came to a head when one victim, who had been on the receiving end of a lot of aggravation, revolted and turned on the leader. He gave him a good hiding which inspired several of the other victims to join in and settle old scores, after which things improved greatly.

Another activity for boys was acting as beaters for shooting parties at 2/6d a day. They met at 8am under the supervision of the head keeper who sent them off in groups, each with another keeper in charge, to be positioned around the woods. They had sticks which they tapped to keep the pheasants inside the wood. Gentlemen of the shooting party took up their positions in the open fields. The main body of the beaters went into the wood to drive the birds out towards them. The boys were lucky if their part of the wood was the first to be driven. The rest of them had to hang around waiting for their turn to take part. Sometimes they were there for several hours in rain or cold with no shelter. So they kept themselves sustained with sandwiches and a flask of tea. Eventually they would join the main body of beaters and were on the move until they stopped for lunch. A catering party led by William brought the Gentlemen hot soup, sandwiches etc and maybe some fortifying alcohol too. If Cecil was lucky enough to be on an early drive he would be with the main body of the beaters gathered at a respectful distance from the Gentry. William would keep an eye out for him and usually was able to pass him something to eat from the picnic table.

Miserden in the 1920s had a church, a pub, a blacksmith, a butcher, a fishmonger and a baker - a lady with a wicker basket who took bread round the village. Although there was only a weekly doctor's surgery, a local nurse, Mrs Minchin, lived in the village and would act as first responder. When Cecil's leg was crushed by a falling log she was on hand to assess the damage and confirm that no bones were broken.

Economic and social life in Miserden were dominated by the Wills estate, which provided so much employment for those living there. Miserden House itself, home of the Wills family, was a typical 'Downton Abbey' setup. William was in charge of the housekeeper, the French tutor, several housemaids, two footmen and an odd job man. They all took their meals in the housekeeper's room, waited on by maids from the kitchen. The housekeeper supervised the cook, who had her own staff of four or five. There were three chauffeurs, a head gardener with a staff of eight and a head keeper with a staff of seven.

A Major Dawson was the Estate Manager in charge of all the outdoor things, such as the upkeep of all buildings and roads on the estate and forestry management. Felled trees were brought to a timber yard to be stacked before eventually being used for maintenance purposes. An old man with a white beard, who was as deaf as a post, operated a steam driven saw in the yard. He would puff away at an old clay pipe as the timber was being cut.

Miserden had a castle that stood on a mound in the woods, with a dry moat and some stone ruins at the top. For a while Mr Wills excavated the ruins with William's help but soon abandoned the project as it was too much hard work. This rather disappointed Cecil who had become quite interested in the excavation.

Mr Wills was very rich and besides his home at Miserden Park he owned a house and grounds at Pitlochry. Now and then William and a few servants had to go up there for weeks at a time. Apart from his duties as butler he would be out during the day salmon fishing with Mr Wills or a guest. He acted as gillie, netting the fish and using the gaff, which was quite a skilled job. They went deer stalking too, with William acting as loader. Mr Wills also owned Holme Lacy in Herefordshire together with fishing rights on a stretch of the River Wye, where they caught several large salmon.

There were no Police Community Support Officers in Miserden in the 1920s. So, when Cecil and other troublemakers used to make a nuisance of themselves after dark, the villagers turned to the local vicar for enforcement of public order. He would disperse them by chasing them round the village with his riding crop, which by fortune or design he never had to use in anger.

The Rev Hodson MC was quite a character who made a name for himself in 1924. In that year the Wembley Exhibition hosted an American Rodeo Show. The cowboys would show the audience how to rope steers and ride a bucking bronco. They also organised a competition for amateurs with a £10 prize for the rider who could stay on a bucking bronco the longest. Rising to the challenge, Rev Hodson stepped forward and, in full clerical outfit, rode a bronco for six seconds, the second longest of all the volunteers. As he staggered from the arena he received appreciative applause from the audience for his courage. He got a lot of coverage from the press too, who dubbed him 'the Bronco Busting Parson.' As a result attendance at his church increased considerably.

One job the boys shared was pumping the church organ with the bellows behind a curtain by the organ. The organist was usually the daughter of the village blacksmith but sometimes a Mrs James, who owned a large house at Edgeworth, took her place. She was a very genteel lady, getting on in years and a bit deaf. She suffered from wind and when she was playing would release the occasional fart. This happened once when Cecil and another boy were operating the bellows. They were reduced to such helpless laughter that they stopped pumping, causing the organ to produce weird notes. Mrs James whipped back the curtain with one hand and gave them such a perishing look that they resumed frantic pumping to keep the organ playing.

But all good things come to an end. Mr Wills started to find fault with William and eventually things came to a head in 1927. William asked, "Would you rather I left your service sir?"

After a few days Mr Wills called him in and said, "Yes, perhaps you had better go."

So William found a new job as butler to Mr Phillipi of Crawley Court near Winchester and the family left Miserden.

Martin Coldicott

The butler, his son and the bronco-busting parson

Twenty seven

"Promises made can be broken.

Dreams can easily fade.

Warnings are sometimes not spoken.

That's how mistakes can be made."

Wise words indeed.

THE RESCUE

"Perfect! Exactly what we have been looking for!"

"But is it within our budget?"

"Annie! Swear box! We promised we wouldn't use that word! THIS is to be an exercise in FAITH and HOPE!"

And probably Charity, Annie thought rebelliously. She'd been dragged into this – 'escapade' wasn't the word for it - if not kicking and screaming, definitely sceptical. Jake had been an avid viewer of Grand House Rescues for nigh on twenty years. He'd been hooked in at the tender age of eleven, and from that moment, had decided that one day he too would launch his dream Grand House Rescue – a heroic quest to bring an old building back from the brink of collapse, and thereby secure its future (and make his name).

"Well, look at it, Jake. It's about to fall down, and a hard hat isn't going to protect us from death by crushing! Please come further away. It's not safe."

"It's fine, Annie." Jake took two strides closer to the ancient wall and banged it hard with his clenched fist. There was the ominous sound of trickling mortar, and an alarmed pigeon flew up from the ledge above his head, scattering debris in a wide ark.

"JAKE!" Annie screamed as a section of the wall began to move and then, seemingly leering at them, peeled away from the rest, and toppled in slow motion, crashing to the ground a few inches away from Jake's foot. Dust exploded into the air from the impact, and for a few moments, Annie could see nothing but dirt and broken brickwork. Jake had totally disappeared. Coughing, and carefully wiping the grit from her eyes, Annie approached the spot where Jake had been standing and tried to locate him. The dust thinned and there he was, sitting up, shaken but, seemingly unhurt, using a far from clean handkerchief to polish his glasses.

"Oh Jake! Are you alright?"

“I’m fine. Stop fussing.”

He scrambled to his feet, shook the worst of the dirt from his cord jacket, and joined her by the boundary wall, whither she had retreated once she knew he was not badly hurt.

“Idiot!” she said.

“OK. So, it’s a bit unstable...”
... “and we can cope with that!” she quoted him.

“Old buildings always throw up a few problems, and we were going to dispense with that piece of wall, anyway.”

“Then why did you go and hit it?”

“Habit, I guess.”

Annie sighed. “Please promise me you’ll be more careful, or I’ll be off with this bump,” (tapping her belly) “and I won’t be back until the project’s finished. If you want to see your son before he starts school, you’d better be more careful!”

Jake grinned. “You win. Come on, let’s head back to the caravan.” The pair turned their backs on the wrecked wall and walked towards the cameras.

“Cut! Great! Got that Giles?”

A thumbs up from the camera man, and Ivan (producer/director) signalled to the lighting team to kill the lights.

“We’ll break now, for lunch. How are you doing, Annie?”

“I’m fine,” Annie replied. She slid her hand under her smock and unfastened the buckle which was keeping the cushion in place. She let out a sigh of relief.

“Lumping this thing around is quite tiring.”

“You’ve done really well, Annie – and this angle of the narrative is important – it keeps up the tension.” Ivan stood up, turned away, and was immediately engrossed in a detailed analysis of shooting schedules and camera angles with the camera and sound teams. Jake and Annie wandered down the lane towards the caravan.

“I suppose it’s worth it...” Annie wasn’t completely convinced, even now.

“It’s our only option. We’re up to our necks in debt – we’ll just have to comply with everything they ask.”

They reached the caravan, unlocked the door, and climbed up the steps into what was left of their previous life. Everything they still owned, was crammed into this temporary home. The cupboards were tight packed with treasured belongings, and one of the bedrooms was a 3D jigsaw of heavy packing cases. Annie feared the weight would unship the caravan in the middle of the night, so that they would wake with the whole thing lying on its back like a marooned tortoise – but so far, no harm had come to them.

“Soup?”

“Great. I’ll boil the kettle.”

Annie added a little cold water to the soup powder and stirred it with a spoon. She continued stirring as Jake poured boiling water from the kettle into the mugs. Satisfied, she handed Jake his mugful and watched as he took up a hunk of bread to go with it.

“No butter?” he asked

“No.”

“Never mind. Better for us.”

Annie joined him on the grandly named ‘sofa’ (a rock-hard cupboard seat with a thin cushion on it) and they ate their lunch thoughtfully.

"How much longer will they be filming this, do you think?" Annie wanted to pin Jake down. What had he actually agreed to?

"Ivan's hoping to complete filming here tomorrow. He's booked a fire engine for the rain scene for the morning. Then there'll be a break of about ten days, and after that, 'The Reveal.'"

"Will the payment cover the overdraft?"

"All but a couple of thousand and Dad has said he'll help with that – just so long as he's allowed to come and visit when they do the Reveal and be part of the shoot."

"Has Ivan agreed?"

"I don't know. You know what they're like – you get an email saying one thing, then another saying something different. I don't know who to believe any more."

"And the product placement – is that all sorted?"

"No problems there. They've agreed all that – and we will definitely get to keep most of it. I think the rugs may have to be swapped, but everything else will stay."

A shame. Annie had liked the rugs, but there would be opportunities to buy that sort of thing once they were afloat once more.

"I'll be glad when it's all over. Do I need the 'bump' this afternoon?"

"No. That's all finished. By the time you've collected Henry from school, we'll be back up to 2026. You'll need to make an appointment to have your hair seen to."

"And you'll need to find your razor!"

"Drat! It's in here somewhere – I've not needed it for over a month." Jake swallowed his last mouthful of soup and went to the tiny bathroom area to start his search.

"Mu-um! Can I bring a friend home to play? Plea-se?"

"Henry, you know you can't. We had to sign that special paper to promise we wouldn't talk about what is happening. Dad explained it to you. Once the filming has finished, we'll be able to have as many visitors as we like."

"Ok – but can I go to Andrew's house instead?"

"Not today, darling. We must get home. Maybe next week."

Henry followed his mother, dragging his shoes in the dirt, trying to annoy her, but Annie was not buying in to an argument.

"Doughnuts..." she said, and Henry picked up his feet.

As they approached the filming site, Jake came out of the caravan and walked swiftly towards them. "Oh, good. You're just in time. We need to go for a rehearsal. Henry can come too, but he can't be seen on screen yet."

"Do I need to change my clothes?" Annie hadn't expected a rehearsal until the following week.

"No. They said 'come as you are,' so grab a snack for Henry and we'll head straight on to the venue. Here's the map." He handed Annie a print-out of the route. It was a place she'd never visited. She hoped she'd like it.

"Can I bring my remote-control car?" asked Henry.

Jake and Annie shook their heads in unison.
"Silence on the set – even in a rehearsal. Bring your Beano annual instead."

"Alright," Henry sighed, and went to fetch it, dropping his school bag on the floor of the caravan as he climbed in, then picking it up again as his parents chorused "No dumping!"
Five minutes later, they were in the car and heading towards the site of the next 'set.' Looking at the map again, Annie reckoned it would take about half an hour to get there. She reached into her

bag and pulled out the promised doughnut and a small carton of orange juice. She handed them to Henry, who was sitting in the back of the car, totally absorbed in his Beano annual. He stirred long enough to take the snack and bite into the doughnut, before going back to his book, leaving the carton on the seat beside him. He'd be no trouble now, just so long as the rehearsal didn't go on too long. They passed through winding lanes, climbing ever higher, until they reached the top, and sweeping views across to the distant coast.

"Not far now," said Jake. "It's in one of the valleys, about a couple of miles away. It's so tucked away that no-one will even notice that we're there."

Annie remained silent. She wished, once more, and along tired tracks, that this was all true, and that their problems would melt away. She longed to be that family, fighting through adversity, following a dream, making mistakes, but somehow emerging, triumphant, to the happy-ever-after home they had pictured, and finally succeeded in creating. The celebrity lynch pin of the series would gasp with awe and wonder at the magnificence of their creation, sliding his hand over perfectly crafted stair rails, gazing through acres of glass windows at the open landscapes beyond, then slipping through hidden doors to courtyards filled with the sound of running water, and the smell of verbena and eucalyptus, lemon grass and lavender...

A question from Henry brought her back down to earth – or rather, car.

"Is this it, Mum?"

The boy was looking out of the window, the Beano forgotten, his mouth dropped open in amazement.

"Is this our new home?"

Jake pulled up beside the catering van, where a small, familiar group of techies were gathering for a coffee break. He pulled the brake on, hard, punctuating their arrival, with a definite "YES!" Annie slowly undid her seat belt and opened the car door. She joined Jake and Henry, who had beaten her to it, and were standing side by side, gazing at the monstrous edifice before them.

No, it couldn't be...

"What is it?" Annie asked slowly.

Jake shook his head. "I don't know," he answered.

The director/producer approached them.

"Bit of a surprise, eh?" His eyes glinted – was it amusement or something less pleasant? "Come with me – the lad can come, too."

Together, they walked away from the familiar clutter of the film-crew, and towards the building, which rose like a cliff face before them.

"It's an amazing opportunity," the producer was saying. "We've never been offered anything like this before. It'll be a first."

Jake had stopped. As he stood and looked up at the tall building, light began to dawn. His mind went back to his student days, when he had joined the college cadets. They had spent weekends training, often travelling long distances to reach remote military camps where they were put through their paces, introduced to hand-to-hand fighting, demolition, booby-traps. The sifting process had gone on for nearly two years, until only the keenest recruits remained committed to the unit. Those who had fallen by the wayside, turned their backs on the rest, and became involved in other things – acting in the college revue, or heading up soup runs in the cold winter streets of the city. But Jake had remained, stalwart and determined, until the day he had fallen, and dazed, failed to roll out of the way of the assault vehicle. It had run over his leg. He would limp for the rest of his life.

"It was here," he said.
Annie looked at him and understood at once what he meant. Henry, who knew nothing of what had happened all those years ago, looked at his father with a puzzled expression.
"What, Dad?"

Jake seemed to come to his senses. "Oh, nothing much. Let's go and see what's inside."

They followed the director, who led them down the slope towards the main entrance to the building. Henry gazed up at the rearing walls, nearly fifteen metres tall. Was it a castle? The doorway was out of proportion with the building, just a simple set of doors, such as could be found in many a village hall across the country. They were incongruous. The building deserved something which made a bigger statement; maybe a flight of steps, bounded by stately columns? The director pushed the doors open and passed beyond them. Jake, Annie, and Henry followed dutifully. What would they find inside?

****

Later – much later, once the court case had been settled, Jake looked back at that day with forensic concentration. Try as he might, he failed to see what they had missed. He, more than anyone there, should have realised the dangers of the location, but he had been totally taken in by its modern façade. Now, in the cold light of his cell, he went over what had happened and sought endlessly for the clues he should have seen but had failed to recognise. They had entered the building cautiously, uncertain of their step as they passed from bright sunshine into the dark, dank interior.

"It smells creepy," Henry had said – just moments before the floor had given way.

In all the chaos and cacophony of screams, shouts, and falling masonry, the moments stretched out for Jake - an elastic limbo. Then - where were Annie and Henry? Were they OK?
In the aftermath of the collapse, Jake had been rescued by some of the film crew, prised out of the corner he had found as a staircase came crashing down. He was relatively unhurt – choking from the dust, scratched, and bruised, but no bones broken. The director had been less lucky. Leading the way, he had fallen first. When interviewed he recounted that he had felt Henry and Annie as they all fell into what proved to be a labyrinthine cellar, but

after that, remembered nothing until he was rescued. His injuries were connected to a blow received to his head. They were to take weeks to fully surface. When they did, he knew he would never work in films again. Henry had been the saving of Annie, her instinct for survival kick-started by his cries of pain and terror. The primaeval need to protect had driven her on and sustained her through the many hours they were to remain entombed together before the rescue party finally broke through the rubble to free them. Henry's nightmares lasted thankfully only a few weeks. He was sufficiently mature to accept the help he needed, and was paired up with a brilliant therapist, emerging much the boy he had been before the accident, only more solemn and considerate. He had learnt, the hard way, that it is good to look before you leap – skills which, in later life, would underpin his successful career in the military – in bomb disposal.

Annie's recovery took time. Her survival instincts may have been powerful and effective at first, but the crash for her came later. As the truth about the whole disaster unfolded, her trust in Jake slowly ebbed until, battling with the highs and lows of recovery, she decided to end the marriage. Two years to the day of the 'accident,' she received her decree absolute. Independent, free, she embraced her choice and trained as a speech therapist – giving a voice to the silent. If not happy, she learned to be content.

****

The programme never went to air, although some of the film clips were shown in court and stills were plastered over the newspapers. Somebody (never identified) placed a particularly harrowing picture on social media – but Henry and Annie never looked at such things – and they were forbidden where Jake was living. Like most scandals, it was a five-minute wonder for the media, soon to be replaced in the public consciousness by the long-awaited death of the King, and a welter of Imperial reminiscence.

The film company was completely exposed. The entire project had been conceived to dupe Jake and Annie. The rehearsal, unbeknown to them, had been filmed. It was 'The Reveal' – there never would have been a magnificent success story: no rescued building, no beautifully dressed interiors, no legacy for the family.

Theirs had always, from the first, been intended as a disaster – with no happy ending. The plan had been conceived as a rebuttal for mounting criticism regarding the false hopes raised by the Grand House Rescues franchise. Too many people had started hopeless projects, spurred on by the fictional ones they had watched so avidly on television. As the courts wrangled out the truth, it became clear that the entire franchise had hoodwinked unsuspecting 'clients,' enticing them to invest in projects that were total scams.

Tied by non-disclosure contracts, and too embarrassed to complain, they had kept quiet. The 'Castle Collapse' case (as it became known) lifted the lid on what had been happening and out flowed a cascade of victims and their horror stories. From the start, the plan had been to film a 'collapse' at the castle, intending it to dash the hopes of the family and see them eking out a meagre existence in a run-down caravan park. The programme was to end in a warning – a sop to the critics. However, the castle (for that was what it had once been) had hidden weaknesses, not known to the film company. Jake had been right to sense familiarity as he approached the tall building. Once a castle, and subsequently a testing ground for the elite army corps of which Jake had been a member, it had been used time and again as a complex booby-trapped location, where recruits were put through their paces. Had the film company done its homework, they would not have taken their cameras within a mile of it. The trickster who had rented them the site, had had no right to do so, and had hidden the KEEP OUT and DANGER notices which had hung there for years. It had been little short of a miracle for the family to enter the building and come out alive. As it was, they nearly didn't!

****

And Jake? His injuries healed, but his life was in tatters. He wasn't to blame for the deception, but his double-guilt – that of pursuing his dream no matter what it cost, and of failing to protect his family, overwhelmed him. He had recognised the place – but only as if through a cloud. Had he properly recalled it, he would never have stepped inside, but the horrors of his cadet experience had been so deep, that he had blocked them from his memory. In so doing, he had been able to marry, have a child, and live a 'normal' life...until that 'rehearsal day.'

He accepted the divorce as punishment – he needed to suffer for what had happened, so he embraced the pain. And later? Well, there are many kinds of prison, but for Jake, the cell he now called home was kind to him. Here, he felt safe from guilt and pain. All that was past. The hours were gentle in their pattern. His fellow inmates quiet, contemplative. They had all lived through bitter, difficult times, but they had paid their debts and were free to live in this safe harbour.

A bell tolled the hour.

Jake put down his pen and stood up. Folding his arms in his sleeves, he left his cell and joined the procession down the ancient stairs to the Abbey Church. Another tall building, but solid, secure. As he limped to his stall, a thin beam of light fell on him.

Peace.

A candle in the darkness.

Then a pang – Henry! But Henry was safe – gently disarming landmines in a foreign battlefield – his life devoted to Rescue

Anne Thomas

The Rescue

Twenty eight

As they sat staring at the large lorry in front of them which hadn't moved for ages it seemed, they were chatting over their coffee and idly reminiscing about their childhood and, in particular about holidays and trips that they had made as children.

The only too often heard phrase, "Are we there yet? came into conversation, uttered by the over excited, tired child in the back of the car.

This story not only encapsulates those moments but also highlights how things can change and the image that we keep in our minds is often the one that disappoints with the passing of time.

THE LAKE

The journey had started full of anticipation and excitement. By the time they reached Birmingham, boredom had set in. This resulted in squabbling. Polly complained that Angus was fidgeting too much and encroaching on her space.

"There is no space," said Angus, which was true. The car was so full of suitcases, gum boots and waterproofs (they were after all going to the Lakes), boxes of provisions and Teddy's pushchair, it was extraordinary really that it had allowed six people to get in. Angus, making fire engine noises, rolled his toy over the back of Ma's seat and onto Polly's legs.

"Do that again and I will throw that stupid truck out of the window." Polly shoved him and he collided with Marigold. Marigold remained impassive, staring out of the window.

"Polly, Angus," said Father. Angus provocatively poked Polly in the ribs with his elbow but Polly decided it wasn't worth retaliating. She was getting anxious. She leaned forward and whispered to Ma.

"Can we stop? I need the loo."

Ma turned to Father, shifting Teddy on her lap as she did so. Miraculously he had fallen asleep within minutes of the journey starting.

"Roger, Polly needs to go to the loo," said Ma.

"Again?" Father frowned.

"She has the curse." Ma's whisper was audible to all. Polly flushed and shrank back in her seat.

"What curse?" said Angus. "Who's cursed her?" His eyes were wide.

"Let's play I Spy," said Marigold. Polly shot her a look of gratitude. Every now and again she caught a flash of the old Marigold.

"Let's have lunch," said Ma.

It was a standing joke in the Manners' family that Father, who built motorways – 'engineered them,' said Ma – would never drive on one – except those he had engineered. Thus lunch, or indeed any stop, involved a detour off the main road down country lanes until a suitable field could be found. Polly was first out of the car, and clutching her bag, marched down the lane until she could no longer see the car. She squatted behind a tree.

After lunch the car seemed more squashed and stuffy than before, smelling nauseously of stale baby milk and warm ham. Teddy was wide awake, wriggling on Ma's lap. He chattered and gurgled, understood by no-one. Polly bit her nails. Angus fidgeted incessantly, singing silly rhymes until even Ma got tired of listening to him. Marigold as before stared out of the window. Polly looked across at her. Small, round, neat, Marigold was fair where Polly was dark, big boned and messy. Before she would have known what Marigold was thinking but after the business with Jerome, Marigold had become inscrutable, though Ma said she was just plain stubborn and sulking to boot; she would snap out of it eventually. Polly was not so sure. It wasn't just Jerome, when Polly thought about it she realised that Marigold had been changing imperceptibly for some time, it was just that Polly had not noticed. She turned away, feeling flat.

Her thoughts turned to Jerome. She did not know for sure what he had done, but it must have been something very bad this time. He had always been difficult, even as a little boy. School holidays were always punctuated at some point with trouble caused by him. On one occasion the police had turned up. Father had been called home from work early, and he, Ma and Jerome had spent an hour closeted in the drawing room with a burly constable and a beat bobby. She and Marigold had tried to listen outside the door but could not make out what was being said. Later, waiting in the local store in the village, she overheard a conversation between the storekeeper and one of their neighbours. They stopped abruptly when they saw her but not before she had heard Jerome's name and shoplifting – common thief, the neighbour had said. With her face flushed she had turned and walked out. It was weeks before she felt she could go back in there again. That was four years ago. Her thoughts wandered. She remembered another time, when she had sat late one afternoon on the grass verge on the corner of the village road and the lane to their house. She was waiting for Father to come home from work, her arms wrapped round her legs, her chin on her knees. The sun was warm on the back of her neck but she felt cold. Jerome had been diabolical all day and Ma had ended up in tears at one point.

Polly wanted to stop Father and get in the car with him, tell him before he got home what had happened, tell him how upset Ma had been. She felt divided by this action. Telling tales was frowned upon, one didn't go running to one parent or the other saying so and so did this to me or so and so said that. But Ma crying was too much. Jerome had just gone too far this time, and Polly wanted to tell Father everything before he got home, before he walked into a house that was rigid with tension and not notice anything at all.

She wanted Father to understand that it was dreadful for them all when Jerome behaved like this. She loved her father, but sometimes she wanted to shake him and shout at him, tell him to open his eyes and see what was happening, because Father very often failed to notice that anything was amiss unless he saw it for himself. He was no good at feeling, Polly decided, that was the trouble, feeling as in sensing, being attuned. She on the other hand felt too much, was over attuned. Was that just as bad she wondered, would she be easier with life if she felt less, thought less and just – what? She could never find the right answer.

Polly felt more and more that Jerome did not belong to the family. He was rude, moody and so confrontational. Polly felt she should know why this was so that she should understand him, but she couldn't. Marigold always sided with Jerome but on that day when Ma had cried, even she had been hurt; she would never admit it but Polly could tell. She knew Marigold, could read her like a book. At least, then she could. Now was different.

They reached the motorway at last, and there was a shift in mood.

"Did you really build this," asked Angus. "Can I sit by the window now?"

Marigold did not respond, so Polly swapped with him. It was not easy. Polly felt the return of the excitement with which she had started the journey. It was four years since they had left the Lakes, and she had not been back since. Marigold had. Marigold had gone last year, and the year before, to stay with Agnes. The year before that Agnes had come to stay with them. Agnes. Polly couldn't wait to see her. Of course, being two years older than Polly she was really Marigold's friend, but Polly had written to her, faithfully, every month, and Agnes had replied, although perhaps not quite so regularly.

"Marigold," she said.

"Mm?" said Marigold.

"Are you excited?" Marigold didn't reply.

"I am," said Polly. "I can't wait to see Agnes."

Marigold turned to look at Polly. "You've spilt tomato on your t-shirt," she said, and turned away again. Polly bit her lip. She tried again.

"I can't wait to see the Lake," she said. "We will get a chance to go to the Lake, won't we Ma?" she asked.

"I expect so," replied Ma.

"Lancaster," said Angus, who had been steadily reading the road signs as they passed.

"You were born there," said Ma. "In the infirmary"

"Eight years ago," said Angus. "I'm eight, Teddy is only one, Polly is fourteen, Marigold is fifteen and Jerome is,"…

"Not here," said Marigold, suddenly, fiercely. "So shut up."

"Marigold!" Father's voice was stern.

Angus looked defiant, bullish. He didn't know what Jerome had done, and why he wasn't coming with them. He felt belligerent. "Why can't we talk about…" he started.

"Just shut up you stupid little boy," shouted Marigold, leaning across Polly and delivering a stinging slap to his leg. Angus reared up and with arms flying tried to hit back at Marigold but only succeeded in catching Polly on the chin. As Polly retorted it seemed as if the back of the car was full of whirling, jabbing, poking arms.

"That's enough, Marigold!" said Pa.

"Children," cried Ma, simultaneously. "Please don't argue. Marigold do not hit your brother. Violence in women is very unbecoming."

Marigold's face was stony as she turned back to the window. Polly put her hand tentatively on her sister's leg, but it was brushed off as if a troublesome fly had landed there. Polly sat back. There was nothing she could do. Marigold certainly wouldn't talk to her now. More pressingly, though, she needed the loo again. She pulled some tissue out of her bag and under the guise of settling herself, carefully slid the tissue under her shorts.

The first glimpse of the Lake caused great excitement. Even the rigidity with which Marigold held herself became anticipatory. Angus decided it was too complicated to sulk and sat up and began asking questions, which Father patiently answered. Polly leaned forward as Ma turned her head and smiled at her. Teddy had fallen asleep again. Polly began to recognise landmarks. She thought about Agnes as the landscape triggered memories. There was something special about her, different. Ma, who had always delighted in making cotton summer dresses and wool winter capes for her daughters, had felt sorry for Agnes.

With three older brothers Agnes was always dressed in their cast offs, corduroy shorts, grey wool socks, black lace up shoes. 'It's a shame,' Ma would say, and, because Agnes was shorter than Polly, would offer her old dresses to Agnes. They were always taken with gratitude but never seen again. But secretly Polly envied Agnes. She would have loved to dress as Agnes did. Only Marigold did justice to Ma's dexterity with a needle. But despite the ugly clothing and unbecoming hair cut – 'I swear Joan takes her to the barber with the boys,' Ma would exclaim – Agnes was, well, different. Polly could not really define how. She had presence, Polly decided. She hugged her arms round her chest, excitement bubbling up.

They turned away from the lake along the road that led to the village.

"Are we really nearly there?" asked Angus.

"Yes, you idiot," said Polly, but with a smile. "Don't you recognise this road?"

"No," said Angus, a worried look creeping over his face.

"You don't?" cried Polly. "But you must, this is the road from the Lake to our home."

"Be fair," said Ma. "He was only four when we left."

"There," said Angus his face clearing. "You're the idiot." Polly hugged him impulsively; she couldn't contain her excitement. Angus shrugged her away, but inside he was pleased. Since Jerome had been sent away, Polly was the only one who hadn't changed. Everyone else had. Except Teddy, but you couldn't count him, he wasn't really a person yet.

The car turned into the driveway and, crunching the gravel, came to a standstill. Before Father had even turned off the engine Marigold had opened her door and in a swirl of skirt was gone. Polly disentangled her legs from the bags in the well of the car and shifting slightly retrieved the tissue from her seat. She pulled her bag over her shoulder and slid carefully out of the car. She looked round for Agnes but only saw Agnes's parents walking towards the car. She smiled at them and said hello, then peered round them towards the front of the house. Who was Marigold hugging?

Polly walked uncertainly towards her sister, stopping abruptly as Marigold turned round, leaving one arm possessively round the waist of a slender, beautiful young woman. Her glossy hair hung smoothly to her shoulders, held back off her face with a tortoiseshell clip. Her sleeveless white shirt fitted over her perfectly shaped breasts. Her bright pink skirt swirled round her knees and red nails peeped out of strappy white sandals.

Polly felt her face flushing. She became acutely aware of her dirty t-shirt, too tight shorts and grubby white plimsoles. She felt ungainly, unsophisticated and too confused to stop the emotions she felt passing over her face. Then Agnes smiled, held out her hand and the moment passed.

As Polly reached for Agnes, Marigold began to laugh.

"Oh Polly," she cried. "Your face! You look, …you look," … Marigold struggled to get the words out as her laughter welled up. "You look…" but she couldn't finish her sentence.

As Agnes's smile broadened Polly felt tears welling. With an effort she tried to smile but found she could not take the perfect hand being held out to her.

Pia Staniland

The Lake

Twenty nine

The coach was filled with football supporters who were usually lively and noisy but were becoming unusually morose and disgruntled as they had been stationary for about forty minutes when Mike turned to his buddy beside him. Both were sipping beers and Mike, rather apprehensively said:

"Did I ever tell you about the time when I was young when……"

In middle England none of us suspects our fellow colleague or next door neighbour of ever being a spy.

This story told by one friend to another certainly raised the friend's eyebrows and made the friend think of his steady, diligent friend, Mike, in a different light.

THE SPY'S STORY

It was the summer of 1976 when it started. That hot, dry summer with lots of ladybirds around, which seemed to bite exposed skin. I was working as a contractor within a government department. My contract ended in mid-September and I decided to book myself a holiday, a camping holiday across Northern Europe, Russia, Poland, East and West Germany. I booked with a company called Penn Overland who provided the coach, tents and a driver and courier. In return the passengers communally provided everything else – food, cooking and cleaning etc. As I was young, I liked to travel cheaply so I could travel and see more.

In June I casually mentioned my plans to my manager. About a week later I was called into the office where two young men in their late twenties, dressed in smart casual clothing, sat. The conversation was quite convivial at first but then started to get probing about my past and present circumstances. It ended with a direct question, 'Would I be willing to assist the UK government during my holiday in Russia?' I agreed, partly out of curiosity, partly a sense of adventure, partly because who knew where it might lead?

Two weeks later to the day I was called into the office again. This time I was faced with an older man who did most of the talking and a younger woman. The conversation was professional and direct. Firstly, I was presented with two copies of the Official Secrets Act to sign. One I kept, the other was filed into a cardboard folder for possible future use against me. I was told that they wanted information about the ten kilometre border exclusion zone between Russia and Finland, specifically the observation posts and checkpoints on that route. They gave me a paperback copy of poetry in which I was to record the information. I was then to hand it in to the British Embassy in Moscow if I got there.

The journey through the border was to be broken up into roughly half mile slots. It was assumed the coach would travel at about thirty miles per hour. I was to open the book at page ten and during a count of five if I saw an observation post on the left I was to turn over the top corner of the page. If the post was on the right it would be the top right corner. If it was a tower observation post

I was to fold over a bottom corner of the page. These would act as checks because they would show up on aerial photographs. After a five second count I had to turn over two pages to page fourteen and repeat the process. This would continue until I reached the Russian internal border.

The book was new, and I was instructed how to age it as if it was a favourite, treasured possession I always carried. I was to put cigarette ash between the pages to take away the new book smell and take the sheen off the printed pages. An old teabag could be dragged over the page edges to discolour them. The book had to be rolled and bent back and forth many times a day to induce creases on the covers, paying particular attention to folding and bashing the corners. The book was to be carried around each day and stuffed into pockets and bags etc.

Over the next month or so I carried out these tasks daily, realising my liberty may depend on it working. Using another book I had a few practice runs. I sat on the top deck of a bus counting to five and randomly turning over page corners before flipping two pages and repeating, just to see what it would be like. I didn't want to mess up my assignment. The hot summer rolled on and my contract came to an end. I said goodbye to my workmates who hoped I was going to enjoy my holiday. They, of course, knew nothing about what I had actually become involved in.

The next day found me in May Place, a small back street in London behind Green Park tube station, where about thirty of us were gathering to board our coach. There were British, Australians and Americans. The coach duly turned up and we boarded. The first thing we had to do was hand over £60 each to the courier to pay for the food and everyday expenses of the trip and then we were off, heading for Dover and the ferry.

The journey across Germany and Denmark passed uneventfully, except for the usual tourist distractions that these countries had to offer. Reality started to dawn at the campsite in Sweden, on the outskirts of Stockholm.

Opposite our collection of tents a black Mercedes sedan parked up, facing us. The sole occupant, a man in his forties, sat in the passenger seat watching us. He had no camping gear, only a couple of blankets to keep warm. He was dressed in ordinary clothes that would not have been out of place in an office. Each morning he walked to the shower block with a towel and spongebag wearing a white vest over suit trousers and lace-up shoes. He came back with a hot drink from the coin-operated drinks machine and ate a cold breakfast in his car. A couple of people in our group said to him *"Dobra Eoota"* (Good Morning in Russian) to which he replied without hesitation.

The black Mercedes and its solitary occupant were on the ferry across the Baltic with us and parked up opposite us again in the campsites in Finland.

On the morning of September 23rd we packed the coach and headed for the border. Our first real sight of Russia was leaving roadside buildings behind us as we drove along a straight road down a slight incline. We saw from horizon to horizon a uniform line of conifer trees. The road headed towards a gap in the trees. Closer to it we passed some eight foot high poles painted red and white, the actual border! Thirty yards further on a solitary guard stood next to a small red and white painted sentry cabin. He wore a light grey uniform of the Border Guards Regiment. He made no attempt to stop us, just watched as we passed.

I wondered if I would leave so easily. After twenty yards the road turned sharp left and I had turned the top corners of pages ten and eleven. My counting continued.

The serpentine road wound further into Russia. The bends meant we could see no further than fifty yards ahead of us. It became obvious why the information was needed. Observation posts line the road, some facing Finland, but many facing into Russia. You can see far more from the ground than you can see from aerial reconnaissance. They had used living plants and shrubs to camouflage them, rather than sandbags and netting. Amongst the woods there were vehicle hides, again made from living tree branches which, using ropes, had been trained to grow into the shape of garage-like structures. Some seemed to be roadways leading through the conifer woods with living branches making tunnels.

After about two miles we emerged into a clearing with a large, low building: the customs inspection building. It was about the height of a two story house with only the lower part being used. Facing us were two large double doors, one pair open and, to the right, a pedestrian entrance. We got off the coach, picked up our luggage and were ordered to file towards the pedestrian entrance.

Our coach, meanwhile, was driven through the open double doors and over an inspection pit. The doors were closed behind it. As pedestrians, we found ourselves in a long, narrow room with a high, girder-frame roof with skylights, the only natural light. Running down the centre of the room was a wooden counter divided into roughly fifteen-foot sections by two -foot -high partitions. Each section was further divided into two areas by a large slot, edged in wood and painted with red and white strips: the confiscated items bin.

We stood and waited and waited, obviously being watched by the moving CCTV cameras fastened to the roof girders. I rooted my feet to the ground and plunged my hands into my pockets so that my limbs would not betray my nerves. The customs staff were dressed in grey uniforms with green patches on the collars but were, unexpectedly, very casual. The men were all clean shaven with short haircuts, unlike many in our party. Some wore their distinctive Russian style, large-crowned peaked hats on the backs of their heads with the peaks just covering their hairline. Some had ties worn loosely. Their shoes or boots were the most notable feature, being in different styles in black or brown (chestnut brown to tan).

The women customs officials wore shoes or knee-high boots in dark blues or greens as well as black. After half an hour of waiting and being watched, about eight customs officers emerged from an office and took up their stations at the counter, each officer occupying one fifteen-foot section. The floor level on their side of the counter was much higher than our side and they towered over us, even those of us over six foot. Each official then proceeded to point at individuals and beckon them forward for the customs inspection.

My turn came to empty out my case and rucksack and spread it over the counter for inspection. My official was a young man in his late twenties who wore a typical Russian rubaha, a jacket which is pulled over the head and hangs loose to the hips. It was in grey with green lapels with the neck unbuttoned to reveal a black and white shirt and black tie. His peaked hat with green band bore a cloth badge of the border guards and was square on his head as he looked down on me. On his right hand was a gold wedding ring on the third finger and a rather expensive looking watch adorned his left wrist. It was chunky with a metal expanding strap. The watch face was black with two supplementary dials. He looked directly at me for a few moments and I stared back at him, deliberately not avoiding his gaze.

He started by looking at my battered, empty case with old travel stickers. My rucksack followed. He patted down my clothing – clean and dirty. We had been warned not to buy books or magazines on polemics, pornography, modern authors , military, modern art and anything critical of Russia. Not only would such material probably be confiscated but it might provoke the customs official to be extra officious towards us.

He paid particular attention to the tourist books I had bought, especially my postcards of Copenhagen. I think it was of genuine interest about what the West looked like. He thumbed through my book of poetry and seemed to read a few verses. He looked at my camera, a Kodak instamatic, and decided I was not a specialist photographer. I had bought a packet of biscuits in Sweden for something to snack on. They went into the confiscation slot.

Next came the customs declaration. At the time Russian roubles had no value as foreign exchange so while in Russia it was normal for tourists to buy goods in *Berioskas* or foreign currency shops. Going into Russia, in addition to travellers' cheques, I was carrying British pounds, U S dollars, German Marks and Swedish Kronor all in small denomination notes. Gold and silver jewellery also had to be declared. This declaration was duly stamped by my official. On leaving Russia I had to make a similar declaration and provide receipts to show I had spent the money legally, not on the black market.

He seemed satisfied and beckoned me to pack up my things while he moved to the other end of the counter and started going through someone else's belongings.

I moved through the door into the currency exchange room and waited in the queue. Like many Communist countries at the time you had to spend a minimum amount of money per day, in this case about £2.50. I would be in Russia for twelve days so had to buy £30 worth of roubles at the exchange rate of one rouble = £1. I paid in travellers' cheques, preferring to keep cash for souvenir purchases where I might get a better exchange rate.

From this room I passed into a holding room with other members of the tour. We waited and waited. After nearly one hour we were allowed out to make our way to our coach. We boarded and found our driver trying to replace panels on the overhead luggage racks. While we had been going through customs so had the coach. It had been run over an inspection pit to look at the underside, the side lockers had been emptied out, including all the tents and camping gear and the interior had been inspected including the air ducts in the luggage racks.

Eventually, we got ourselves sorted out and prepared to leave, escorted by a Russian Zil car with three occupants. It had taken us four hours to get through customs.

My five second count continued. We soon emerged from the forest into open grassland extending for a mile or so. Some yards from the tree line, and parallel with it, ran a witness track. This was a strip of bare earth ploughed and harrowed to provide an even surface in which the tracks of anyone crossing it showed up. Equally spaced on this open grassland were three ditches running parallel to the border. Each ditch was about twenty foot wide and four feet deep. It contained rusting coils of barbed wire all overgrown with brambles, weeds and the like. This vegetation had been cut off level with surrounding ground thus providing a barrier to vehicles and pedestrians but without obstructing views. At intervals, tower watchtowers sat astride the ditches. Some were of the older type with four legs, like truncated electricity pylons, about forty foot high with a square observation cabin on top. Others were of the modern type of a concrete cylinder with a circular observation cabin at the top which had no corners to obstruct the views.

The road had two very pronounced zigzag bends which slowed the coach right down. A leg of these zigzags ran parallel to the border for a hundred yards or so, enabling the watch towers to get a good view of the vehicles from front and back.

Just before we entered the dense woodland again, we passed another witness track running parallel with the tree line. The now familiar serpentine road took us through the forest. We passed through two very visible checkpoints with moveable barriers. Our escort car was obviously controlling our passage and speed through this part of the journey. Occasionally I saw, on the side of the road, armed guards in camouflage clothing who stood and watched us. A few miles further on and we emerged from the forest and into arable fields with tractors harvesting the crops. We were now out of the border exclusion zone and into Russia proper.

Up ahead were a few houses where we parked while our courier went in search of the Intourist guide who would accompany us on the rest of our journey. *(Intourist is the state-run company providing leisure breaks for Russians and foreigners alike.)* Our coach with bright colours and company name was like a magnet for the locals and they stared at us. When we got out to walk, our clothing also set us apart. I was approached by an unshaven and dishevelled young man with a wad of roubles in his hand. He asked if I wanted to change one US dollar for six Russian roubles. He spoke grammatically correct English without a trace of an accent; obviously professionally trained; was he a blackmarketeer; or a police agent provocateur?

In Moscow I went to the British Embassy as instructed. I made my way to reception and said I had run out of money and could they help: my cover story in case I was overheard by any Russians in the Embassy. They took my passport and showed me into an anteroom where a young woman clutching a notepad duly joined me. I told her who I was and could I see a particular, named, person. I was soon joined by a young man to whom I handed my poetry book. We exchanged a few pleasantries; I was given my passport back and I soon found myself back on the streets of

Moscow savouring the joys of Red Square and Gums department store.

Later, on our first night back in the West at the campsite in Berlin we were visited by two USAF 'Snowdrops' military police. They spent about two hours chatting and walking around the group. I often wonder if someone else on the tour had been collecting information for the Americans.

As a legacy, I often travel with a paperback book of poetry. I find it is better than a novel because I can read a few verses and allow my mind and imagination to digest them while my eyes and senses can take in what is around me.

Mike Stewart

Thirty

Pat is often asked which of the travels that she has made in the world is her favourite and she will reply that each one is different, rarely has there been one that she hasn't liked and life is full of wonderful memories, especially those made in the few short years she had with her late husband Bob. However, there is one trip that is the most poignant, a trip that will stay in her mind and in her heart for ever. A true story recognising man's inhumanity to man, a message that history cannot hide.

She tells it here, just as she told it to her friend Sheila as they travelled together on a coach trip to Bath Christmas Market, barely able to keep the emotion from her voice and the tears from her eyes.

WHEN A MEGALOMANIAC FANTASISES

Arbeit macht frei! - work makes you free!

The news attracted my attention. Today was the anniversary of the relief of Auschwitz and all the memories came flooding back........

The rain fell steadily. The dreary day highlighted our sombre surroundings. It was Christmas Eve one year ago. My partner and I, in pursuance of finding a different approach to everything, were in Auschwitz. Auschwitz Birchenau, a concentration camp where Germany, in search of the perfect Aryan race, had rounded up Europe's Jewish and gypsy minorities for slaughter, where man's inhumanity to man knew no boundaries, where innocent people were taken like raw materials and placed on the conveyor belt of the factory of death.

We set off on our tour, a shabby little group of tourists. The rain which had begun in Zakopane, our holiday resort, as pure white snow, was now a dirty grey. It felt funereal. Auschwitz really fulfilled only one function: mass extermination, be it by torture, execution or starvation.

I stepped in a puddle.

Our guide, although extremely attractive, never smiled. She gave her commentary with an air of knowledgeable resignation. It had happened and it had happened there.

The forlorn little group followed the guide to the Death Block, with its wall of execution, to Crematorium 1 with its Gas Chamber and to 'Rollcall' square, with its collective gallows. Not one word was spoken as she described the carnage that evolved from the bloodbath of collective butchery.

She was a Polish Jewess. If I had tried to say something the words would have got in the way.

Stupefied, we stumbled through blocks 4 and 5 where we came face to face with the story of mass extermination. Piles of human hair were heaped on the floor, products of the factory of death woven into cloth for the pure Ayran race. Mountains of suitcases held wretchedly together with time worn straps. One particular case, slightly apart from the rest. Labelled '*kind———-,*' the name now escapes me. A child whose life was hopelessly abandoned at the point of no return. Piles of suitcases removed because they were no longer needed. Soft embroidered baby shoes, lives that never began! Towers of artificial limbs, poignantly significant, Jewish prayer shawls!

Blocks 6 and 7 showed exhibitions of life in the camp. Dressed like convicts, the emaciated bodies cried out to us in pain. Drudgingly on to the train head, the halt, the train that went to nowhere but the train that went to hell. Those that survived the journey of deportation underwent selection, where families were wrenched, husband from wife, mother from child, and on to the pond where prisoners' ashes were dumped.

Finally, a memorial to all those who perished. We took no pictures. It was not necessary. We will never forget the aura of death and depravity that clung to us on that day. We needed no memorial. It was Christmas Eve in Poland and a new dawn brought a new birth. In Zakopane a fall of snow covered the cold-blooded ruthlessness of years gone by, but snow melts and bares to the world the bleak depravity of man.

In Auschwitz it only rained.

Arbeit macht frei.

Pat Mabberley

The gates of Auschwitz

Thirty one

The conversation from the back seat passengers in the car, who were being careful not to annoy the frustrated driver, who had been sitting in an overheated car, bumper to bumper with the car in front of him for far too long, turned as usual to the 'good old days.'

"You hear such terrible things these days. I remember the days when courting was courting, when a lad asked a girl out, escorted her back to her home afterwards and genuinely behaved in a courteous manner."

Sue sighed as she said these words.

"So true," said her companion, "Exactly; only last week I heard the most awful tale........."

HE WON'T DO IT AGAIN

"You're very quiet tonight, Geoff said to his sister, Emma. You seem miles away."

Emma was the barmaid at The Dove, one of the few hostelries left in the town.

"Maybe I'm just wishing I was." she replied.

"Oh dear, that doesn't sound too good. Do you want to talk about it?"

"Yes, and no."

"So, what am I meant to understand from that?"

She didn't reply.

"Knowing you like I do I'm guessing that's a yes, with a 'but.' Am I right?"

"You know me too well."

After a pause she said,
"Let me ask Ted if he'll let me have a five-minute break and we can pop outside for a fag. But before we do I want you to do something."

"Anything to help, sis. You know me."

"Well, don't look now but at the table by the fireplace is Sharon, you know, Kevin's sister."

"Yeh, I know who you mean."

"The bloke she's sat with, in the blue polo shirt. Tell me if you've seen him before."

"I tell you what, I'll go for a pee while you see Ted and I'll have a quick butchers. What's so special about him?"

"I'll tell you in a minute."

"Ok. Hang on here till I come back, though."

Geoff took another swig of his pint of Old Peculiar, got down from his barstool and headed towards the gents. As he passed the table where Sharon and her escort were sat, he waved her a greeting, which she reciprocated. After leaving the gents he stopped at Sharon's table and said,

"Forgive me for interrupting."

This was addressed to the bloke. He was about Geoff's age with short, blond hair and several tattoos on his left arm. He looked as if he wasn't too pleased about the interruption but Geoff ignored him and said to Sharon,

"Have you seen Kev lately? Only he was going to bell me about the game on Saturday but I haven't heard."

This was a complete fabrication but Geoff had to say something. Sharon gave him a puzzled look.

"I don't know what you mean, but I'm a bit tied up at the moment. I'll see him tomorrow and ask him to give you a shout, yeh?"

"Ok, fine." Geoff replied.

He repeated his apology to Sharon, nodded at the bloke, who just glared at him and returned to the bar.

"Ted's just changing the barrel of Guinness and then he'll relieve me for five minutes. I can't be any longer, though."

Once they were outside Emma lit a fag and, after a deep inhalation, she asked,

"Have you seen that bloke before?."

"No. new one on me. Why do you ask?"

"I guess he didn't recognise me." After another drag, she added, "I don't know what the bloody hell he's doing in here."

She sounded angry.

"So, you know him, then?" Geoff asked.

Emma looked away and chewed her bottom lip.

"Come on, sis. What's going on?"

"If I tell you I don't want a word of it getting back to mum and dad."

"Ok."

"You promise?"

"You're getting me concerned now." he said.

"Do you promise?" Emma repeated.

"Ok, I promise."

Emma took another long drag and began,
"I was out with the girls last week and at the end of the night there was only two of us left and we ended up at Wally's."

"Yeh, I know it. Not my sort of place but carry on."

"Well, cutting a long story short, we ended up chatting to two blokes and one of them was the bloke that's in the pub now with Sharon. Susie left with the other one and I stayed chatting to Gary, that's his name, by the way, or so he said. Anyway, he seemed quite nice and bought me a couple of drinks. Later he offered to walk me home as he said he had to get back to relieve his baby-sitter. I remember leaving Wally's and heading back towards my place. I guess that's when whatever he had put in my drink kicked in."

"What, he spiked your drink?"

"He must have done because I woke up at three am, in the rec, freezing cold."

"I'm really not liking this, sis."

"Hang on, there's more. I managed to get to my feet and that's when I noticed my underwear had been re-arranged."

"You ain't telling me that he…"

"Yeh, I'm sure he did. A woman knows this sort of thing."

"The bastard. I'm going to go and push that glass in his face."

"No, hang on. Don't do that. I have to work here remember. But we do have to stop him doing the same thing to Sharon."

"Too right we do. How many drinks have they had?"

"They were on their first when you came in."

"Ok. Let's go back inside and see if we can warn her somehow."

"That may not be easy, but I do have a plan I've been thinking about. I'll tell you at the bar."

As they re-entered the bar area, loathsome Gary was just finishing his pint. He stood up, picked up his and Sharon's glass and went to the bar. Sharon headed towards the ladies and Emma followed her.

"Same again," he said to Ted.

He took both drinks back to the table. Emma returned to the bar, but Sharon didn't re-appear.

"Where is she?" Geoff asked in an undertone.

"I told her what I thought, and suggested she get home quick. I let her out the back door."

"I wonder how long our lover boy will wait."

"I'm guessing no longer than five minutes, then he'll come and ask me to go and find out if she's alright. In the meantime, I want you to phone Kev and get him to meet you outside, urgently, with three or four others, including big Dave, and to bring either some long cable ties or a length of strong rope. I'll tell you the rest in a minute."

Geoff looked perplexed, but he did as he was asked and when his call was over, he said to Emma,

"They're on their way; Kev will cover the back entrance, big Dave out the front but the others will stay outside in the motor. He won't get away."

"Nice one."

"Ok, what's next?" he asked.

"I'm gonna make sure he won't do it again."

Geoff returned to his bar stool and a few minutes later, just as Emma had predicted, Gary came to the bar again. Geoff didn't look at him but made a play of messing with his phone. A text came through to tell him the guys had arrived and he went outside to relay instructions. Emma told Gary that Sharon had gone home with 'ladies problems.' Gary then became aggressive and said,

"Well, she might have had the effing decency to tell me."

"I don't want that sort of language in here," Sharon told him and added, "Will you kindly leave."

"I know you from somewhere, and I ain't going anywhere"
.

"Yeh, you do know me and yes, you are leaving.

"Who's gonna make me?"

Geoff sent Kev a text to warn him of Gary's imminent departure. "Ted," she shouted, "Could you help this offensive chap find his way out."

Ted appeared and said to Gary,

"Are you leaving of your own account, through the door, or do I put you out through the window?"

Ted's menacing presence was enough to persuade Gary to choose the former option. As soon as he stepped outside big Dave approached him and said,

"You got a light, mate?"

Gary reached into his pocket but as he did so his midriff became exposed, and Dave's huge fist gave him a crushing blow to his solar plexus. Gary doubled over as the blow took effect. Things then happened quickly. Dave pushed him over, turned him on his front and held him down. Kev appeared, pulled Gary's arms behind his back and secured his wrists, very tightly, with a cable tie. Dave then lifted Gary, still struggling for breath, onto his feet and he and Kev half- marched, half-dragged him to the car where Martin quickly opened the boot, and Gary was roughly bundled inside. All done in twenty seconds and, thankfully, there were no witnesses.

Kev sent another text which read, "Turkey is trussed. Awaiting next move."

Geoff relayed this message to Emma who grinned and said,
"We'll have to wait for me to finish in half an hour. Then we can put part two into action."

"Which is?"

Emma quickly outlined what she had in mind.

"You know what, sis, that's bloody evil. But I like it."

“Here’s four bottles of beer,” she said. “Take them out to the lads. If the sod’s becoming noisy then ask Big Dave to stick something in his mouth. While he’s doing that, get him to search for the phial of that knockout juice, he’ll have it on him somewhere. Use whatever method is necessary.”

Geoff went outside with the drink for all the lads, said,
“Well done, guys,” and also asked Martin if he knew Cooper’s farm.

“Yeh, it’s about five miles away, but it’s deserted.”

“Exactly,” Geoff replied, and added “See you all there in about half an hour.”

Muffled shouts were now emanating from the boot. Geoff relayed Emma’s instructions. Big Dave got out of the car and took off one of his socks. He opened the boot to be met with a stream of obscenities.

“You’ll pay for this you bastards,” Gary shouted.

“I don’t think so, now shut up,” Big Dave told him and stuffed his sock into Gary’s mouth. Big Dave soon found the small phial in Gary’s shirt pocket. Dave closed the boot again. The car arrived at its destination in about ten minutes. It was pitch dark apart from a subdued glow from the amber signal light of the nearby railway line.

Inside the car Martin asked, “So, what has he done?”

“He spiked Emma’s drink and took advantage of her when she passed out,” Kev answered, and continued “It looked like he was going to do the same to my sister. But Geoff managed to stop it occurring.”

“What a frigging lowlife. I hate buggers like that.” This was the first comment that Frank had made. Kev’s phone went off and was answered immediately.

“Let me speak to Dave,” Geoff said after establishing that all was well. Dave took the phone and Geoff said to him,

"Listen, mate, I really appreciate you all doing this."
"Glad to help, mate."

"Did Kev tell you about him spiking Emma's drink?"

"He did, and that you stopped him from doing the same to Sharon. Well done mate. Sounds like the sod deserves anything that's coming to him."

"The bottle of jollop you found…"

"Hang on a minute."

Dave had to wait the few seconds it took for a train to go hurtling past.

"Sorry mate, you were saying?"

"Yeh, the bottle of jollop you found, you have to persuade him to drink it himself. Use whatever methods you have to."

"Consider it done."

"Cheers. Me and Em should be there in about fifteen minutes."

"Right, see you then."

Big Dave relayed the message to the others.

Kev said,
"Dave, can you drag him out and chuck him on the grass?"

Dave did as he was bid and the four of them gathered around Gary. Frank shone the beam of a small torch in Gary's face and smiled at the look of fear on the man's face.

"So, what are we gonna do with him?"

"Emma has a plan, evidently, but in the meantime, I know one thing we could all do. Anybody need a piss?"

They all murmured assent, and Gary made a perfect latrine for all four men. His muffled protests went unheeded. When they had all finished Kev approached Gary and asked Frank to shine the torch on him again. Gary was breathing hard now, whether from fear or anger Kev wasn't interested enough to ascertain.

"So, what's this for?" Kev asked showing Gary the small bottle.

Gary's eyes were bulging and he vigorously shook his head.

"Well, you're going to drink this," Dave added.

Again a shake of the head from Gary.

"Oh yes you are," Dave reiterated. He got behind Gary and viciously yanked his hair so that Gary's head went back.

"Move the sock to one side, Kev."

"What you want me to touch your sock?"

"Just do it."

Kev did so, and the small amount of liquid was poured down Gary's throat.

"How long does it take to work," Kev asked.

"About half an hour or so," Martin said.

"So now we just wait for Geoff," said Kev and asked, "Oily rag anyone?"

Martin took one, the others declined. They had stubbed out their butts on Gary's jacket when they heard a car approaching. They all hoped it was Geoff and Emma. It was, and Emma stopped her car not far behind the other one. She got out and walked towards the other car with another small torch.

“Right, boys, this is my plan.” Emma spoke in a commanding tone; she was one woman that not many dared to cross. She continued,

“Once you’ve heard it, if any or all of you want to walk away, I will understand, and I won’t condemn you at all. If you do, me and Geoff will finish the task. There’s a nice drink in my motor for all of you for what you’ve done so far, which is yours whatever you decide. Geoff’s taking charge of that. I want to speak in front of lover boy here so he knows what’s coming.”

She moved over and spoke into Gary’s face.

“Yes, you do know me,” she said to him, “I’m the one whose drink you foolishly spiked last week. And I’m gonna ensure you never do it to anyone else again. If you live, you won’t be able to.”

It couldn’t be seen in the dark but Gary had wet himself.

“Martin, can you go through his pockets and remove anything that might show who he is?” Martin did as he was asked.

“Right, I’ll make this quick because we don’t have long. I‘m sure you all know that there’s a railway crossing just ahead. It’s made up of those wooden boards that stretch across the tracks. What I want to do is to lay Casanova down on the boards then ‘m going to tie his hands to one of the rails. You got the rope?”

“In the boot, nice strong nylon cord.”

“Isn’t that a bit drastic?,” asked Frank.

“Nah, I don’t think so, but like I said, if you want to walk away then do it now.”

Nobody did, but Frank continued, “Have you thought about the repercussions?”

“I’ll cross that bridge if and when” was Emma’s curt reply. She checked her watch.

“Right, Kev, you get the rope and Dave, you drag him to the rails. We’ve got eight minutes till the last inbound train passes.”

The effects of the drug were beginning to kick in so Gary put up no resistance. Dave dropped him heavily on to the boards and knelt on his back. Martin used his pocketknife to cut the cable ties from Gary’s wrists.

“Martin, cut me off two lengths of rope, about two foot long.”

Martin did so. Gary could feel the effects of the drug slowly beginning to take effect; he was drifting between fantasy and conscious reality. He guessed, no he knew, what this bunch of animals had planned for him and he really didn’t want this to happen. Yet he was powerless to put up any resistance to them dragging him towards the railway line. What a relief to have those cable ties removed.

“I should have done that mouthy bitch good and proper while I had the chance” he thought to himself. Not that she was any different to any of the dozen or so girls he had treated in the same way. She was nothing special. Anyway, once they were incapable of resistance then the whole act wasn’t as exciting as having a willing and active participant. It was just the feeling of power that the act gave him which he found exciting. But the bitch was right; he wasn’t going to be able to do it again.

Gary could still feel someone sat on his back as the woman grabbed each of his arms in turn and unceremoniously tied both wrists to the 10cm wide steel rail. It was very cold. He tried to shout, to summon assistance, but all he could manage was a garbled guttural noise.

So, this is it – the bastards are going to leave me here to bleed to death. I hope they get caught. This really wasn’t fair. Why couldn’t they just have beaten him up, or broke his legs or something? Anything but this. He could feel himself weeping.

"Right," Emma said, "You guys go and wait in the motor. There's only three minutes to go, and I'm going to have a wee chat with him before the train comes. Give us a fag, Kev."
Kev lit one and passed it to her. She walked towards Gary as the others returned to the vicinity of the vehicles.

"Well, lover boy, not so brave now, are you? she said. She put the cigarette close to Gary's mouth.

"Every condemned man asks for a last cigarette" she said, in a mocking tone.

Gary found the wherewithal to pull his head away.

"Please yourself," she said. After a pause she added,

"You shouldn't have done it, arsehole. You chose the wrong girl."

She took a deep drag on the fag before saying,

"I'm going to leave you now. You just lie there and ponder what life's going to be like with no hands."

In his dreamlike state he heard her walking away. He also began to feel a vibration in the rail and realised the train was on its way.

"No, you ain't having it all your own way' he thought.

Somehow, he found the strength in his arms to pull his body closer to the tracks. He could hear the train now; it was only seconds away. With a final, massive effort he managed to drag himself up so that his neck was also on the rail. The thunderous roar of the train was now upon him, and he closed his eyes for the final time.

Sallee Beardfish

"He won't do it again"

Thirty two

Sheila and her husband had taken their group on a trip to the seaside and on the way home on this midsummer day, they had stopped for a drink as the inevitable traffic jam was slowly building up.

"There were some interesting looking fossils on the beach today" said one of the group.

"I'm not surprised that some people find a lot of enjoyment in searching for them."

"Let me tell you a true story," said Sheila……

A FOSSIKER'S TALE

A fossiker is someone who seeks to find something mislaid, hidden or just beyond their reach. But in the Australian Outback a fossiker is one who is lured by something more maddeningly elusive , the chance 'find' of a beautiful gemstone.

Chance will play a big part in my tale because it was by chance that my husband, Nick and I had been selected for teaching posts in Cairns on the Great Barrier Reef in 1973. Living in this tropical wonderland was reward enough, but to have the exciting but legendary expanse of the North Queensland Outback to explore as well, was beyond our dreams. Stories abounded around us of fortunes made and lost by prospectors there; of the fabled Coober Pedy opal mines, of garnets, topaz and sapphires lying undiscovered in the ancient ground below your feet. And then fate played its hand when Chas, a local prospector that we had got to know, told us he was planning to head out quite soon to search for some lucrative tin deposits in remote bushland beyond Mt. Garnet. He must have sensed how desperately keen we were to explore the Great Outback, as we would often pump him for tips about coping with the heat; the dangers we might face, from poisonous spiders, snakes and getting lost, of knowing the kind of terrain that gemstones might lurk in, and how we would recognise them should we amateurs venture out there.

"I'll tell you what," he said, "If you want to try your luck at a bit of fossiking, you can tag along with me, if you like. I can lend you a couple of sieves and shovels. While I'm gone surveying for tin, you can make your way to some of the old creek beds I know where there might still be a few topaz hanging around."

With a frantic nodding of our heads and a shake of his huge, leathery hand the deal was sealed.

So here we were in the wilderness of the Outback at last, the eerie silence broken only by the crunching of our feet as we trudged along the rutted, dusty track under an unforgiving sun. Stumbling on over rocks and dead tree stumps, with the rasps of dry grasses plucking at our clothes we heard the magical sound of trickling water ahead. And then, through the scrub, the creek was suddenly upon us; a sinuous pathway of boulders and sparkling rock pools; so surprisingly beautiful in its harsh, parched setting. Down the rocky bank we scrambled , no time for pondering, we were here to fossick, to get those shovels working and live the dream.

After a quick, thirst-quenching drink we hunkered down in the stream scooping shovelful after shovelful of stones and shale into the sieves, eagerly swirling them around and riddling among the grains with our fingertips to spot anything unusual. Over and over, we repeated the process, mopping our brows, swatting away flies from our eyes, and easing our backs. Two hours of relentless digging and dredging had gained us nothing. We rested against the bank, wafting our big sunhats against our hot, clammy cheeks, soaking up the primeval sounds that punctuated the silent wilderness around us. We decided trying a different part of the riverbed would improve our chances of making that lucky find, so snatching up our tools we heaved away boulders and soldiered on. The sun relentlessly bore down on us, but whenever we felt like giving up, we became even more determined to have one more try. The repeated rhythmical scrape of a shovel , the splash of water, the rattle of stones in the sieve, was all that could be heard in the stillness, when Eureka! Suddenly, there it was, a small glass-like shape gleaming in the sunlight, unlike anything else we had unearthed that day. We scooped it under the water again and held it up high against the sky, screwing up our eyes and seeing the clear transparency of what surely must be a topaz. It matched the samples others had shown us. We were awestruck.

We jumped at the sound of Chas's voice above us,

"Any luck then?" he shouted. I passed my sieve up to him, holding my breath for his opinion.

"Yep, that's a topaz alright," he chortled.

"It really is!" I squealed, smacking my forehead in disbelief.

Nick passed up his offering of gritty waste.

"Well, mate, it's your lucky day alright, you've got a couple of little beauties in there too," said Chas with a grin.

We camped under the starry sky that night beside Chas's rustic shack that night , thinking how incredible it was to be the first people ever to set eyes on those beautiful gemstones since they were formed in the creation of the world many millions of years ago.

Two years on and we are soaring skywards looking down through the aircraft window, as the vast brown bushland shrinks from view. I think of the many wonderful hours of fossiking we had spent there and the precious gems we had unearthed now in their leather pouch stashed securely above my head in the locker. As the pouch had been too bulky for my handbag, I had tucked it innocuously into the duty free polybag from Sydney airport, along with a few other gifts and goodies. Alongside the topaz in that pouch you would now see gorgeous garnets and smoky quartz from our many other fossicking days and a slice of iridescent opal we had doggedly dug out from the old pioneers' mine workings. Looking deeper into the pouch you would find a necklet and rings inset with our gemstones now cut and polished to their sparkling intensity that I had fashioned at a jewellery making class in Cairns.

The landing gear rumbles, we descend, then it's touchdown on a blazing hot London morning and then the countdown begins to our homecoming reunion with our family.

The family gathering was to be at 1 pm that summer day in 1976 with Doris and Rex, Nick's parents from Plymouth and mine, Ernest and Eileen, from Manchester, below the clocktower at Reading station, so that we could all then zip on to a train down to Devon for our special welcome-home party. Would our much awaited rendezvous work? Of course it did… like magic! There they were arms outstretched and faces beaming as we sashayed between the milling passengers to get those longed-for hugs. All bustle and chat, we awaited the arrival of the train. Rex would look after all the luggage and load it into the rear guard's van while we found our seats. The train squealed to a halt, door were flung open, people piled out and up we stepped. An overheated Rex tossed his jacket towards Doris before heading down the platform with the bigger cases to the luggage van at the rear of the train.

We relaxed into our seats, full of news to share, ready for Rex to join us when to our disbelief the train suddenly began to pull away. There, at the window, was a horrified Rex, his mouth agape. I can picture him now disappearing away from us on the edge of that platform, still helplessly waving his arms in the air.

In stunned silence we shook our heads, trying to take it all in. We were all talking at once, conjecturing how this awful situation could possibly have happened. Surely the stationmaster would have seen him reaching for the door before signalling the 'all clear.' There were more 'What ifs' and 'Maybes' but none resolved the sad truth that our joyful gathering had been deflated.

"He'll be fine," Doris optimistically reassured us, "He'll catch a later train."

But all wasn't fine with me. I had mislaid my duty free bag. I was inwardly frantic. It was nowhere in sight. Furiously, I tried to piece those last hectic moments on the platform together. I had had the bag with me , then laid it down beside the cases to help my mum lace up her shoe. Beyond that, it was all just a blur of excitedly helping my parents on to the train.

"Does anyone remember seeing my duty free bag?" I asked the family, trying to disguise my panic. No one had. I searched around the seat wildly, then rummaged through the luggage racks, convinced it just had to be there somewhere. But no, no sign of it.

"Rex will have it," was the general consensus. Ah yes, the chances are that he will have gathered it up with the cases, I assured myself. But, unbelievably, worst was to come. As we neared Plymouth Station Doris began to fold Rex's jacket, only to find his wallet and return ticket inside. Rex would now be stranded!

Real concern set in.

Once home, the shrill sound of Doris's telephone made a harsh interruption to our subdued conversation but were delighted to see her smiling as she lowered the handset.

" That was a neighbour," she told us. "He said he had had an unexpected call from Rex earlier, saying he had not been able to get in touch with you, so could I let you know that all was well, and he would be home on the late evening train." What an immense relief that was.

Some anxious hours later, the doorbell rang, and a weary Rex ambled in, Were we relieved! With the taxi paid off and a warming drink in his hand, he spilled out his tale. He described how terribly shaken he was and had flopped onto a nearby bench to try and get himself together. He realized he had no jacket, return ticket, or money to buy himself a drink. He could see no way of getting himself home and would need to go and get help. He had stood up to steady his legs, and find some fresh air, when by pure chance, he had walked straight into an old naval friend, Clive, a fellow officer he had once served with in Malta some twenty years before. Despite the grey hair and slacker jawlines, they instantly recognised each other, and clapped each other on the shoulder with delight.

As they were both heading for Devon, and with an hour to spare before their train, they had decided to pass the time in the café, where much to Clive's dismay, Rex's alarming story unfolded. Without a' by your leave,' his shipmate had quietly placed enough money into Rex's hand to pay for his return ticket. With the few coins in his pocket, and desperate to spare our obvious worries, he had managed to make a call to his neighbour whose number, luckily, he could remember.

The two naval veterans had passed the journey amicably swapping stories of the action aboard HMS Ausonia, and what their paths had been after the war had ended. As Rex stood to leave the train at Plymouth, his discomfort on accepting the money had been waved aside by his friend. 'Perhaps look me up in Liskeard sometime and treat me to a drink' was all he had said with a farewell wave of the hand.

After letting him catch his breath a little, we timidly asked about the whereabouts of the Duty Free bag.

"Duty free bag?" he replied, with a bewildered look, and shake of his head

"It was left with the cases on the platform," I chirped up.

Rex shook his head,

"I remember the kerfuffle on the platform, and yes, there was a bag, but I think I must have rested it on the bench when I went to pick up the cases. Then I met my friend and forgot all about it. I am so sorry. Was there anything very important in it?" he asked with concern.

Secretly I was devastated, and Nick too, but this was not the time to cause further upset by telling them the real value of what was really in it.

"Oh, just one or two things we wanted to show you all," I replied fleetingly, before being swept along in the happy family chat and laughter.

By now it was nearing midnight, and we headed off for a welcome sleep, agreeing to make some vaguely hopeful enquiries at Reading Station the next morning. But sleep eluded me, as I pictured the tough, dangerous, exhausting, but joyful things we had done to achieve our mission, and now we had lost it all. It would hardly be worth making that call the next day; our chances were nil. Hordes of passengers would have passed that by that everyday bag, or even sat beside it, duped by its ordinariness. The platform cleaners would have tossed it as litter into their machines. The curious would have looked inside and helped themselves to our precious hoard. We wouldn't see our jewels again.

How ridiculously foolish it sounded when we spoke to the Lost Property manager at Reading Station the next morning describing the loss of an open plastic airline bag, with no identification, left on a platform bench in that huge, busy station containing a considerably valuable number of gems, and gold items. But we couldn't be too harsh on ourselves, as the whole upset had been caused by totally unusual, and unforeseen circumstances, rather than our negligence.

We stood with bated breath.

"Well actually madam," came a voice, "remarkably, we have your bag. It was handed in yesterday afternoon by a lady who told me she had noticed the contents and realised it might be of value to someone. Consider yourselves very, very lucky."

We gasped and gaped at each other, dumbstruck at what we'd heard.

"If you let us have your address we can try and get it to you, but it will be at your risk. We can get it down to Plymouth Station on a train in the guard's luggage compartment, then it's up to them to see to it. But you realise that lots of people will be in and out of there collecting cases. "

We were a bit crestfallen, but felt it was worth the risk, and still held out a hope that it would somehow survive.

Three days later, as we were eating our breakfasts, the doorbell rang, and we heard Doris call us. There at the roadside was a Western Rail van, and stepping towards us was a smartly dressed man with our treasured duty free bag dangling from his fingers.

It was the stuff dreams are made of!

Jubilantly, we sat everyone round the table, and slowly took out the leather pouch. Now we could own up to the hundreds of pounds worth of jewels that simple bag had actually held. We spread out the garnets, the opals, the andalusite and topaz, then the rings and pendants I had made.

And do you know what?... . Every single one was still there. Beautiful, shimmering and intact !! Now what were the chances of that? So did my tale come to the happy ending you had hoped for us, unknown reader?

Well you see, yet again by chance, this was not the final conclusion of my tale at all. Step forward some decades later to 2017, when one of my rings began to feel uncomfortably tight, so I took it to a Taunton jeweller to be adjusted. After the arranged collection date had come and gone, and with no news of my ring's progress, I popped into the shop to see if there was a problem with it.

"Well yes there is," the assistant confided. "You may not believe this, but your ring is being withheld as evidence in a police court case in Devon. It seems that an employee had been found with some stolen mail bags concealed in his house, and your ring was among those."

I was rooted to the ground. Now what were the chances of that!

I am typing my story looking at the very ring glistening very, very securely on my finger!

Sheila Tucker

A fossicker's tale

Thirty three

Sometimes, things are not what they seem, as this next story shows.

Heather told it to her friend Amy in confidence, as they were impatiently waiting for the traffic to clear at the roundabout just off Junction 25 one summer evening.

THE ORCHID

Heather was in a very bad mood. She had had a very irritating day at the bank dealing with difficult customers and incompetent managers and was feeling grumpy already when she decided in a moment of madness to take the motorway from Taunton down to Wellington instead of her usual route on the A38. When the accident happened she was just past the Taunton Deane services and could almost see her exit. She had sat there in the motionless traffic for more than an hour, fuming at the wheel. She watched as all the blue-light vehicles passed her on the hard shoulder.

When they traffic finally started to move and she passed the spot where the accident had occurred she saw a caravan on its side and in pieces. Some family's holiday had been ruined and motorway workers were still sweeping the remains of their holiday 'home' into piles on the hard shoulder.

Her face broke into a semi-smile as she finally opened the door of her little cottage in Pinksmoor. She loved her little house and felt so comfortable there. She was looking forward to a quiet night in with Nick and then a lovely, lazy weekend. As she moved into the tiny hallway she noticed her answer machine blinking at her. She closed the front door behind her with one hand and, at the same time, pressed "Play" on the machine while throwing her coat on to a hook..

Her face darkened as she listened to the only message on the machine.

"Hi 'H,' it's me, Nick. Look I'm really sorry but I can't make it tonight, something has come up at work. Actually, er .... I'm not going to be around anymore. I'm sorry to have to break it to you like this, er, ... but I guess this is goodbye. Thanks for the good times and take care."

Heather slammed the phone down, stormed into the kitchen, opened the fridge door and took out a bottle of wine. Then she put the bottle back and instead picked up a bottle of vodka from the worktop. She poured herself a hefty slug, took a mouthful, winced as the fiery liquid burned her throat and moved into her tiny sitting room where she threw herself on to her sofa.

"What on earth is going on?," she wondered aloud.

She poured herself another hefty slug, her mind struggling to comprehend Nick's words. What had happened? At breakfast this morning he had been fine. They had eaten together as usual and, as he left, he had kissed her and said,

"I'll see you this evening then, 'H.' I don't think I will be too late."

She had smiled and whispered,

"Let's have a quiet night in. I'll get something for us to eat on my way home."

"Sounds great," and, with that, he was gone.

As she sat there Heather wondered, 'Has he taken his things with him?' She dragged herself to the bathroom and saw that his few bits and pieces were still there, where he had left them. Automatically, without thinking, she tidied things away and then did the same in the bedroom they had shared.

She stumbled back down to the sitting room, the effects of the vodka beginning to show. Back on the small sofa they had shared for many an enjoyable evening she picked up her mobile.

"Of course! I'll ring his mobile. Stupid woman, I should have thought of that straightaway."

She clicked on his number,

"The number you have dialled is not available," she heard in disbelief.

"What?"

She tried again but with the same response.

"I know, I'll ring his workplace, maybe they will know where he is," she said to herself as she dialled the number.

"The number you have dialled is not available," she heard. Frustrated she dialled again,

"The number you have dialled is not available," came the response once more.

Nick had told her he worked for a large consortium out on the edge of the city of Exeter "Over on the Marsh Barton side." She had never bothered to ask him for any more details but, later, had suggested he might give her his work number "Just in case."

Angrily, Heather threw the phone on the coffee table and poured herself another hefty slug of vodka. Pulling her legs up beneath her she drank a large mouthful of the spirit, and then another, emptying the glass. She loosened her hair, then threw her head back against the cushions and felt herself beginning to cry.

"Hold it together," she told herself and glanced again at the by now almost empty vodka bottle.

Sighing heavily, she again tried to work out in her now befuddled state what on earth had happened.

The piercing ringing of her doorbell startled her awake and she realised after a few moments of confusion that she must have fallen asleep on the sofa. She looked at her watch and saw the time was now approaching nine o'clock. 'Wow that vodka must be stronger than I thought' she muttered to herself, conveniently forgetting that she had consumed more than two thirds of a bottle. The bell rang again. She forced herself on to her feet and made her way to the front door, automatically checking her make up and her hair in the hallway mirror.

'If it's Nick,' she thought to herself, 'I'll really give him a piece of my mind.'

But it wasn't Nick; she hadn't really expected it to be.

Standing before her were two well-dressed strangers - a man and a woman. Immediately Heather's still befuddled mind thought, "Jehovah's witnesses" but before she could say anything rude or otherwise the man spoke:

"Good evening. Heather Wilmot?"

"Yes, who ….?"

He held an identity card featuring an impressive badge up to Heather's face and said,

"I'm D.I. McKinley and this is D.S. Robertson. We are from Scotland Yard and would like to ask you some questions, if you don't mind."

Heather gaped at him. She saw that the card he was holding was, indeed, an identity card.

"Sc.. Scotland Yard?" she stuttered, "What on earth do you want with me?"

And then she stopped, 'Oh my God, two police officers, soberly dressed … someone has died'

She stumbled and leant against the wall to hold herself upright.

"Are you OK?," asked the woman.

"Yes, yes, er just a bit of a shock, you know, police officers at the door at 9 o'clock at night," she attempted a rather pathetic smile.

"Of course," said the man. "May we come in? These things are better discussed in comfort. You don't want all your neighbours nosing into your affairs do you?" He smiled disarmingly.

"Yes, of course, of course," Heather stammered. "Please do."

She led them through to the small sitting room, embarrassed to see the vodka bottle and glass standing prominently on the table and the sofa with its crumpled cushions. She quickly plumped the cushions and picked up the bottle and glass and, as she made her way to the kitchen, called behind her,

"Can I get you a tea or coffee, detective?"

"No thanks, we're fine," D.I. McKinley replied. He took advantage of the short time Heather was away to scan the room noticing that there were no photographs, family or otherwise, some 'arty' prints on the walls, a vase of flowers, a couple of those large jars with orchids in that he had seen in garden centres and various 'knickknacks.' He got the impression of a very feminine room which was tasteful and uncluttered.

"Please sit down," said Heather as she returned from the kitchen. She guided them to the sofa and took the armchair for herself. She looked enquiringly at the detectives who were squashed together on the small sofa. Heather felt she had the upper hand as they looked decidedly out of place in her sitting room.

D.I. McKinley began:

"Am I right that you are the sole owner of this property Ms Wilmot?"

"Well me and the mortgage company," replied Heather quickly, probably giving away her nervousness.

"Am I also right in believing that you have had someone staying here recently, a man, a man called Nick Garwood?"

"Yes that's right," replied Heather before adding anxiously, "Has something happened to him?" Then realising that she was sitting opposite two police officers she added,

"Oh my God. It has, hasn't it? Is he dead? Has he had an accident? Please tell me he's OK."

"Calm down Heather," said Sgt Robertson quietly, "It's nothing like that. Let D. I. McKinley explain."

Heather did as she was asked and Inspector McKinley continued,

"It's not like that Heather. But I do have some bad news for you I am afraid." He looked at Heather's pale and anxious face and suddenly felt very sorry for the young woman. In spite of all his years' experience he still disliked moments like this.

"I am afraid you have been the victim of a cruel deception. Nick Garwood was not who he claimed to be. He was an undercover policeman. We are investigating the bank where you work and he was under orders to get close to someone there and try to find out what is going on. He should never have allowed a relationship to develop between the two of you. He has a wife and two children in Enfield."

Heather felt shocked and relieved at the same time …… then she began to feel cheated and abused ….. and finally she became angry.

"Well, the lying bastard!" she exploded.

Sergeant Robertson intervened,

"Heather, we understand how you feel. We are here to ask you if you would like to make a formal complaint against him.

Twenty minutes later the two officers left her having given her all the information and documentation she needed for the complaint and having offered her "The force's" sincere apologies for the way she had been misled. They also told her the investigation into the bank was concluded.

Heather sat back in her chair again and sighed heavily. She picked up one of the jars with an orchid in. Carefully, she removed the orchid which was an artificial one from IKEA and thrust her fingers into the 'soil' in which it had been 'planted.'

She withdrew a small mobile phone which had been concealed there. Flipping open the device she speed-dialled the only number the phone contained and waited.

A voice said, "Go ahead."

"They've gone. We're safe. They know nothing," Heather replied, then closed the phone and put it back in the jar.

Then, for the first time that evening, she smiled properly.

Keith McGinhal

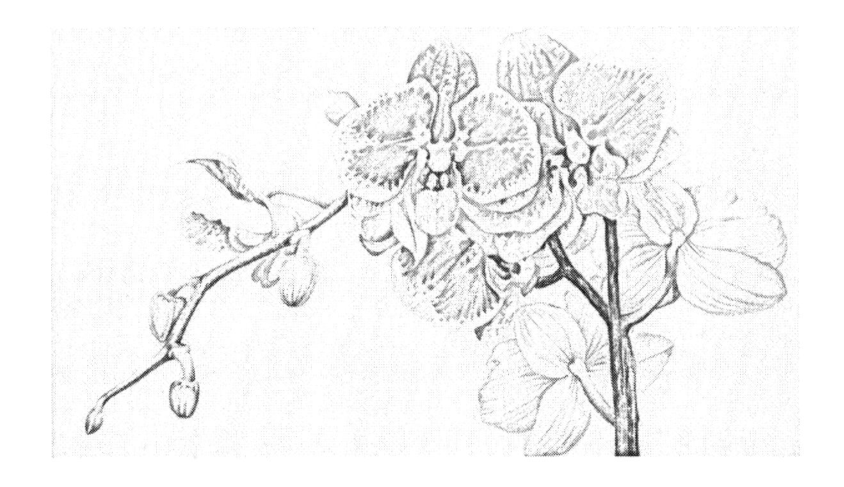

The Orchid

Thirty four

And finally .....

Fate works in a mysterious way some times. It is not really for us to ask 'Why?' or 'Why me?'

Our role is merely to 'Keep calm and carry on.'

SNAP

Lost in thought, she was thinking of the 'snap' he had taken with him, that meal he took away with him on every shift. It never altered much, but there had to be plenty in his snap tin. Once he stepped into the lift to go down to the coal face, he didn't surface again until a good twelve hours later, and only then after he had crawled back along the seam about half a mile to the lift, to wait in line for the ascent back to the surface. Black as tar; no washing facilities at the pithead. No, the coaldust had to lie,
covering every bit of exposed skin, until he had walked up pit lane and was stood upright in the galvanised tin bath, naked as a jay, while she struggled to sluice off the accumulated filth of the long shift. It took a fair few rinses before he turned, again, into the man she had seen off at the start of his shift. Clean as a whistle. Not a mark on him. Except for the smattering of black spots on his back, permanently embedded, that she knew would never shift.

He didn't talk much about his time down there. None of the men did. But you picked up enough from the idle chatter in the Demi, the Democratic Working Men's Club, to give it its full title, beer-sloshed on weekends when the place heaved, men letting down their guard a little, to know that conditions were dire. The long shifts meant you spent the whole of the working week barely clapping eyes on one another, except for eating and sleeping. Strange then that, having looked forward all week to spending some time together and having smartened yourselves up for the occasion, once you got to the Demi the wives and girlfriends would invariably gather together in clumps around the room while the men tended to cluster together at the bar. Together, but separate. It had always been like that. It would probably always be. As they say in Yorkshire, "There's nowt so queer as folk."

It was particularly hard for him down the pit, him being so tall and broad-shouldered with it. Down there it was searingly hot, the seam narrow, barely head height in places, not a fit place for a dog, let alone a human being. But her man, all the men, had no choice. There was no other work. Son followed father; father followed his father. And so on. You reckoned, when a boy was born in the village, that mining was in his blood.

She had let out a huge, silent, sigh when he wasn't called up to serve. Coal mining was a protected occupation. His work was vital in hacking out the coal that was needed to stoke the fires that ran the railways and the munitions factories. Safe from German guns, he was serving his country as surely as any man on active combat.

Life's a funny old business. He was on a night shift, working like a slave while the rest of the village slept like babies. But, if truth be told, the wives and sweethearts never completely relaxed until their men were home safe again. He had taken his 'snap' with him, as usual, the 'snap' he took away with him on every shift. Despite wartime shortages, there was still a decent hunk of bread, plenty of cheese and pickled onions and a hefty slice of fruit cake. And because his allotment was overflowing with fresh vegetables and there were still plenty of root vegetables that he had stored over the winter, there would be a good stew for dinner. Not much meat, mind. But enough to fill a belly or two.

The whole village heard it. It turned their hearts to ice. The siren's wail. Almost as one, those who had been in their beds just seconds before, now spilled out and filled pit lane, snaking their way to the pithead. They stood, heads bowed, stoic in their despondency, hope almost, but not quite, lost.

Oh, the bitter irony. Safe from a German bullet; felled by a falling roof.

She looked at his coffin, waiting in the parlour. She pulled her black shawl more tightly to her body, as if to hold in her grief. Slowly, relentlessly, they came through the door. They were ready now to take him away. Barely conscious, footsteps moving mechanically, she stumbled forward, head bent, heart shattered.

Snap

ACKNOWLEDGEMENTS

Our thanks are due to all the contributors of these stories.

In addition we are grateful for the support of Mike Tompsett, Pat Iles and Lauraine Newcombe who took the time and trouble to read the stories and comment upon them.

The logo of the u3a is "Learn, Live, Love" and within that context Pat Mabberley established a writing forum for members the purpose of which was to enable those u3a members who wanted to write to be able to meet together for their mutual benefit.

Malcolm Godfrey, Pat and Michael Knight are members of that writer's forum and this collection was conceived and collated during their meetings together.

Although Mike is listed as the editor Pat and Malcolm also made major contributions.

Other publications on Amazon by Taunton u3a members are:

"From Son to Father"
A memoir, by Malcolm Godfrey

"Here, There and Everywhere, a journal of discovery and misadventure"
A travelogue by Michael Knight

"Wells Farrago"
A novel by Malcolm Godfrey, Michael Knight and Oat Mabberley

Printed in Great Britain
by Amazon